AF507963

To my brothers, Greggy and Lukey. To the journeys you are
still in the middle of.

Diamonds are created under pressure.

To Forge a Fate

One dream.

That was the first domino to fall, causing an

inevitable

chain

reaction.

Dream and Reality

My footsteps echoed through the empty neighborhood. The colors of the setting sun stretched across the sky, a mosaic illuminated by the dying light. The glow softly lit the empty houses around me—a neighborhood freshly completed from construction but not quite lived in yet. My family thought I was a little odd for strolling in a "ghost town," as they called it. But I was always around people, and being around them twenty-four-seven absolutely drained me. Finding a quiet place to collect my thoughts was a necessity every now and then.

Cool wind brushed against my face, sweeping my worries away with it. I ambled down the sidewalk, carefully avoiding the cracks, although there weren't many on the new pavement. Crisp air surrounded me, not chilly enough to be cold, but just enough to be refreshing.

The sun lowered beneath the horizon. I needed to head back, but I couldn't bring my walk to such an abrupt end. Plus, I could already hear the demands of my foster mother, which she would surely shout to me as soon as I returned.

Maybe I'll stick around here, just a bit longer.

Even though I was alone, I didn't find myself lonely.

The trees and wind and sunbeams were better friends than most classmates could be. Odd, how nature could be better company and less draining than being around some people. Being alone was better sometimes.

Only now, I didn't feel quite alone.

A shiver crept up my spine as the unshakable feeling of leering eyes fell upon me. Someone was watching.

I looked across the street. The person standing there wore a black cloak swaying softly in the wind. My eyes stuck to them, and I wondered if they were really there.

The wind grated against my panicked eyes. I made the unfortunate decision to blink. The person was gone, as if they had been a figment of my imagination.

My ribs shook while my heart pounded. I continued walking, darting my eyes. *Okay, time to relax is over. I should probably head home…*The shiver lingered in me, as if the person was still watching me, even though I couldn't see them. My senses were on high alert. Walking accelerated to a jog, then a run. That was when I heard it: heavy footsteps following me.

I bolted.

I ran as fast as I could. Empty houses watched me run, and I almost wished I was in a populated area. For the safety, if nothing else.

Okay, maybe I'll stop hanging out in ghost towns.

An unseen force shoved me into an alley between houses. When I looked up, the cloaked person blinked into sight, like magic. I couldn't think of a way out. Cold hard brick pressed against my back.

"Do not move, and I will make this as painless as possible," he said. His soft voice was gentle but edged with venom.

I just sat there in terror while he walked closer. Though I wanted to do something to defend myself, I was only a kid. What could I possibly have done?

His shadow crept closer along the ground. A new silhouette joined the scene.

Great, who else now?

The cloaked man didn't seem to notice.

The newcomer ran up behind the man and pushed him into the wall, knocking him to the ground. When he fell, the newcomer swung around a pole, ready for their opponent to bounce back.

The new person wore a white hoodie with blue jeans, black and white sneakers, and leather gloves. Nothing about them seemed out of the ordinary, but their face was shrouded in shadows.

They bent down toward me, the concealment thick even as they came closer.

"Are you okay?" the newcomer asked. His quiet voice was masculine and filled with worry. It felt strangely warm and familiar.

I knew him, but I didn't. Though I wracked my brain, I just couldn't remember.

Before I could react or say anything, the cloaked man got back up and tackled this hoodie guy, knocking him down. He popped right back up like a spring. The hoodie guy used his glowing staff, and the cloaked man pulled out a dagger that lengthened into a sword. They fought, one trying desperately to kill the hoodie guy and get to me while the other just continuously keeping him at a good distance from me.

Yeah, this was getting pretty weird.

What did *I* do, pray tell? I sat. Sat and watched.

The hoodie guy seemed to be winning, but no matter who threw an attack, their faces stayed hidden. Somehow, nothing could move their hoods back. I didn't understand. It didn't feel real.

Soon, the cloaked man fell to the ground.

The two began speaking in an odd language. It sounded different, lilting and quick in a way I had never heard before. Definitely nothing like English.

The hoodie guy picked up his staff and pointed it at the man. Once the cloaked man saw this, he pulled out a handful of crystals and threw them into the air. They formed an oval floating in front of him, and the space in the middle began to ripple, as if it were liquid. He walked through and disappeared. The crystals seemed to get sucked inside, and it all vanished.

I was stunned. By now, the night had consumed the sky, and a part of me—the only sane part—knew I needed to get home. The rest of me was freaking out, trying to comprehend everything that had happened. Distracted, I barely noticed the hoodie guy pick up the cloaked man's sword and head in my direction.

"Sorry about that. Are you all right?" he asked, kneeling to my level. He wouldn't look directly at me.

Still in shock, I gave him a quick nod. He tapped the tip of the sword twice on the ground. The metal warped and shrank into a dagger. The man placed it in his pocket.

Wouldn't the blade still hurt him through his clothes?

There were so many things I wanted to ask him, all of them swirling around my mind in a hurricane, but only one question made its way to my mouth. "Who are you?"

He wouldn't respond. Instead, he fidgeting with his glove.

"All of this will make sense soon. Just look here." He

gently pointed to the palm of his hand.

I didn't know what else to do, and he *had* just saved my life—as it seemed—so I obeyed. A white light seared into my eyes, forcing me to close them.

When I opened my eyes, I was in my room, in bed, still in my clothes, shoes and all. The fresh sunlight shone on my face, warming me. It was morning, and the Cruzes were running about. I was stunned.

Was it all just a dream?

It had felt so real when it happened, but whenever I looked back on it, it truly felt like a dream.

But if it was a dream, how did I get home?

Before I was fully able to think about it, Luna, my foster mother, opened my door, startling me out of my train of thought.

"What are you still doing in bed? *Andale!* We need to be at the docks in fifty minutes, and it takes forty minutes to get there!" she yelled. Her eyes went up and down, scanning me. "*Que es esto?* Are you still in your clothes from yesterday? *Sabes que*, never mind. Just be out here in five minutes. We'll eat once we get on the cruise, so don't even think about bugging us for food."

She slammed my door shut with the final syllable of her last word.

Grasping the blankets around me, I collected my

thoughts, worrying about the night I had.

Do I try to remember what happened last night, or should I get my luggage to the living room before Luna bursts a blood vessel?

I shivered at the thought of what she might do to me if I disobeyed her. After all, I had already slept in, and she had sounded pretty angry. I decided to push what might or might not have happened the night before to the back of my mind to deal with later, preferably after the cruise.

I swiftly de-wrinkled my bed, grabbed my stuff, and ran downstairs to the living room. We were on the road in three minutes, ready to take our vacation cruise — the birthday party for my foster brother.

***

Crash.

The boat rocked with every wave. I would have been dreadfully seasick had I not gone to the front deck. The diluted sunlight shining off the mist comforted me. My family was probably also happy, considering I was nowhere near them.

The only reason I had been brought along was because it would have been illegal for Luna to leave me home alone. Plus, she didn't trust me that much to leave me around her belongings without supervision.

Despite this, I was having a great time. I let my mind wander while I watched the sea. Each sway was graceful but powerful, everything quiet and simple. I could have stayed staring at the sea forever. Unfortunately, I was only able to stand there for about fifteen minutes.

A chill shivered up my spine. Someone was staring at me. A wave of familiarity flashed through me, reminding me of my dream.

I started to look around but saw no one else there, yet I felt them, could sense their warmth. It was like playing "hot-and-cold," but the heat or lack thereof was palpable. No one else was on deck. Everyone was inside, partying or making bad decisions.

Yearning to find this person, I focused on the heat signature and followed it.

Whoever it was must have noticed my awareness of them because their heat ran away. I chased the invisible trail all around the deck and inside the boat, despite my upset stomach. There were other spots of heat, but I didn't care. I just focused on that one trail.

Right when I thought I might catch the person, I ran into Juan and Luna, knocking all three of us to the floor.

Luna was the first out of the three of us to get up. I was the second, mainly because she pulled me up along with her. She had grabbed me by my elbow in a tight vise grip.

"What do you think you are doing?" Luna scowled at me.

I was still looking around for the ghost while she held

me, but the trail had disappeared. Now I was just hot, as if I could feel *everyone's* temperatures, especially Luna's.

"One more thing, and I swear…" Luna hissed, balling her right hand into a fist.

Juan placed his hand on her shoulder and began to whisper into her ear. Her expression softened, along with her clenched fist, but her grip did not.

"This is your last warning, *muchacha*. Leave us alone, and we will all be happy. And I mean throughout the *whole* trip."

"Go on now," Juan said sweetly with a sad look. The pity in his face was embarrassingly apparent.

Luna let go of my arm, leaving a red wound on my elbow. When I touched it, it was still raw.

Once my "parents" walked away, I rolled my eyes and began roaming the boat, searching for the invisible person I had lost. This didn't last long, however. Well…my stomach didn't like me, and I polluted the sea some more.

After I finished feeding the fish, I felt it again. Although I wasn't oddly super sensitive to heat anymore, my gut told me I wasn't alone. I looked around and found them.

Someone appeared out of thin air in the shadows. The figure wore a black cloak—once more akin to my dream—which helped them blend into their surroundings. Similar to the person in my dream, but not the same. They had a smaller build.

My curiosity led me to follow and sneak into a room around the corner — the wheelhouse. At the front of the space, looking out the window, was the captain, steering the boat. The cloaked person started whispering something to him.

"Speak up. There is no one here. Plus, take off that hood. You are making me sweat just looking at you." The captain's voice was identical to the man from my dream: the cloaked figure who had tried to kidnap me.

The captain had slicked black hair, combed and gelled immaculately. It contrasted his pale skin but brought out the dark in his thin almond eyes. He had on a formal white shirt with golden trim, tucked into his black pants. On his neck was a metal circle, stuck to his skin, although I couldn't quite tell what it was.

When I got a good look at his face, it seemed stiff, as if he could only feel sheer apathy.

The cloaked person took off her hood. She had wavy amber-red hair pulled back into a low bun. Her eyes were a dazzling green, blazing like frustrated emeralds.

"I do not think —"

"You are to address me as 'Captain.'" The man shrugged. "Well, just for another couple of minutes or so. Only until this boat's pieces scatter." His voice was as stern as his face, but a slight empty grin appeared. A malicious gleam shone deep in his eyes.

They both had an unrecognizable accent, not

matching with any region I was familiar with.

"Ugh, I do *not* care. Can we just get this going? I think that she is starting to get suspicious. I was keeping track of her when suddenly, she looked at me. She *looked* at me! I do not know how. My shield kept me invisible."

"That is odd."

"I know! I do not know what happened. The cloak must have glitched, but once I began to run away, she *followed me*. It was as if she could see me!"

"The technology does not glitch. Ever. Plus, she does not even know that such technology exists. If she saw you, then that must have been *your* fault. Where is she now?"

"I do not know," she said with a sliver of fear.

His cold eyes shot a glare toward her. "You seem to not know a lot. Just remember that I can dispose of you at any time. Boss's orders."

"Listen, all I know is that I lost her in the crowds. How much longer until we leave? I do not want to be part of the debris once this boat bursts."

"Are you scared of that little girl? She is a *child*. Suck it up. She will be dead soon. But that does remind me…We got" — the captain stopped to look at his watch — "forty-two seconds now."

"Great. Let's go."

The lady took crystals from her pocket and threw them into the air. The space seemed to liquefy in a floating oval, identical to the portal from my dream. They stepped through the rippling area and disappeared, the crystals zooming after them.

My mind was racing everywhere while I tried to comprehend their suspicious conversation and departure. They were breaking the laws of physics, nature, and just about everything in between. *Who were… How did they…?*

Questions flooded my mind for the next few seconds until one thing they said brought me back to reality: "Once this boat bursts."

The boat was going to explode.

I ran as fast as possible, faster than I actually thought I could run, scouring the boat, looking for the bomb—as if I could disarm it. Wishful thinking. There wasn't enough time to do anything or tell anyone.

Then everything went black.

I blinked into groggy consciousness, finding myself lying on the shore. Everything hurt, and the gritty sand only made it worse when it pressed into my wounds. My breath was labored, and I couldn't move. My head was pounding, and the misty air scratched against my throat. Or maybe that was the sea, which had previously filled my lungs. My vision was stinging and blurry from the saltwater.

Right before I fell back into the darkness, I saw a

blurry image of a man approaching me, his brows knit
together in worry.

Stranger Danger

"**Is** she all right?" a muffled voice asked.

"For the last time, don't worry! Her wounds are cleaned and will only take a short amount of time to heal. You know I tended to her," someone else said.

I tried to open my eyes, but it took a lot more work than I expected. My lids felt like stone. Peeking them open, I was in a white room, with two people standing in front of me. It was a hospital room, and I was in a patient bed. Panic rushed over my body. I jolted up.

"W — Where am I?" I asked.

My body began to register the delayed pain. I began rubbing my healing wounds, feeling as if every one of my bones were bruised.

The man had slightly wavy raven-black hair, combed to the back. He wore an emerald-green tunic and black greaves, like he had just come from some historical convention. Surely, he couldn't have been any older than twenty.

The woman was obviously a doctor. She wore a salmon blouse and tan pants underneath her white coat. Her strawberry-blond hair was tied back in a low ponytail. Softly, her chestnut eyes examined me. The lady looked only a couple of years older than him.

Whoa, youngest doctor on Earth.

"Calm down, sweetie. You're in my clinic. I'm Dr. Taylor. This here is the man that found you on the shore and brought you to me. Mr. Anderson." She gestured toward the man. "What's your name?"

Her voice sounded fun and sugary, with a slight but beautiful accent. Although something about it felt recognizable, I couldn't quite place her accent.

However, this wasn't the thing that stuck out to me like a sore thumb. *The man…*His face felt familiar but out of reach.

I have seen him before, but where?

"Elena Cruz," I said absent-mindedly.

Mr. Anderson gave me a weary grin, and it tortured me even more. He felt like a part of my past, but he had never been in any of my foster families.

Could I have just passed him in public or something?

A more pressing matter entered my mind. Within a couple of seconds, I remembered what had taken place…mostly. Mixed emotions filled me while I tried replaying everything that had occurred.

"What happened?" My heart was pounding out of my chest.

They glanced at each other before anyone spoke.

"He found you, washed up on the shore. He wasn't sure why you were there, but then the news said that a cruise ship had just been blown up. It seems like a bomb was placed inside the boat. They think it was an act of public terrorism," Dr. Taylor explained.

"Wait, why? Have they caught them?" I asked. Before she could respond, it dawned on me that I was the only patient in a room filled with empty hospital beds. "Where are the other survivors?"

A sorrowful silence struck the two of them. It took a little bit, but after some hesitation, Mr. Anderson came to the left side of my bed.

"I found only you. *Only* you. No one found any other survivors…or at least reported any. You were alone on the beach when I saw you, all marred and battered."

Mr. Anderson sounded wise and experienced, having the same accent as Dr. Taylor's. But a worried tone rang through it. His voice echoed in my head. It dug deep to a well-worn memory.

I sat there on the bed, staring at him for a few minutes, trying to locate the memory with him in it. We were all quiet until Mr. Anderson seemed to get bothered by my staring.

His eyes were deep with sadness. I wasn't sure if he was grieving over the lives lost in the explosion or because of something older. To try and hear his voice better, I brought up another question.

"What about my family? Did you find them?" I asked. The familiarity of his voice was driving me insane. Akin to the torture of having a word at the tip of your tongue.

"No, I am sorry. You must miss your family a great deal," he said.

I wasn't listening to the words. Rather, I was absorbing the low registers in his tone.

I grew tired of trying to remember him and scoffed. "Do I know you?"

His expression changed. It registered a glum "yes" right when he whispered, "No."

Mr. Anderson turned away, avoiding eye contact. He had the *worst* poker face, but he also would not admit that he did, in fact, know me. It didn't matter, though. His hushed voice snapped the memory of him right into place.

"The alley!" I said. "You were the man that helped me!"

"What? I am sorry, my dear. I do not know what you are talking about." Confusion tainted his face.

My hope began to disappear. *Was that not him? Had it all really been a dream?*

No, I told myself. *It couldn't have been. How could that man's voice be his if I had not met him yet?*

My eyes drifted to Mr. Anderson's. I might have wanted answers, but I needed *real* ones, not lies, and I was determined to call him out for it.

"It had to have been you. You're *lying*."

"I am sorry. We have not met before," he insisted.

I wanted to yell at him more, but he was standing by his fib, no matter what. Before I could say or do anything else, Dr. Taylor inserted herself.

"Well, you must've had a long day today, Elena. I suggest that you rest." Her voice was as sweet as honey.

Mr. Anderson began to seem skittish. He pulled Dr. Taylor over and whispered into her ear. Something fishy was going on, not just with him lying.

While I wasn't sure what he told her, she seemed conflicted. I, on the other hand, was overwhelmed. A storm brewed in my head. I wasn't sure what to feel or think. My mind was a rubber band stretching, and it was threatening to break. But I had to push on. I needed truth.

Dr. Taylor headed to the door. "I have something to tend to. Tell me if you need help." Her eyes batted between the two of us. "That applies to both of you."

Without another word, she stepped out of the room. Her absence left me and Mr. Anderson alone. I wanted to interrogate him as much as I could. Once I opened my mouth, almost every question that had been badgering me blurted out.

"What are you hiding from me? How was I the *only* one that survived? Who was that person with the cloak in the alleyway? Why—"

"Okay. Calm down. I know that you have a lot of queries, and I will answer them as soon as I can. But you need to understand something before I explain anything." Hints of apprehension staggered his voice.

He is going to tell me? Just like that? There has to be some kind of catch. Something…

But even if there was a catch, it might be the only chance I would have to get answers to the most ridiculous of my questions. So, I took a deep breath, calmed myself down, and nodded.

"All right. Let us see. Where do I start?" Mr. Anderson mumbled to himself.

Every movement of his just made me more restless. He rubbed his temples, sitting down in the doctor's rolling chair with a nervous look on his face.

Why is he nervous?

"Listen, what I am about to say is going to sound crazy, but it is the truth," he warned me.

Curiouser and Curiouser

"**What**?" I tugged my hair, playing with it while I rested my head on my hand. "I don't even know what a fae is."

"A fae. The fae is a sentient species, just like humans. We look quite similar too. However, humans live much shorter lives than us, and we naturally have an abundance of Essence."

I stared at him blankly, bewildered. There wasn't any doubt or hesitation in his eyes. He was serious.

"And…I am a fae? Um, Mr. Anderson, are you okay?" I whispered, genuinely concerned.

"I know how this sounds, but please, you have to believe me," he insisted. "You should know about fae, although we have been called by different names through time: elves, fairies, genie, seelies….I believe that there are many human myths about us. However, the fact that we have pointed ears is *not* a myth. You will get yours in six years, but mine are already in."

"Really?" I decided to try to use logic against him. To help him see the truth. "Okay, show me them."

He quickly nodded and pushed his hair back. Mr. Anderson stroked some invisible thing above his ears, and when he lowered his hands, I could make out their pointed tips, extending around an inch or from where his ears had previously stopped.

I was astonished, speechless, and dumbstruck…for a minute. Before common sense kicked in. The man had just pulled off one of the oldest tricks in the book: *Watch while I make something appear out of thin air!* Who was this guy trying to fool?

"How impressive," I said sarcastically. "Come here."

"Why?"

"Because if those are real, then they should be warm with blood."

He chuckled, as if I were the most adorable thing on Earth. With an internal groan, I was ready to tell him that he was wrong, respectfully or not.

"All right," Mr. Anderson said. "Just be careful."

He knelt to the left of my bed so I could reach him. I scooted over to the side and put my hands on his ears.

"See this? If these were real, then—" I stopped.

Confusion flooded over me when I felt warmth in the tips of his ears. Hastily, I examined them. Sure enough, there were visible *veins*.

"Okay, you have had your time. I do not want you to rip them off my head," he said with a smirk.

I searched my brain for an explanation or any reasoning I could use to prove he was wrong and I was right.

"Um, if—if those are real, then how come I didn't see them before? You have really short hair. They should've stuck out..."

"Oh, now you want to get into *specifics*. Well, fae are given Gifts once they turn ten years of age and perform a Ritual," he explained. "Gifts are abilities that allow you to tamper or control an Element. The kind of Gift you are granted varies depending mostly on your lineage."

He placed a hand on his chest.

"I am an Illusionist—a fae that can create facades from light—but my Gift is a little more, eh, complex. You see, I can also trick the senses of others to make my illusion almost reality, making me a Sensorial Illusionist. This is how I conceal my ears in human public."

There! Some dirt that I can use against him!

I chuckled. "*Gifts*? Do you mean *magic*? Magic is as real as—"

"Fae?" he interrupted with an arched eyebrow.

I growled softly, ignoring him. "There is no science to prove it. And an illusionist is a type of magician. What do you do? Make appearances at kids' birthday parties? And really, if all of what you said were true, then why don't *I* have a 'gift'? I am almost twelve years old."

"First of all, an Illusionist is what we call someone who can tamper with or bend light, making something akin to hallucinations—or more simply, illusions. Second of all, you did not do the Ritual. Skipping the Ritual is a first for our species, but that *should* explain why the seemingly lack of a Gift."

I put my hands on my hips, perhaps with a slight hint of petulance. "Well then, how did you make your ears disappear?"

"Easy. I twisted the light so it would make them invisible to the mortal eye."

I couldn't believe it. The guy had an explanation for everything.

Mr. Anderson sat beside me on the bed. "Really, my dear…Why do you think you never seem to fit in? Or why you are separate from others in your class, no matter what?"

It made no sense, but this little voice in my head recalled every time I had been rejected from anything, especially families.

Wait, he just described my life. I haven't met him before

today!

"How do you know those things about me?"

Mr. Anderson's eyes jolted wider in surprise. I knew right then that I had him. He glanced around, trying to find an answer.

"I—Um..." he stammered.

"This makes me think that you, Mr. Anderson, have been stalking me. That would kinda explain that night in the alley." A smile slowly stretched across my face. "I *should* turn you in to the police, especially since it looks like you just kidnapped me. However, if you let me go, then I won't include everything that I should charge you with."

As a kid, I would bluff as hard as I could. I was rather full of myself at the time.

"I did *not* stalk you. In fact, I was unaware of all of it until recently. It is...pretty complicated," Mr. Anderson murmured. "But I certainly did not kidnap you. You were injured. I brought you to a doctor that I personally knew."

"If you didn't kidnap me, then you should've called the authorities to tell them that there was a survivor or something. If you did that, then I should've been taken back a long time ago. Even if *that* had not happened, I would currently be surrounded by news reporters or whatever right now...since I would be the only survivor. But if you look around, you can see that I am not in *any* of those situations."

He was struck silent.

In such an event, any normal kid would have been scared about what their kidnapper might do to them. But because of the situation, I felt confident throwing my words around as much as I wanted, using whatever expectations I had as probable outcomes. I was ready to walk right out of there, find a phone, and call the police. But he interrupted me before I could continue.

"All right." he told me, with a newfound expression of courage on his face. "I understand what this looks like, but if I could show you good, undeniable evidence against the obvious, would you believe me?"

"Of course. I'm not unreasonable."

But he had no proof. What would he possibly show me?

Mr. Anderson walked back a few steps in front of the bed. I stood up by it, with my back leaning on the frame. He grinned and waved his hand to the side.

Instantly, the whole room changed.

The environment seemed to melt away and change from a hospital room to a forest. I was no longer leaning on a bed but a tree. This odd energy touched me, like adrenaline rushing through my body, but it wasn't the same. I was frozen in shock.

The scenery was gorgeous. I was surrounded by pine trees and luscious grass. The sunlight was tinted green, shining through the needles, but it couldn't have been real.

Magic isn't real. Right?

I slowly walked toward a shrub that was in between me and Mr. Anderson. When I bent down to touch it, my hand went right through it. I gasped, and my heart skipped a beat.

"Fascinating, right? Try touching it again," he said.

I was beyond baffled, but without thinking, I did as he instructed, expecting my hand to disappear into it again. I stumbled back a few steps when the soft leaves brushed my hand. My mind was spinning. I darted my head up at him.

He had a gleam of exhaustion in his eyes. With another wave of his hand, he made it all go away.

We were in the hospital room again.

Mr. Anderson crossed his arms, and his chest heaved while he tried to steady his breathing. "Do you believe me *now?*"

I shook my head and slowly walked backward, questioning everything and anything I had ever known to be true.

This...isn't just a trick, is it? It's real...

My mind was dazed, in disbelief, until I hit the wall behind me, overcome with confusion. My fight-or-flight instinct kicked in, and I began to run. All I knew was that I needed to get away from him.

I sprinted out of the room and through a white-tiled hallway, passing by a person or two. Not as many as I thought there should be in a clinic. The hallway wasn't very long, with only a few rooms connected to it.

What didn't make sense to me, on top of my crisis, was that there was nothing there that would make me think of this as a medical center. I went through a hall and right to the front room, where I stopped.

There was an elevator. Across from it was a slick desk a slightly cooler white than the room. Behind it, Dr. Taylor was holding her arm in front of her.

She was talking to a hologram of a person projected from her bracelet. The language she spoke was the same one Mr. Anderson had used when he spoke to the cloaked man in the alleyway.

That's what their accent sounds like.

It was right then that she looked at me.

Dr. Taylor said one last thing and turned her hand over, closing the hologram.

"Hi there, hon." She spoke slowly in English.

Dr. Taylor began walking toward me as if I were a startled animal or something. I mean, she wasn't far off from the truth. She hadn't left her desk yet before Mr. Anderson came into the room, breathless. He leaned on the wall.

"I am…sorry," he said to Dr. Taylor in between

breaths, appearing more worn out than before. "I…did not think that she would react that way."

Dr. Taylor put her hand on her face and rubbed her temple. "Did you show her your Gift?"

"I had to. She was thinking that I kidnapped her."

More evidence was presenting itself, proving that what he had said was true, but I just couldn't comprehend it.

"Ugh, well, no wonder she's freaked out. You overwhelmed the poor girl." Dr. Taylor turned toward me. Her voice was sugary. "Calm down, sweetie. We aren't going to hurt you."

I didn't know what to do.

Well, I *knew* I could use the elevator to get out of there. But that would have gone too slowly if they insisted on following me.

Instead, I closed my eyes, took a deep breath, and tried slowing my thoughts. I was *not* going to freak out madly any more, like an idiot. No, I was going to get my answers and freak out in an *organized* manner.

The elevator opened behind me, and out came a girl. Strawberry blond hair hung to her jaw. She had pointed ears, just like Mr. Anderson's. The girl seemed a little younger than Dr. Taylor and Mr. Anderson—around eighteen. She wore a brown leather outfit and a band of cloth in her hair.

The girl, looking troubled, walked past me, probably

not even realizing I was there. She started speaking to Dr. Taylor in that same foreign language.

Dr. Taylor painted on a nervous smile. Her eyes darted back and forth between me and the fae. "Um, Shaeli, dear. We have a visitor."

"Uh, why are you speaking English?" Shaeli asked. She turned around and scanned me with slight disgust. "Who is this wik?"

"Shaeli! This is Elena."

"But really, what is her name?" Shaeli asked.

"You are so embarrassing," Dr. Taylor muttered, frustrated. "Um, Elena, this is my daughter, Shaeli." she said with a small smile.

I looked at Dr. Taylor, then at Shaeli. They had the same color hair and chestnut eyes. But it *could not* have been her daughter. They seemed around the same age. It felt much more likely that Sheali was her sister or something.

"Uh, not to be nosey or anything, but I don't think that's possible," I said shakily. I couldn't help sounding a little nervous.

"And why not?" Shaeli asked, her hands on her hips.

"Oh." Dr. Taylor giggled. "Fae don't grow much physically after turning the age of eighteen. I'm really one hundred and thirty-one years old."

I stood, staring.

Sure, why not? Magic is real. Fae are real. Why not have her be one hundred and thirty-one years old?

"Wait, did you not know that?" Shaeli asked. This girl was *really* obnoxious. She began laughing. "Wow. You must be the dumbest fae ever! How could you not know that?"

"Shaeli!" Dr. Taylor snapped. She jerked her daughter toward her. Dr. Taylor began whispering in the girl's ear.

Shaeli's face dropped in confusion. Her eyes widened in revelation.

"You mean she—um, okay." Shaeli took one suspicious look at me before she stepped into the elevator and left.

I didn't understand. Couldn't understand. Didn't *want* to understand. There were too many bombs being dropped. Just trying to comprehend everything was giving me a migraine.

Before anyone could say anything more, I decided to speak up.

"Please," I said, turning toward Dr. Taylor and Mr. Anderson. "This is all…Just let me leave, please."

"And go where?" Mr. Anderson asked. "To another human foster family that will just reject you in a year? Listen, I—*we*—finally found you. Apparently, so have those people. You are no longer safe."

"I don't under—"

"You can no longer be with the humans," he said, interrupting me. "We should have…should have taken you out earlier so that you could do the Ritual, but we did not know where you were. We have arrangements ready to be able to take you into our village. You need to be with others like you. You need to be with fae."

Was the guy really asking me to let him take me to his village?

I believe that this is the epitome of kidnapping.

"Sweetie, try to understand. We are only trying to help you," Dr. Taylor said.

I squeezed my wrist.

This is all too much. It can't be real. Should I give him a chance to explain and—no. I can't do this.

"I'm sorry. I just *can't*. Please, let me leave, and then leave me alone."

"But—" Mr. Anderson began.

Dr. Taylor put her hand on his shoulder. "Let her go," she said softly.

His expression dropped, and his eyes became glassy. He seemed distraught. Mr. Anderson backed into the hall behind him and turned away from us so we couldn't see his face.

"You can go. Do you want to be taken to the station?"
Dr. Taylor asked me.

Was she really going to let me go? Just like that?

Maybe these people aren't really as bad as I thought.

"No, thank you. I can get there myself."

She gave me a simple nod and then went to talk to
Mr. Anderson. I stepped toward the elevator and pressed the
one button on the outside with an arrow pointing up. When
the doors automatically closed, with me inside, I could see
Dr. Taylor trying to comfort Mr. Anderson.

Why is he so upset?

The elevator took me to the surface, but I felt the
slightest bit of guilt.

Am I responsible for his distress?

World Upside Down

The "hospital" must have been below ground. Exiting the elevator, I found myself in an abandoned house. A totally *not* creepy place those people had taken me to.

I was numb and confused. It was hard, while I tried to ignore the previous events, to focus on getting to the police station. I waited by the side of the road, wondering what to do.

After standing around for about an hour, an old guy pulled up beside me and asked if I needed a ride. I ended up hitchhiking with a total stranger, which was freaking me out for, well, obvious reasons. But I didn't know where I was, so I wasn't exactly given a choice.

He tried talking to me, but I couldn't focus on anything. I was barely able to whisper where I needed to go. My eyes just stared blankly at the window while my head went crazy with theories and thoughts. Thankfully, he didn't steal me or anything.

After I got to the police station, I sat in a chair in the waiting room, seeing if anyone would notice me there.

Other than resting in shock, I didn't know how to proceed. I wasn't sure if I should have gone up to someone, seeking help. There was a lot of hustle and bustle going on around me. Apparently, there had been multiple acts of terrorism, not just the exploding cruise ship.

Everyone was running around, crossing my line of sight. Yelling echoed through the building. The officers were mad at forensics, and the civilians were complaining that nobody was paying any attention to them. The stress and panic in the air was palpable.

While I sat there, perplexed, I began thinking about those people, what happened on the boat with the captain, and my dream. The world around me seemed to be out of reach, out of sight. I looked around, but nothing felt the same.

It took a while before anyone noticed I was there. A lady came over to me, wearing a uniform. At the corner of her uniform, it said "Social Services" right above her name, "Ellen Rose."

"Miss? What are you doing here? Where are your parents?" she asked.

Her voice sounded like an echo to me. It didn't feel real. Nothing did.

"I am a survivor of a cruise ship explosion," I

murmured. My words seemed to fade as soon as they left my mouth.

The lady's face dropped as soon as I said that. She was trying to talk to me, but with everything going on, I couldn't pay attention to what she said. Maybe she told me just to wait there. It looked like that was what she was gesturing. At least, that was what I thought. She kept on waving her hands downward, like she wanted me to stay.

What happened next felt like a blur.

She left, returned with another officer, talked to them, left, and then came back within what felt like a few seconds, with me so caught up in the past events repeating in my head. I was still sinking in the ocean, with a multitude of my bones broken, still standing in the hospital, watching while Mr. Anderson turned the room into a forest.

Nothing drew my attention, that is, until she touched me. It took a little bit of shaking, but when she finally broke through my daze, I looked up.

"Okay, let me explain what's going on. Um, you seem to be the only survivor from that incident. Some people will be coming to ask you questions. Are you okay with that?" she asked, concerned.

With everything going on, do they seriously want my answers?

"I'm sorry. No," I muttered.

What would I tell them? Someone found me, took me

to their friend's, and then said that they were fae? That I was a fae? That everything I ever knew had been wrong? I tried telling myself that perhaps it had all just been derived from my imagination—I mean, I *was* just a kid. But I knew it wasn't true. It was all real.

"All right. That's going to be difficult. Okay, because you don't want that, we are going to just take the next step and return you to your family. We'll have to ask you questions later on, though. We can give you a week to recoup, max. Where do you live?"

I softly groaned. I had almost forgotten the problem that was the foster system.

"My foster family is dead."

The lady's face instantly fell. "Oh, sweetie, I am so sorry. That's right. They died in the…incident, didn't they?" She looked around, trying to find an answer. "Foster family, huh? You're in the foster system?"

I sadly nodded. As if it wasn't enough to be confused by all the recent revelations, I was forced to deal with the problem of fostering.

"Um, okay. I suppose the next step will be to put you back into the system. Follow me."

Great. I get to spin the wheel again for what kind of family I'll be placed with next.

Ms. Rose pulled me over to her desk to see who I would get next. She pulled up a phone number and tried to call, waiting a while for someone to pick up, but she kept on being sent to voicemail. Eventually, Ms. Rose gave up and instead pulled up an address on her computer. She wrote it down on a piece of paper.

"We're going to get into my car, and I'll escort you over to your new home."

"Who am I staying with?" I asked.

"Um, well, it's a change of pace for you…I—I'll tell you about it on the way there, 'kay?"

*All right, then…*Maybe she meant that they would be an entirely nice family. Or just mostly nice. Any change of pace had to be good.

She led me over to her car, and I climbed into the backseat. Not everything seemed out of focus anymore. No, it just seemed useless. Meaningless. I doubted everything and anything I had known.

My lack of understanding left me in a heavy gloom, but in spite of the futility, I went along with it anyways.

I thought I would ask Ms. Rose what she had meant before once she started driving, but she beat me to the chase.

"Listen, dear…You've been in a lot of families. I'm not gonna lie. The system says that you have been in around eight families." Her words faded out, and she looked through the rearview mirror at me. There was pity on her face. "And, um, well…you aren't going to another foster family."

I shot a look at her.

"Wait, what?" I asked, leaning forward. "Where am I going?"

"You're going to a group home, Elena. We think that this, perhaps, will be a better solution for you."

"'We' who?"

"'We' meaning me. I read your files. You have been—eh—*transferred* out of a lot of families," she said, acting like using a different word would hide the one she was trying to avoid: rejected. "In fact, every family you have been in, you've been transferred out of. And each time you are transferred out, there are fewer and fewer people willing to take you, especially since you are growing older. People are more likely to take in a two-year-old rather than a tween. By the way, you *are* twelve now, right?"

My heart sank. This lady was literally saying that no one wanted me.

"You understand, don't you? I don't mean anything against you. I just think you could be happier in a group home."

I fell back into the seat. A group home. That would mean I would be crammed in a house with a bunch of kids. Apprehension pulled at me. I knew in the bottom of my gut that this wasn't going to go well.

We pulled up to a really fancy house that could have only been owned by rich people. It was sandy tan, with a mahogany roof. Eight windows graced the front of the house. On the right, a double garage extended. The house had two stories, at least. In front of the house was a green—most likely fake—lawn, with spots of dirt holding different plants.

Great. Snooty rich people. Maybe since the kids are orphans too, they'll be nice.

Ms. Rose led me out of her car and toward the house. We knocked on the right door. I slowly moved behind the officer.

What if they don't accept me?

The door slowly opened a crack, and a man peeked his head out. His hair was a messy mop, and he had a tense smile. Through the crack came a bunch of clamor and children screaming. I couldn't tell if it was with laughter or pain.

"Um, morning. How can I help you?" he nervously asked Ms. Rose.

The man was Middle Eastern, with a slight accent. He darted his eyes down to me. Immediately, his body relaxed, and he opened the door a little more, revealing a wrinkled white shirt and tan khakis. His eyes widened and his smile grew, shy but kind.

"Oh, hello. Who are you?" he asked.

"Hello, Mr. Amin," said Ms. Rose. "I understand that this is very short notice, but I tried to call and couldn't get through. I was wondering if you were willing to, perhaps, take in another?"

I didn't even get a chance to speak.

"Oh, um, well…Yes, this is quite sudden." Mr. Amin looked at her wearily. "We are really full. Sophie is about to move out. Could you maybe wait a couple of weeks?"

Seriously? Another rejection. *Wow, just my luck.*

"Mr. Amin, she has nowhere to go. We cannot wait two weeks. Again, I do apologize for asking you this so suddenly, but she needs a place to stay *today*. If you can't hold her, I completely understand. We have more than one group home. I only came to you because I know that you are always willing, but if we had been taking advantage of that, then I will move on."

Mr. Amin appeared troubled. The gears were turning in his head. "Uh—uh," he stammered. "Give me a second."

He closed the door and went inside. I looked up at Ms. Rose. A smile was growing on her face. When she glanced at me, she bent down and whispered into my ear.

"That's how you get things done. This man is very nice. I have no doubt that he'll take very good care of you."

Mr. Amin came back out, and Ms. Rose straightened. He opened the door all the way.

"I am sorry for my hesitation. Of course, she can stay here. The more, the merrier! We have a space for you here."

I let out a relieved sigh. Mr. Amin put his gentle hand on my back and led me inside.

Smile for the Bruises

The interior was even more sleek than the outside. Before me was a white staircase leading to the second floor. Slick black rails lined the steps up, and each step had a plate of polished wood. Hundreds of pictures hung on the white wall curving along the staircase.

Every picture was of a different child Mr. Amin must have fostered. But none of his wife.

Man, one parent and tons of children? No wonder he looks burnt out.

"Let's get the others. I would like you to introduce yourself to us," he said.

Right then, he whistled with a piercing shrill. I was surprised I didn't go deaf. Almost immediately, a herd of kids—seemingly ages four to eighteen—came from all around the house. They ran in like a stampede and gathered in front of us. There were so many of them that I felt like I was right back in school.

"I would like you all to do introductions. Each one of you will take turns saying your names and ages. Let's start from youngest to oldest," Mr. Amin said.

The smallest was a girl. She had black pigtails and lightly tanned skin. Her smile glowed between two dimples.

"My name is Evy, and I am four years old, and I can't wait to play with you!" she said.

I couldn't help but grin.

The next child stepped up. He was a little boy with hazelnut skin and bushy black hair. "I'm Diego. I am six and a half years old, and I am really cool," he said with attitude.

I chuckled softly. "Of course, you are."

He nodded sharply in agreement. Seeing each of them was a much needed break from the stress I had been in. Each kid took a turn, one at a time. Yet it got a little less cute and more awkward the older they were.

A girl cleared her throat. She was a little older than me.

"My name is Kylie, and don't think that I'm a kid." She gave me a glare that froze my blood. Her voice eerily reminded me of one of my classmates. She instantly sent shivers down my spine.

Another kid stood beside her. "I'm Kyle. We're in charge." He looked exactly like his sister, just the male version. "We're thirteen."

They walked back in tandem.

About five more kids introduced themselves. A few seemed as vicious as Kylie and Kyle. A couple were in their teens. Even though the little ones were cute, the others were like giants to me.

After all the children presented themselves, Mr. Amin said, "Very good. And I am Yussif Amin. I will not be sharing my age." He gave me a quick wink and a smile. "What's your name?"

"Oh, um…My name is Elena. I'm twelve," I wearily answered, avoiding eye contact with the others.

"Thank you. It is nice to meet you, Elena."

Mr. Amin seemed genuinely happy that I was going to be with them. I could not say the same for the teenagers.

"You may all go," he told the children.

Immediately, chatter ensued, and the little ones ran. The house returned to its chaotic state.

Mr. Amin turned to me and said, "Let's get you situated, hm?"

He led me up the stairs to a small room. In the middle, taking up half the space, was a bunk bed.

Oh great. I have to share such a little room?

But no, it was worse than that.

Kylie snuck up behind me. She was so silent that I didn't even know she was there until a low growl came from behind me. My heart quite nearly jumped out of my chest.

"What? This is mine and Kyle's room!" she screamed, almost blowing out my eardrum. *"Kyle! Get over here!"*

He arrived so fast I almost thought he teleported. On the other hand, it wouldn't have been the weirdest thing I had just gone through.

"Why is the new kid in our room?" he asked, glaring at Mr. Amin.

Mr. Amin gave him a strained grin in return, but it seemed odd. It was almost as if he was afraid of the twins, but then again, those two were much scarier than Tweedledee and Tweedledum.

"She…will be staying here," he hesitantly told them.

Instantly, the rants, complaints, and insults began.

Mr. Amin winced. "Oh—okay, okay. Let's calm down now, shall we?" he squeaked between words.

They shared a nasty look and temporarily stopped.

"Good. Thank you. Now, the three of you are around the same age. And this is the emptiest bedroom we have. You both know that the others share rooms with three of their siblings. Can we try to get along?"

Again, they looked each other in the eyes, but this

time, they shared a malevolent smirk. My stomach sank. I had a feeling if they were happy, then someone was about to get hurt, and I was the new kid.

"Sure...We'll share." Kyle perked up. "Don't worry. We'll take good care of her."

Mr. Amin gave a small smile and left us. He left *me*.

Great, I am all alone with Scary and Scarier.

They brushed past me with those ghoulish grins and walked into their room. I knew I would never be able to relax again. It wasn't like I just had to sleep with one eye open. No, I would have to sleep standing up, with a wooden stake in my hands.

***

Exhaustion, fatigue, and fear riddled my face, along with a few bruises and a black eye. It had only been one day since I arrived, and I had been "welcomed" into the family with punches and bullying.

Of course, I couldn't tell Mr. Amin. He was a pushover, just as scared of them as I was. All the kids had him wrapped around their little fingers.

The younger ones were sweet and kind, but they were innocent and only saw the best in everyone, including their siblings. It was the kids who were thirteen to sixteen who didn't like me. The older ones were too cool and mature to get into such trivial problems. Either that or they were too busy with social media.

I couldn't just sleep it off either. The twins loved taking shifts throughout the night, just to make sure I didn't get any rest. Their favorite tricks would include kicking me by "accident" or dumping a cup of water on me in passing.

That didn't really matter, though. Even if someone hadn't been there, I wouldn't have been able to sleep anyway.

Not only was my mind always at work, trying to absorb this big change in my life, but I had to sleep on the floor. The cold, hard floor. I didn't have any pillows or blankets, thanks to the twins.

I found out Mr. Amin was almost always on the phone or in his study. Apparently, he worked from home twenty-four-seven. This didn't mean that he kept himself from helping us, though.

While he meandered around the house on different calls, every now and then, he would break up a fight over a toy or something between a couple of the younger kids. Due to this, the teenagers knew better and would deal with matters in a room behind a locked door.

That was where my torture would happen.

It was the weekend, so thankfully, I didn't have to go to school. But that was not to say that place was any better than school. There were times when I would have preferred to be at the place where I would be bullied by my classmates. At the very least, in school, there would be witnesses. "Home" didn't have that.

By the time dusk came, I was covered in injuries. The others would intercept me before I could go outside, so I was trapped inside the house. I had to watch the sunset from the window of my tiny room. My stupid, crowded, freaking tiny room.

At least the colors that painted the sky comforted me. I leaned on the windowsill. No one was bugging me.

Heh. The twins must be busy with something.

I had silence and peace. With the beauty of nature relaxing me, my eyes drift closed.

Before I was able to dream, a memory came back to haunt me.

I remembered the alleyway and Mr. Anderson. They had a place ready for me. *Had they really assumed I would just leave with two weird strangers?*

Then I thought about the house. I would probably go into a new school on Monday, where I would be pushed around for no reason if the past was any indication of the future. And I would come back here, where I would be bullied *again*, but this time, by "family."

A desperate idea sparked.

I opened my eyes. The night had fallen, and the stars shone like fireflies. *I can't do it tonight. It's too late.* I hugged myself in reassurance. *Tomorrow. I'll get Mr. Amin to let me go on my walk.*

Hope comforted me. That night, I slept soundly, despite the failed attempts from the twins.

Everything happened just as I expected the following day. I got beat up, insulted, and bullied. Others forced me to do their chores for them. I pushed through, hoping for light at the end of the tunnel.

Later, I told Mr. Amin about my daily habit of walking at sundown, and he said I could continue if it made me happy. There it was. My permission to go out by myself, completely and utterly alone. I could get away from my "family" forever.

I couldn't wait until dusk.

A Desperate Idea

Beads of sweat rolled down my back, and my lungs worked overtime. I ran as fast as I could for as far as I could. The sand slowed me down a little, as did the lack of light from the half-set sun.

I tripped several times, but I forced myself to get back up, unwilling to stop for anything. Of course, I was only able to go so far. I soon stumbled on my own feet and fell hard on the gritty ground.

Wow, I really need to work out more.

It didn't matter if I got up. I was backed against the wall of sand and rock.

My lungs heaved for more air.

Any minute now. Any minute now…

Mr. Anderson appeared out of nowhere, wielding his staff. He was wearing the same hoodie from the time in the alleyway. I couldn't see his face—his hood cast thick shadows on it—but I knew it was him.

Mr. Anderson darted his head back and forth, trying

to find the person who was chasing me.

"Wow, you are really gullible." I chuckled and stood up, brushing the sand off and straightening my posture.

"What?" Mr. Anderson asked, cocking his head to the side. "Is there not someone after you? Or—"

"Well, let's take a look, shall we?" I mockingly looked left and right. "Gosh." I feigned surprise. "It seems like no one is here." Pride filled my chest, and a smug smile grew on my face.

"You faked it? Why would you fake this?" Annoyance sounded in his voice.

"Why?" My smile disappeared as I gathered the courage to voice the pains I harbored. "The truth is, I've been placed in a group home. Now, it's like school but all the time. Hated everywhere I look. Really, I would rather be in a stinkin' foster home, but I've been rejected too much. It's also bugging me that there is a whole lot of stuff that I don't know about. I mean, if there are other intelligent species, and they live right here on Earth…And we just think that they're fairy tales."

He lowered his staff. "All of the theatrics were because…"

"Because I remember you telling me that you are watching me—which is really creepy, by the way. But because of this, I thought that the only way to get your attention was to—"

"Pretend like you were in trouble," he said, finishing my sentence.

He pulled up his sleeve and clicked a button on his watch. The shadows covering his face instantly lessened, and he flipped his hood back.

His black hair was messed up, thanks to his hood. Mr. Anderson's smile was sweet and comforting. It melted me. I knew it then. He *wanted* me to choose to be with him. That was why he had been so disappointed when I rejected him before.

But his grin was a little odd. It made me think he was proud of me or something. It creeped me out a little. But if I gave him a chance, maybe I would find a better solution than that group home. A break from the cycle I'd been stuck in.

That was how much I wanted things to change. No matter what would happen, I was never going to be the same. I yearned for that.

He turned away and waved for me to follow. "My dear, are you coming or not?"

Okay, I thought. *Here we go.*

Some Proper Introductions

Nope! This was a bad idea!

My knees were shaking, and my stomach was doing somersaults. Mr. Anderson had shown me to his motorcycle, where I was clinging to his back while he rode away. I was trembling. Neither of us wore helmets. When I asked him why, all he told me was that his cycle was much safer than any normal human vehicle—whatever that meant.

He pushed a button, and crystals were launched from the cycle. A portal—much like the others I had seen before—formed in front of us, and we drove right through it. When we went in, every fiber of my body tingled. It was as if a wave of electricity had passed through me, channeling to a part of me I hadn't known was there.

After we came out, my head pounded, and my stomach lurched. I slowly got off. It would definitely take a bit before I could walk straight.

Mr. Anderson tried to help steady me. "I forgot to tell you…Going through a rift for the first time is usually hard on a fae. You will get your bearings in a minute."

I gave him the best sneer I could muster. "Oh, really? 'Hard'? Man, well, I didn't notice anything between the intense *nausea* and *dizziness*."

"Sorry." He scratched the back of his head and stared at the ground.

His eyebrows gathered together, and a slight frown formed on his face. Mr. Anderson really did seem sorry, which made me feel a little guilty for yelling at him. Just a little, mind you. This guy seemed determined to put me through every mind-blowing and disorienting experience possible, so I had every right to be mad at him.

"Well, I know that was an unpleasant trip, but I would like to welcome you to my home," Mr. Anderson said, trying to change the subject.

I looked up and nearly gasped. His house was two stories tall and made of stone. It had clean-cut wood for the roof and stairs leading to the door. A porch laid beautifully in front of the main door. Most of the walls had at least one floor-to-ceiling window.

The inside was lit by yellow lights, showing off the interior through the windows. Even an evergreen forest peeked out behind the home. The whole place had an aura of security.

Oh, yeah. I could get used to this.

"Do you like it?" Mr. Anderson asked.

"This place is *amazing*. I didn't know you were rich. Although, I guess I should've known something along that, seeing how you dress. Especially at that hospital."

"What is wrong with how I dress?"

He unzipped his white hoodie, revealing his cream-white tunic with metallic green filigree adorning the trim. It was tucked into his blue jeans, which appeared tacky combined with his top.

I rolled my eyes. Mr. Anderson looked at his tunic, then back at me. I, on the other hand, was wearing a wrinkled white T-shirt and powder-blue denim jeans, both of which were a size too big since they were Kylie's clothes. All my stuff had been lost in the explosion.

Mr. Anderson chuckled. "Oh, I see. No, I am not rich. Fae do not have different classes in terms of money. My tunic is normal clothing. Well, by our standards. The jeans were to blend in with humans."

"No different social classes? No poor or anything?"

Sounds kinda utopian…

It probably shouldn't have surprised me so much, but it was hard for me to imagine a society without the struggles.

"I did not say that. I said that we do not have

different classes in terms of *money*. Currency isn't as important to us as it is to humans."

"What? But you have money, right? How do you get essentials? Do you not buy things?"

Mr. Anderson wasn't paying full attention to me. He was looking away, taking out a hexagonal glowing tile from the dashboard of the cycle and putting it in his hoodie pocket.

"For the most part, we do not *buy* things. Everything is shared. Well, I guess that is more accurate for the Tribes. For Independents, we each produce something to be traded."

He walked over to his home. "For example, as you can see, I have a forest behind my house. When needed, I can forage for items there. Whatever I do not use, I share with other Independents, and they do vice versa. Other than that, if I am in need of food that I cannot get from my community, then I use money to purchase from Tribes. Or I use human money to buy something in their stores."

"That can't possibly be a reliable system."

"It *is* much harder for Independents because we do not have the Ancients providing for us. However, this also means that we do not have them breathing down our necks, fitting us with others who have the same Gifts and documenting every movement we make. They give us some freedom, and we get to provide for ourselves." Mr. Anderson stared forlornly at his house. "It is also much easier when you live by yourself."

His shoulders sagged, and a gloomy aura surrounded us. I wanted to comfort him. He looked like he needed a hug or something. But really, considering that this was still a stranger who had basically kidnapped me and made me doubt everything, I thought it would be a little awkward if I hugged him.

Fortunately, we didn't stand there for long. Soon, Mr. Anderson looked at me and gave me a smile.

"But now, I will be taking care of a sweet girl. I am up for the challenge if you are."

I cracked a grin. Was I up to the challenge? The question wasn't if *I* was up to the challenge of dealing with *him*, but rather, was *he* truly up to the challenge of dealing with "sweet" old *me*?

I chuckled. "I'm up to any challenge. The harder, the better." I gave him a glare and a smirk as a playful warning.

I didn't think he understood, though, because he stared at me. "I do not think I—"

"Don't worry about it," I said, interrupting him. "So, are you going to show me into your house or not?"

Mr. Anderson shot me a curious look, then led me toward his home. He pulled up his sleeve, pressing his thumb on the face of the watch. It flashed green, and a lock clicked. He turned the knob, opened the door, and walked in.

Even though I was able to see the interior from the outside, it still felt like walking into a different world. There was a couch and matching chairs on both sides, all of it surrounding a glass coffee table. The walls were a birch color, and dark oak beams supported the ceiling. However, there was an apparent emptiness. Despite the furniture, there was an abundance of negative space.

A wooden staircase led to the second floor. To my left was the kitchen. Externally, the place had felt inviting, but I could tell that despondency had taken root inside. Even though I hadn't known Mr. Anderson for long, the place instantly reminded me of him. But I was confused about something.

"Do you live in this giant place all by yourself?" I wasn't sure if fae just liked living alone in big, empty houses, but it didn't make sense to me.

He stared at his feet. "Yes, but that wasn't always true. We bought this land with the aid of the Ancients and had built this place when we got married."

I was surprised. "Married? *You* are married?"

He is only what, twenty? That feels a little young to be married.

Mr. Anderson gave a sad chuckle and a slight grin, almost reading my mind. "You *do* realize that I am one hundred and twenty-four years old, right?"

Oh, that's right. Fae stop aging at eighteen or something. Isn't Dr. Taylor over a century old as well?

"Sorry. You just—"

"Look nineteen? Twenty? That sounds right in human eyes. But to answer your previous question, yes, I was married." The smile disappeared, and his features softened.

"I'm sorry. *Was?*"

He slightly tilted his head away so I couldn't see his face. "That's right. My wife died a few years ago."

Oh… It was no wonder he owned the house but lived by himself. *He and his wife probably wanted to have a family when they first moved in.* My heart felt sorry for him.

"Before we continue, there are two things I want to tell you." His voice was solemn, and the gloominess almost entirely melted from his face. "Number one: Do not go around pitying me. And do not deny that you are. I can see it. It has been years, and I try *very* hard to not linger in the past." Mr. Anderson gave me a slight grin. "Two: You should know that my name is not actually Gabriel Anderson."

"What do you mean? So you lied?" I asked, although it wasn't like I knew his first name earlier anyway.

"Well, *I* technically did not. Kaylessa did, and she did not even say that was my name. She just introduced me with that name."

What? All right. Now he's just throwing names around.

"Who's Kaylessa?"

"Oh, I meant Dr. Taylor. Okay…Maybe we should sit down before I get into this. I am sure you exhausted yourself with that little act at the beach."

He took off his sweater and hung it on a hook behind the front door. Mr. Anderson—err, *not* Mr. Anderson—led me to the couch and sat at the end, waiting for me.

Oi, I really have to relearn everything, don't I?

I sighed and dragged my tired butt over to the couch.

"Okay. I sat down. Happy? Now, what are you talking about?"

He cracked a small smile. "Kids today are impatient. You should learn how to wait. Patience *is* a virtue."

Dude, seriously? Okay, now I can see how he's over a century old. "Yeah, sure. Whatever." I said it with such an extreme eye roll that I almost saw my brain.

He gave me a hearty laugh. My annoyance increased exponentially steadily as his entertainment did.

"Okay, okay. Calm down." He looked me in the eye but retained his smile. "Now, my name is Gabriel Anderson just as much as Dr. Taylor's name is Catherine Taylor. These are our human names. So, when a fae turns ten years of age, they create a human name, in case they would ever need to work in the human public. But these are not the names we are given at birth. My real name is Leorn Lavadan. Dr. Taylor's is Kaylessa Heiwys."

"Wait, wait, wait. So, your name is Lord Lavadon?"

He stifled laughter before correcting me. "No. You are pronouncing it wrong. My name is pronounced more like 'l-OR-n LA-vah-dahn'. Leorn Lavadan."

"Right…I'm going to call you Mr. Lavadon 'cause your first name just sounds like 'lord', and I really don't want to call you that."

He shook his head. "You are still not quite pronouncing it right, but I am good with that."

Yeah, I wasn't really happy with Mr. What's-his-name. This guy was basically full of contradictions.

He looks nineteen, but he's really over a century old. "Mr. Anderson"? Now, why would I think that was his name? It's not like he told me that it was. Oh, wait. He did. Instead, his name is something that no one can pronounce.

It felt as if he was trying to somehow confuse me more than I already was. But on the plus side, it was fun to mispronounce his name.

"You will live here, with me, in one of the guest bedrooms," he said.

"Well, why do I have to stay with you? Why can't I live with Dr. Taylor?" I didn't understand why I had to stay here and not with her. In my defense, she was really nice, soft, and sweet, whereas he was kind of odd and uncomfortable to be around.

"Oh, do you want to live with Kaylessa? She does not live alone, you know. She lives with her husband, Taelin, and with her daughter, Shaeli. You have met Shaeli already, so I think you will agree with me when I say that she is pretty, esh, *difficult*. But if you want to live there…"

"Well…" I pondered. Even though Dr. Taylor was really nice, her daughter was pretty obnoxious. It also seemed like their house was crowded enough without me in it. "I think I would like to stay here."

His shoulders seemed to relax. "I would like that too."

It wasn't just because of Dr. Taylor's full house that I wanted to stay. I remembered what Mr. Lavadan had gone through and felt for him. This guy had lost his wife and then lived alone. I was hoping my mere presence was comforting. But if it all went wrong, I could probably wiggle out. My ways had yet to fail me.

"I should probably show you to your room. Come with me." Mr. Lavadan got up from the couch.

I followed him up the stairs. When we entered the hall, I noticed all the lights were already on.

"Did you really leave your house with everything on?" I asked.

"Well, I did not think I would be long. I did not expect the 'emergency' to be faked and you to come back with me." He looked at me and chuckled. "You know, you are pretty unpredictable."

"I'm taking that as a compliment." I gave him a grin, and he cracked up.

There were four doors around us: two to the right and two to the left. The walls were walnut brown, and there were torch-like lights at both sides.

"I hope you can make yourself comfortable here. This one's yours." Mr. Lavadan led me down the hall and opened the door to our left.

As soon as I saw the room, a warmth sparked in my chest. Whenever I moved in with a new family, I was always given the worst rooms. They were either too small and cramped or barely insulated and next to the washing machines. One time, I had to sleep in the living room because the house didn't have another bedroom. But this room wasn't anything like that. It was spacious and beautiful.

Light flooded the room, thanks to the floor-to-ceiling windows making up the entire right wall. The rest of the room was a light tan, almost white, with brown wooden lining. A mint green twin bed faced the door, framed perfectly by a sheer metallic gold curtain draped over it.

At the left was a tall bookshelf, but something was off about it. When I looked closer at the titles on the spines, I noticed they were in a different language. It seemed as if they had runes on them. They were simpler than hieroglyphics but definitely more complicated than the English alphabet.

Of course, they would be in a different language. I wonder how many fae speak English.

My curiosity got the better of me, and I asked Mr. Lavadan, "What kinds of books are these?"

"Why, they are history books."

"History? How boring," I groaned. "Do you expect me to read all of these?"

He chuckled. "Maybe one day you will read them all, but I do not expect you to read them right away, especially because you cannot read them. My expectations *will* go up after I teach you our language, but please, do not be so against the idea of studying them."

He walked over to the books and touched a few. "The stories in these books are not the history that you are thinking of. I can promise you that."

"Whatever. History is history, and history is *boring*."

Mr. Lavadan seemed slightly disappointed. I decided to change the topic.

"What language is this anyway?"

"They're written in Voliun. It might look a little odd to you, but I will help you."

"Voliun?"

He nodded. "Fae language. You will learn how to speak and read it…later." He walked toward the door.

"Listen, it has been a long day. There is a lot to get to, but it can wait until the morn."

"'The morn'? Seriously?"

"The *morning*. Does that make you feel better?" Mr. Lavadan began closing the door. "There should be a set of pajamas in your closet. Good night, my dear." He turned off the lights and shut the door.

The crisp moonlight was the only thing illuminating my new room.

The snark melted away from my face, and my sarcasm faded. I stood there, in the middle of my room, soaking it all in. Now that I was by myself in silence, I could process everything.

Since I was always in a new home, I shouldn't have been so shocked, but this was different. I had left everything for this opportunity, and I wondered if Mr. Amin even noticed I was missing.

After staring at the closed door for a minute or so, a fog rolled into my mind. A fog of new memories. My brain tried playing every recent second all at once.

One thing at a time, I told myself. *Just take it one thing at a time.*

I looked around me but saw no closet. With a sigh, I grumbled to myself and began the search for it.

I swear, if there's no closet, I'm gonna make sure Mr.

Lavadan regrets it.

But soon, I found it. One small handle was attached to the wall between the bookshelf and the corner of the room. I opened it, and a light turned on, temporarily blinding me. When I regained my vision, I walked in.

A mirror stood in front of me, with an empty clothes rack to my left. To my right was a set of drawers. Yet the whole closet seemed empty.

That makes sense, seeing as this was no one's room before, but didn't he tell me that there were clothes for me?

I began looking in the drawers, where I found a light blue dress, folded up.

What? I thought that he said there were pajamas in here.

I closed that drawer and opened the one below. It contained a leather vest and cuffs, a dark blue tunic, and navy blue pants. I laughed to myself.

What kind of clothing is this? It definitely wasn't pajamas.

I put on the dress. Immediately, it was incredibly uncomfortable. The material was thick on my torso yet didn't keep my legs warm at all. I had never sweat and shivered at the same time before. And the itch was instant, surely giving me a rash. I hated it and decided I would cut my losses and sleep in Kylie's clothes. At least those were somewhat comfortable.

I got redressed and flopped on my bed, no longer sitting in stagnant anxiety. I didn't have any more mental strength to harbor any apprehension. With a bit of surrender, I quickly decided that whatever would happen from there on was out of my control. Worrying did no good, except to burden me more.

The exhaustion and fatigue set in. It only took a few blinks until my eyelids shut. I turned to my side and felt the coolness of my pillow on my ear. The tension that had built up in my limbs relaxed. I took one last look at the moonlit forest out my window while I sank into darkness.

***

My whole body was trembling. Cloaked people were chasing after me, wielding weapons, cornering me. The pain of the debris and fire hit me from the explosion. Fear and anxiety filled my body. It was never-ending torture caused by my own mind.

I didn't have nightmares much, if at all, and I almost never dreamed. Every second was as though I was reliving the destruction, with the terror and agony amplified tenfold.

I sat on the floor, holding myself, in the corner of my mind. My eyes were clenched shut while I tried to escape my own memories. Then, to my surprise, everything went silent.

I slowly opened my eyes in apprehension, wondering what awaited me, but all I saw was black. Had I not been able to make out my hands, I would have thought my eyes were still closed. I was the only thing with color in this place.

In fact, it seemed as if I was glowing. A slight pearly aura consumed my body, leaving me the only source of light.

I glanced down at the reflection of myself in the cold, hard floor. It was so crisp and clear that it seemed like there was no ground. I tried to stand up, but the lack of orientation in the complete blackness caused me to be wobbly. Once I finally steadied myself, I noticed something rather off-putting.

Out of the corner of my eye, the darkness was moving, but if I tried to look at it, I could see nothing. The whole place gave me the creeps. Even though it wasn't the chaotic and horrifying pain I had just been in, I could have gone insane from the pure amount of fear the place instilled in me.

"Well, that was traumatic."

I instantly jumped. My heart skipped a beat. My landing wasn't quite so graceful, and I struggled to rebalance myself. My chest pounded while I turned around to see who had spoken to me.

The darkness twisted and accumulated until it created a blob of sorts. The shape formed itself into a woman.

She had completely pale skin, resembling a corpse. Her hair was straight and so black that I couldn't differentiate it from her surroundings.

The same thing happened when I looked at her clothes. They reminded me of a raven. She wore a one-shoulder Renaissance dress, which only went as far as her mid-thigh, but the tail in the back hit the floor. Underneath, she had on black tights and no shoes; her pale stood in complete contrast from her surroundings.

It was as if she was completely grayscale. Fitting with the theme, her lipstick was black, and she had raccoon-ish eyes. They were surrounded by a smokey black, like she had way too much messy eye shadow. However, the more I looked at it, the more it just seemed natural.

Something strong radiated from her, but I couldn't tell what it was.

"Did I frighten you?" she asked, staring at me.

Her eyes were deep and dark. When she looked at me, a shiver went up my spine.

Her voice was as empty as her eyes, but yet it still held an odd sound. It wasn't like Mr. Lavadan's, but was instead akin to whispering. She barely pronounced any harsh letters and over-emphasized the soft syllables. Almost like a snake.

I hesitantly nodded, and a grin grew on her face.

"Didn't mean to," she said. "Although, it was quite fun to see you jump."

I mustered my breath enough to ask, "Who are you? Where am I?" My voice trembled with every word.

"Oh, please. Stop." She winced as if I had hit her. The woman rushed up to me until only an inch of breathing room remained between us, with me still frozen in place. "I'm really trying hard to leave you be, so don't you go making it difficult."

She backed up a bit and crossed her arms.

"I probably should've led with my name. You can call me Umbra." She placed a hand on her chest. "And you probably already know this place." Umbra gestured toward our environment and rolled her head to follow her hand.

"W-what do you mean?" I asked.

She rolled her eyes and sighed. "'The Abyss,' 'The Void,' 'Shadow Realm'…This place has many names. You can call it Afautiya." She once again locked eyes with me. "It is my *prison*. You were trapped here just a bit ago."

Almost dismissing me, she looked away and placed her hand on her hips.

"What can I say, though? Your nightmares were so overly dramatic, and you were suffering too much from them."

That's right. I am dreaming. My heart settled down with this comforting thought. *None of this is real, and it is definitely better than it was a moment ago.*

I looked at her once more with fresh eyes, silently chuckling to myself.

I've been through a lot recently. Why not relax a little and play along? What can she do to me?

I straightened myself and fixed my clothes. "Well, thank you for whatever you did. It was kind of you to help me."

"Ha! You think I did that for *you*? Do you know how hard it is to resist it when you make it so strong?" Umbra turned toward me and scanned my face. "Huh, you actually got it under control right now. Now, *this* is how a guest should behave."

"What?"

She was full of riddles and ambiguous words. Even though her vernacular wasn't very sophisticated, it was plenty cryptic. Breaking my train of thought, my skin's glow intensified.

"What's happening?"

"Why, you're waking up. You had spent most of the night in that nightmare of yours. *Tsk*. I do hate how the day enslaves people…heh, says the slave." Umbra turned around to walk away, but then she stopped, barely turning her head. She glanced over her shoulder at me. "Do come back here. I've got a good feeling that those nightmares aren't gonna stop haunting you."

Somehow, I could tell that there was a grin on her ghost-like face behind her curtain of hair.

Her tone changed. "Can't wait to see what you do,

Hasha."

Her whole figure proceeded to morph back into black sludge and then evaporate away, becoming a puff of smoke.

Time for Assimilation

I jolted up in my bed with a sharp intake of breath. It was difficult to calm my heart down. When I touched my face, a thin layer of cool sweat coated my skin. Its abnormality startled me.

I quickly snatched the blankets and wiped it off. The night had not been restful, and a part of me was relieved to be awake.

My dreams were normally odd and mysterious—no doubt about it—but despite this, something felt unusual. No matter how much I told myself my dream wasn't real, some part of me believed otherwise. After all, my previous dream had been real.

I shoved the concern to the back of my mind.

I can't worry about every little thing. If I do, then I'll never get anywhere.

I looked over to my left and was greeted by the

morning sun shining through my window. Orange and yellow rays peeked through the multitude of trees, stretching out to push away the night. The sight calmed me in the same way sunsets did. My windows quickly became my favorite part of the room. I slid off my bed with a stretch.

My stomach grumbled, so I made my way downstairs to the kitchen. The room seemed normal enough, complete with a sink across the room, a stove and cabinets to my right, and a counter in the middle. The only thing missing was a refrigerator. I found Mr. Lavadan prepping breakfast.

"Oh! Good morning! I just came back from gathering and trading, so food will not be served for a little bit. I hope you are okay with that."

His back was to me when he greeted me while he focused on cooking. Beside him was a basket full of leaves, berries, and eggs. He took the eggs and cracked them into a pan atop a stove.

"Hi...I didn't expect you to be up," I said.

"Why would I not be up? The sun has risen, and even the birds chirp as they awake."

I shrugged. "Well, it's really early. Especially since it's summer, and it's only dawn."

The sizzle of the eggs was satisfying, and the aroma of the cooking food was almost enough to make me drool. Quite to my own embarrassment, my stomach growled again. I quickly clutched my abdomen, but when I looked up, it didn't seem like Mr. Lavadan had noticed.

"Ha! Your attentiveness surpasses your age, as do many other aspects of yours. However, you are missing an unforeseen factor." He opened the top cabinets to grab two plates.

Mr. Lavadan continued talking while he plated the food.

"Now that you live in my house—and will be living among fae—you will learn to live as we do. We have our own way of telling time that is quite different. To start off, for us, 'hours' are 'phases,' and 'minutes'—"

Mr. Lavadan stopped and turned around to look at me. He scanned my outfit, confused.

"Are you still in those human clothes? Did you sleep in that?"

"Huh? Oh, yeah. I found the pajamas you left for me, but they were so itchy. I thought I would find myself scratching a layer of skin off after two seconds in it. Since that didn't sound too fun for me, I just stayed in this."

"Ah, that is my own fault. I…I do not know how to shop for girls. Kaylessa warned me, but I hated to bug her to help me. She is so very busy nowadays. Later, perhaps, the two of you—and maybe even Shaeli—can go out to help your wardrobe."

He brought the plates to the counter and placed them in front of two chairs before going to the other side of the counter and grabbing items from inside.

"Before I forget, we are going to need drinks."

Mr. Lavadan brought out utensils, cups, and a glass bottle of orange juice and finished setting up.

A bit of warmth seeped into me. I couldn't remember the last time someone had done something nice for me—exempting the times Mr. Lavadan himself had saved me. This was a simple act, but it meant a lot.

I sat down beside him. An omelet each had been set in front of both of our chairs. The aroma was so heavenly that my mouth watered and my empty stomach grumbled in unison.

I happily went to grab my fork but was stopped by Mr. Lavadan clearing his throat. When I turned to him, he looked at me with a slightly disappointed frown and expecting eyes, as if he was waiting for me to figure out what I had done wrong.

"What? What'd I do?" I asked, slightly annoyed that he was treating me like a naughty child.

"Do you not give thanks before you eat?" He seemed genuinely confused, and his scowl deepened.

"Ohhh. Yeah…I've never been really religious," I said, fidgeting with my fork. "It's hard when you're always going in and out of different families practicing their own religions. Don't know why, but I didn't picture you as that type of person. No offense, of course."

"I understand your position in this, but you are a fae. We do not have religions like humans. Fae despise religions, believing them superfluous and not even adherent or consistent. But we do have lore and legends that we respect. A history that we venerate. Taking a couple of seconds to give thanks for having food should not be an inconvenience. Would you care to join me?" Mr. Lavadan seemed genuine, but I still felt rather uncomfortable.

"I—I don't know. I still don't know your customs or anything, so—"

"It is not hard. Because you do not have the ability to actively join yet, all you need to do is observe. And you will not see me saying this often." Once more, he flashed me a welcoming grin. "Please?"

Touched by his desire to share his culture, I gave him a subtle nod.

He closed his eyes and held his hands together. "I will speak in English so that you can understand." Mr. Lavadan separated his palms, creating a ball of light between them. "Thank you for providing us with nourishment on this day. Allow us to use our Gifts to further provide ourselves with continued favor and prosperity." He closed his hands, smothering the floating light, and opened his eyes. "We can eat now."

The omelet was surprisingly good, filled with herbs and…meat?

Every aspect of the meal was flavorful. I couldn't

remember the last time I had tasted something so fresh.

"Okay…So, do fae worship a god or something?" I asked, taking another bite of food.

He shrugged. "Um, not exactly a deity. We acknowledge the Elements."

"The Elements? You mean, like the periodic table? Or like earth, fire, water, and air?"

"The latter, kind of…According to our legends, there are actually ten elements. They are Light, Darkness, Technology, Fire, Plant, Water, Air, Body, Emotion, and Mind," he explained between bites.

"Light and Darkness? Technology? Seriously? Those aren't elements. Those—"

He shot me a frustrated glance and gave a sharp sigh. "Do you want to learn about our folklore or not?"

"Yeah, yeah. Go on."

Geez, touchy much? I went back to silently enjoying my food while I waited for him to continue.

"Anyways, we do not worship the Elements. Although contrary to our myths, they are currently not believed to be deities or immortals, but enigmatic forces. They were originally thought to favor the fae, giving us Gifts at the age of ten. For the last millennia, we have come to understand this as rather a surge of Essence for our young, finally manifesting into a Gift. We do not pray often, but when we do, it is in acknowledgment of their 'presence,'" he explained, making air quotes with the last word.

"So, you do or don't believe they exist?"

"Yes, they exist, just not in the same way as we previously believed. We used to treat them like entities. Fae used to believe them to be beings of great power. The Elements have since lost that sense of personification. Mainly because we have seen no proof of their existence as anything other than categories of matter and life in this world. Just different building blocks—or *elements*—of reality. No apparitions, no individualism."

"If fae don't believe that they are people, then why do you pray to them?"

Mr. Lavadan drank the rest of his orange juice, picked up his now empty plate, and headed to the sink.

Wow, he's been talking this whole time but still finished before me?

"First of all, we still pray in respect of our traditions. Unlike humans, all the other evolved species hold onto their traditions and customs for as long as possible. That might be partially because we all live much longer than humans. Thus our cultures are not easily destroyed." He looked back at me, seemingly a bit proud of his people. "Instead, we value building up from our traditions, not just letting them fade away or assimilate."

I wagged my utensil at him. "Wait…You said 'all

other evolved species.' Are there other species besides humans and fae?"

A huff came from near the sink. "My dear, there are both demibeasts and fae, but that is a discussion for another time. May I continue my train of thought now?"

I sighed. "All right, yeah. Sorry." It was going to take some time to get used to how behind I was in this world.

Mr. Lavadan nodded at me before flicking a towel over his shoulder and proceeding to wash the dishes.

"Thank you. Second of all, we rarely pray to the Elements. That prayer you heard me say was a daily one. I am not going to recite it again today. Lastly, you will notice that most of our traditions fall into this odd category of being exercised just for cultural respect. Like, for instance, Rituals.

"I briefly explained these to you before, but Rituals are big milestone events done for every fae. They show the Elements that the young fae respects each individual Element. Nowadays, we just perform it in reminiscence of our history, to celebrate the child's growth and maturity, and to give them the opportunity to amplify their Essence so as to manifest a Gift."

He laughed over his shoulder.

"Technically, most theories suggest that fae can still get a Gift without a Ritual, just with a massive amount of focus. I mean, they have not been proven since no fae wants to delay their Ritual, but our theories are usually very solid."

I finished my meal, and he instantly came over and took my dishes. "Thank you," I said.

"You are very welcome. It has been a while since I cooked for someone else. Now..." He halted. Mr. Lavadan leaned on the edge of the sink. "You should go get dressed. We are going to meet up with others soon."

"Others? Who?" I asked.

"Friends," he said simply. Mr. Lavadan took a brief pause. "I talked to them last night. We have some time, but I think that you need to meet them sooner rather than later. You might have come upon your other clothes last night when you were getting dressed."

"Other clothes? You mean that leather stuff?"

"Oh, um, yes. Humans do not do this commonly, but fae wear leather quite often. Our youth don leather the most, but as we grow, we tend to use it less." He waived his hand dismissively. "Do not ask me why. I think leather can be rather dull as anything more than an accessory, but that is just me. They certainly do not think that."

"Seriously?"

With a huff, I went to my room and pulled the clothes from my closet. I tried on the tunic and pants, which seemed to feel just fine. In fact, they were soft and light. Even the boots were flexible and fit me well despite being made of leather.

That wasn't the problem.

No, the problem was the corset. It constricted around my torso, choking my lungs, and I hadn't even tied it yet! I snatched my cuffs and stormed down the stairs.

Mr. Lavadan was in the middle of the living room, straightening up a vest he had just put on. My heavy footsteps echoed through the house and caught his attention.

"Oh, do you need help tying the corset?" he asked sweetly, all innocent-like.

"No! This is horrible! I can't breathe in this, let alone function!" I shouted. Indignation flowed out of every word.

"Heh. Seems you have enough breath to yell at me." He arched an eyebrow.

"This. Isn't. Funny," I spat through gritted teeth.

I tried walking in his direction to reprimand him but failed. My chest was pulled back with a tug, and I hit the floor. Mr. Lavadan broke into laughter, leaving me on the ground.

Frustrated, I looked behind me, only to find that the ribbon I had left unattended had caught on the rails of the staircase.

This stupid corset!

"Are you done yet?" I snapped at him.

"I—I am sorry…This is ludicrous," he gasped between laughs.

Mr. Lavadan gathered himself and came over to untangle me from the staircase. He gave me his hand, helped me up, and proceeded to tie my corset.

"My dear, you have given me more joy within the last day than what I received within these past few years."

"Hey, not too tight!" I slipped in a breath between my teeth.

He turned me around and helped me put on my cuffs.

I grumbled once more. "Why must I wear this?"

"It is as I said before. You are a fae, and if you are to attempt to fit into our culture, there are many things that you must be attentive to, like dressing as we do. Specifically, how our youth does." Mr. Lavadan tilted his head a bit, frowned, and began messing with my hair. "This truly looks as if you rolled out of bed. Just because you have short hair does not mean that you can be lazy in appearance."

I would have protested, but he was done just as quickly as he started. When I looked at my reflection in the window, examining what he had done, every strand of hair was neatly placed into an immaculate hairstyle.

"There we are. Now…" He extended his hand. "Let us go, for we do not want to keep people waiting."

Others. More fae like me.

Apprehension and anticipation vied for space. This would either go very well or very, very badly.

I hoped for the former, but expected the latter.

Judgments and Admiration

Nausea, my old friend, twisted my stomach, and a storm of a headache shook my head once more. I decided something right then: Portals were officially my least favorite type of transportation. Mr. Lavadan took my hand, assisting me off the cycle.

"Apologies once more, my dear. Do not worry. You will get used to the sensation over time, I assure you." He set the cycle to lean against the nearest wall and took out the tile from the dashboard.

While my body regained its bearings, I noticed that my environment looked familiar. I was in the same white place as I had been when Mr. Lavadan and Dr. Taylor—I mean, Mrs. Kaylessa—revealed what I was. Nostalgia flashed through my mind. A ghost of myself ran into the main room, searching for a way out. A bit of unease sank into my gut.

"Ain tikan veel!"

Yells of a foreign language caught my attention. In the corner of the room, by the desk, were three people: Mrs. Kaylessa, Shaeli, and some other guy. Shaeli was shouting at Mrs. Kaylessa. The guy was rubbing Shaeli's shoulders, trying to calm her down.

"*Hai shai balih*," the man said soothingly into her ear. A mop of messy dark hair sat on top of his head, with two pointed ears emerging from the curls. He had a sharp mouth contrasted by his other soft features.

"Do not be afraid. They do not bite," Mr. Lavadan whispered. "Unless you deserve it…" He turned toward the three, greeting them in what I assumed was Voliun.

We walked closer as he conversed with them. Even though I knew nothing about the language, I was able to understand a few cues. Shaeli seemed worried and frustrated. Whenever she talked, she seethed. Meanwhile, Mrs. Kaylessa, the man, and Mr. Lavadan all chatted as old friends would, seemingly briefing each other.

I felt as if I was back in school again. Like an outsider looking in. It didn't help that I couldn't completely understand what they were talking about.

Mr. Lavadan gestured to me, then chuckled a bit. In response, the other man nodded and headed behind the desk, rummaging through its contents. While we waited for whatever he was retrieving, Mrs. Kaylessa caught my nervous eye.

"It's nice to see you again, Elena. Don't worry. My husband is just making sure that you can be included in our conversations." Her smile was warm and soft, a comforting sight.

"Finded it!" Mrs. Kaylessa's husband shouted, holding up a gadget. The man spoke with the same accent as the rest of them but much heavier.

He came over and showed me the thing. It seemed to be a patch with what looked like earbuds attached.

"This is translator. Put it here," he explained, touching my neck. I pulled away instantly, not fond of the contact, but it didn't bother him. "These wires go in eyes."

"What?" My eyes widened, and I took a step back. I turned to Mrs. Kaylessa.

"I am so sorry. My husband cannot speak English quite well. This device is a translator. It will allow you to understand and speak Voliun." She chuckled. "He also meant to say ears, not eyes. The speakers go in your ears, allowing you to hear Voliun as English. The patch will change whatever you say in English to Voliun. Try it on."

She peeled off the plastic covering the sticky part of the patch and handed the translator to me. I gently stuck it to where her husband had touched on my neck, and I put the earbuds in. As soon as they were both situated, white noise filled my ears. It faded as quickly as it had come.

"Can you understand me?" her husband asked.

The weight of his accent hadn't changed, but it seemed to flow well with his words, actually allowing for clearer communication. What I was hearing from him was foreign and unknown, but my ears told me otherwise, that he was just speaking to me in my language.

"Yes. You are speaking Voliun right now, aren't you?" I asked.

I knew what I had intended to say and what I had said, but it didn't quite sound like that when it came out of my mouth. My tongue formed the words in English, but what came out was clearly in Voliun.

"Ha!" he exclaimed. "Yes, I am, and so are you! Now that we can clearly understand each other, allow me to introduce myself. I am Taelin Heiwys. It is clear that you have already met my wife, Kaylessa, and my brother, Leorn."

Ohh, I thought. *That's right! I knew Mr. Lavadan told me her last name before. Just couldn't quite remember what. Yeah, it's gonna take me a while before I can memorize it, though.*

"Oh, Mr. Lavadan's your brother?"

"What? I don't understand..."

I shrugged. "It's just...he doesn't quite look related to you. I get it, though. I am a foster kid—or I was."

Mr. Lavadan was undoubtedly Asian, and Mr. Taelin was certainly not, although I couldn't quite tell what his race was.

Wait, are races still applicable to fae?

"*Pft*, that's because he isn't," Shaeli said. "Is your translator not working right? He just called him his *brother*."

I stood there for a second while a loading sign played in my mind. "Um, maybe something *is* wrong with it. It keeps on translating what you're saying to 'brother.' Isn't that what you're saying?"

"Oh, that makes sense," Mr. Lavadan noted. "You see, there mustn't be a word in English that exactly means what we're saying. The word that we've been using means something close to 'brother,' which would explain why it is translating it to that. The word actually means 'brother of your spouse.'"

"Um, do you mean 'brother-in-law?' That goes by the same definition."

"'Brother-in-law'? But why 'in law'?" Mr. Taelin asked.

"Well, because once you're married, then that is through the law. All family from your husband or wife is considered 'in law' because through the law, you are related to them. Mother-in-law, sister-in-law…Really, it applies to all of it."

Mr. Lavadan nodded. "Ah, that must be a human thing. Marriages for fae don't involve the law almost at all. Well, except for them taking record of who is married to who." He laughed. "Huh. I guess it does involve the law a little. Our word is just closer to 'brother,' making it a more personal title."

Someone came in from the hallway, interrupting our conversation. She came up to Mrs. Kaylessa, whispering into her ear. After a couple nods, the strange person left.

"Well," Mrs. Kaylessa said. "She's right. Come on, Elena. We mustn't keep our friends waiting."

***

Everyone was quiet and staring at me. We had walked into what seemed like a conference room without any furniture. When we got to the doorway, the room had been full of chatter, but as soon as I walked in, it all seized.

There were forty to fifty pairs of eyes fixated on me solely. I had felt pressure before, plenty of times at school, but this was suffocating. It wasn't enough that my organs were being squished and my lungs were compacted by my stupid leather. At this point, it was a miracle I was even able to stay standing.

My heart raced, and my limbs froze. Everyone's collective body heat only made the number of people present more apparent. Instinctively, I hid a bit behind Mr. Lavadan, hoping that putting him in the way of their eyesight would lessen the strength.

94

He glanced at me and whispered, "Don't fret, my dear. They mean no harm." Mr. Lavadan turned to face the intimidating crowd. "This is Elena Cruz. She will be staying with me."

"Is she the one?" someone shouted from behind the crowd.

"Um, well, yes," he sheepishly replied. That simple answer set off tons of murmuring, along with protests.

"She doesn't belong here."

"This isn't right!"

"Let her be with her own kind!"

Each comment was a dagger thrown. I was disappointing them, and they had only just seen me.

"Calm down! Please, calm down!" Mr. Taelin foolishly attempted to help with a bit of a nervous laugh, but failed. He glanced at Mr. Lavadan, who nodded in response.

"Stop!" Mr. Lavadan shouted.

With a wave of his hands, what appeared to be tape appeared on everyone's mouths. The silence that followed was immediate, as was the quiet surprise and frustration. This didn't last long, however. Mr. Lavadan very quickly began trembling and fell to his knees. Instantly, the tape disappeared.

Before the commotion began again, Mrs. Kaylessa

spoke up.

"Listen, we aren't here to cast our opinions on the poor kid. No one here even knows her yet! We brought you here to welcome her into our village, just as we do to any newcomer. If I see even one of you merely side-eying her" — she turned to the corner — "Cainaris, that includes you, then I will refuse my services for you for up to a month, varying on how much I deem necessary. That doesn't just include injuries, but any superficial help. Do I make myself clear?"

No protests continued from that point on. Mrs. Kaylessa turned to Mr. Lavadan and picked him up.

"Come on, Leorn. I can't believe that you would attempt to use your Gift on so many at once." She looked at me before she left. "Listen, Elena. Go ahead and mingle. You are here to be acquainted with our village. If they give you any more problems, I trust my husband will take care of that."

"For sure," Mr. Taelin said, putting a hand on my shoulder.

Mrs. Kaylessa exited the room with Mr. Lavadan, leaving me alone with her husband and a bunch of people who apparently hated me.

"Come on, kiddo," Mr. Taelin said.

It took a second, but I obeyed. Most of those in the room were adults, but the other third were children of varying ages. I didn't see anyone seemingly over the age of thirty.

Psh, Fountain of Youth in here.

I decided that if no one wanted to talk to me, then I wouldn't speak to anyone. Unspoken unless spoken to. Less work for me. However, my plan was foiled when a girl ran right up to me.

"You're her, aren't you?" she asked. "My name is Darunia Qikian. What's yours?"

She wore a wide grin, which complemented her button nose. Her hair was in a short afro, pinned at one side. She seemed to be practically glowing, radiating with joy. A tight leather corset constricted her too, but she didn't seem the least bit bothered by it.

"Um, Mr. Lavadan said my name. It's Elena Cruz."

"But isn't that—Ohh! We're going by our human names! Odd, but okay. Then my name is Joanna Lee."

At that moment, I remembered Mr. Lavadan's comments on human names versus fae names. "Know what? I'll—I'll just call you Daroona, and you can call me Elena."

"Uh, okay, but it's Darunia. Dar-oo-nee-ah," she enunciated for me. "But sure, we can do that. I'm sorry I didn't speak up earlier. Some might think badly of you, but not all of us. I don't! We can just be quiet in such situations, waiting to see how it turns out."

"My daughter is right," a woman said. She looked very much like Darunia, only a bit more ragged. The fae seemed young, but she had faint circles under her eyes. Her hair was fairly unkempt, and her smile was weak. "We support you—uh—somewhat. I'm sure we'd all be a bit more willing to welcome you if we knew a bit about you."

"Thank you, Imra," someone else added. "So, how old are you?"

"Who's your family?"

"What school do you go to?"

Everyone began asking their questions, trying to survey what kind of person I was. Explaining my foster families to them was a bit hard, but they got it. Although, it was quite surprising to them when I explained how kids were often raised by others instead of by their own families. That rippled through the room like a bad taboo, but this wasn't the most shocking thing I said.

Even though they all had plenty of prejudice against humans, the question that startled everyone was the one I could not answer: "What Gift do you have?"

"Um, I don't—I don't really have...a Gift."

Confusion filled the room, causing murmurings once more.

"What? But every fae has a Gift," someone said.

Another scoffed. "Come on. What are you? Don't

mess with us. Are you a Luminary or a Tenebral?"

"No, no, she looks like an Igniter."

"No, I think she's a Hacker."

Guesses were thrown, and arguments began over what Gift I had. They started out simple enough, just suspicions and hypotheses, but things escalated very quickly. This was a very temperamental crowd.

"She's an Empath!"

"No. She's a Biokinetic. Don't subjugate her to your standards!"

"How dare you? The girl is a Polyform! We need representation!"

"I would rather dissipate than let you take away from our dignity anymore!"

Multiple different people were talking over me, yelling about a topic I was no longer included in. Mr. Taelin was shouting, pulling people away from me, and begging for no one to use their Gifts. The building pressure made me want to crumple like a piece of paper. I had never wanted to go find a dark corner and crawl into a ball so much before.

The faint sound of laughter caught my attention. A boy stood in the corner of the room, cackling to himself. I sneered at him but was quickly brought back to the enveloping arguments.

Right before I gave in to their fighting, my saving grace appeared. A portal formed behind the crowd, and someone stepped out.

"What the Ether is going on here?"

Everyone stopped and turned.

The person crossed his arms. "Someone better give me a good explanation, *now*."

I've Had Better Days

Relief calmed my mind when the fighting ceased.

Because everyone had dropped like flies, I was able to see who had helped me.

A tall man stood at the back of the room, holding his head high. His black hair was pulled into a ponytail, sleek and immaculate. Silver and black markings were scattered around his narrow and deep-set eyes. Immediately, his gaze fell on me — the only person left standing in the room.

Mr. Taelin elbowed me, gesturing for me to kneel.

I fell to my knees, going down as quickly as I could, bowing as the others were.

"Get up," the mysterious man hissed to the crowd.

His eyebrows were furrowed, but his frown was slight. Everyone rose to their feet instantly, and I followed suit. No one was focused on me anymore. Fortunately, the man had become the new center of attention. He strode to me, with each person giving way. The compliance of the others made one thing clear: *This is a man of power.*

He lowered himself to my height, never breaking eye contact.

"I asked: *What. Is. Going. On. Here?*" His voice was emphasized with disgust. The gratitude I held for him vanished with every word he snarled.

I was gently pulled back toward Mr. Taelin, who proceeded to speak for me. "She is being introduced into our village. Just like any other new fae we get."

The man straightened slowly and turned his attention to Mr. Taelin, scowling. "Oh, is that so? Then what was the violence I was witnessing? I may not be totally accustomed to Independent gatherings, but surely, that is not how any fae should be welcomed." He looked at the surrounding crowd. "Is it? Or was it instigated?"

"Things just…got out of control. But these are our problems and are not under your jurisdiction. What are you doing here, *Ngahn?*" Mr. Taelin asked.

"First of all, I am not implying that it is your fault. After all, it's not like I know who is…"

He shot me a quick glare. I had seen this look before, particularly when a teacher was ready to pin something on me just because I stood out.

"Second of all, I came here because of certain *rumors* I

have heard about a certain *someone*. I didn't wish these claims to be true, but I had to come see for myself. However, just from what I saw, I have reason to believe that they are more than just rumors. Heiwys, look me in the eye and tell me that they are false."

Mr. Taelin's grip on my shoulder tightened slightly.

"So what if they *are* true? This girl is an Independent now, whether you like it or not. Additionally, she hasn't done any wrong, so what's so scary about her? What has she done to incriminate herself?"

The man scoffed. "You know as well as I do that her very upbringing is incriminating. And I am not scared of a youth. No, I just refuse to stand by to see the things she will do. Must we wait until the hurricane destroys the land before we contain her? Shall I wait to see everything crumble in her hands before I do anything about it?"

I was back in my old life again. My past foster parents lectured me and prosecuted me, convicting me of crimes I had not done.

The man continued to rant in complete disdain. "No. This child is anything but innocent, both past and future considered. She grew up with humans. *Humans* of all species! Who knows what things she was taught and raised with? And we don't know her! What if she does things just like humans, with their violent and self-destructive ways? Their immorality, discrimination, and egotism could already be ingrained within her!"

I remembered my classmates bullying me, making fun of me for growing up without a family.

Voices gathered into one solid brick, battering my self-esteem. I clutched my arms, trying to brace against the blows. My breath shuttered. Words began forming like stone in my throat.

The man continued. "This child deserves to be put down before she wreaks havoc! I will not support her—"

"*Stop!*" I yelled.

His eyes shot to my face. He was obviously confused by my outburst.

"I can't take it anymore! I have been bullied every day of my life. My foster families, my classmates, and almost everyone in between has had their turn! Not a second has gone by where I haven't been accused of being a smart alec or a mistake! My own family didn't want me!"

Every bit of withheld anger rushed out of my mouth. My filter had been blown to pieces.

"So just stop. I have had it with others talking flak about me. I won't stand for it anymore, whether you're an adult or not. Now, I believe a saying I have heard before could be useful for you: If you have nothing nice to say…Say. Nothing. At. All."

Everyone was stunned, except for the man, of course.

His eyes were wide in shock, akin to the others', but

his grimace was wrinkled with offense. Aghast by my lecture, he searched for words but failed.

Confused as to why everyone seemed so startled by my claims, I looked to Mr. Taelin for answers. To my surprise, he, too, held a dismayed stare. His mouth was hanging open.

What's so shocking? I didn't even fire off any insults yet.

"Listen here, and listen good," the angry man said. His look of appallment had only worsened into wrath, and his eyes seared into my confidence. The scowl on his face had deepened greatly. He waved a finger in my face. "This lack of respect will only turn people like me against you. I can't believe how evident it is that you were raised by humans. If you wish to live a normal life in any regard, I suggest you take your snark and protests and stuff them in a pile of *tee'ilih!*"

I fortified my position, throwing as many daggers as possible into my stare. Leaning toward him, I lessened the distance between the two of us, even though I was a good foot or so shorter than him.

"Well, thank you for that, but if having a normal life means having to abide by what *you* say, then I'd rather stuff myself in that pile of *tee'ilih*. Go ahead. Do your worst. I don't need you for anything."

He gave me a small malicious grin. "I'll remember that."

The man stormed off, pulled out a bag of crystals to

make a rift, and left without another word. The grumblings started as soon as he left.

Further frustrated by everyone's reaction, I turned to Mr. Taelin.

"What is going on? Why is everyone so restless by what I said? I was just sticking up for myself."

Hesitantly, he answered, "Elena, that fae was one of great authority."

"Really? I never would've inferred that by everyone kneeling," I said sarcastically.

"Hah!" Shaeli said. "Are you kidding me? That was *Ngahn* Nylian Sarkis, one of the ten Ancients."

"Great. More to learn. Who the heck are the Ancients?"

Shaeli scoffed. "Our *rulers*. You just made enemies with one of our *rulers*. They are in charge of everything we say, do, and how we live. And yet, you treated him like trash!"

My heart dropped to my feet. Everything clicked in place. *I thought that he was just...Was this dude really the equivalent to a king or something?*

"You mean…"

Mr. Taelin rubbed his temples. "I know he's a—a *wik*, but it's a different matter when dealing with Ancients.

Everyone was startled because we aren't supposed to directly say a word against them. And you went ahead and scolded him like a petulant child."

He shook his head, turning his attention back to the crowd.

"Listen, I think it's time we all go home. Like my brother said, she will be staying with Leorn if you have any more questions. Good to see you all."

People began to leave, shooting me quick glances of contempt or concern before stepping through their portals.

Regretful of my actions and words, I sulked a bit, letting my head dangle.

How could I have been so stupid?

Mr. Taelin sighed and combed through his messy hair with his hands. "Come on, kiddo. What's past is past. We'll try to fix it later. Let's go home."

He and his daughter began walking away. I followed slowly, still soaking in what I had done. But a hand yanked me back, turning me like a top.

"Why, you're horrible at this!" A boy, seemingly around seventeen or eighteen years old, was laughing at me.

His eyes were dark green and framed by off-black strands. His hair was unkempt but effortlessly gorgeous, complementing his hazelnut skin. He wore a Greek tunic, as if he had been plucked right out of the myths. A cuff of rubies was clasped to his upper arm.

I recognized him instantly.

"You're—You're the kid that was laughing when the fights broke out!" I frowned. "Hey, what's wrong with you?"

He chuckled, obviously enjoying every moment. "I was just appreciating the entertainment! Your social standing has sunk from 'somewhat uncomfortable' to 'my Ether, someone get water for this fire!' Seriously, the bar was on the floor, and you brought a shovel. How could I not have fun by watching you obliviously dig that hole, thinking you were in the right all along?"

This guy's insane! What a jerk!

"Elena, what happened—" Mr. Taelin came over but stopped once he saw the boy. "Oh, are you still making friends? No offense, but I think you've done enough for today." He flashed a wry smirk to the boy. "How are you, Akkar *Gee*?"

Still beaming, Akkar replied, "Perfect! In fact, I just had the time of my life!"

"That's great, but I'm afraid we have to go. If you want, you can come visit Elena whenever, no prior notifications required. You know your family is welcome in our homes anytime."

I was astonished by what I was hearing. *Why on earth are you allowing this prideful oaf in your home?*

"Thank you. I might take you up on that, if more for her than for me. I think it's evident that she needs quite a lot of help." Akkar looked at me with a lifted chin, a puffed chest, and a condescending smile. "A word of advice: Try to make friends, not foes. I mean, unless you *want* to be the villain."

Not Ready Yet

Mr. Lavadan was thunderstruck by the news. "She did *what*?" He looked at me, rather disappointed. "What have you done? You were not there to make enemies."

Regret floated around in my mind like a swirling gust. I stared vacantly at the floor, remembering the things the others had said.

"An Ancient of all people! I understand how snobbish they can be, but to confront him so? It is imperative that you gain their trust if you are to enter into our society."

The last sentence sank in as soon as it hit my ears.

Regret switched out for realization. *But why do I have to in the first place? Why was I put in this situation?* I glanced toward him.

"We'll have to fix things somehow. Perhaps the other Ancients will only take this event with a grain of salt. Maybe they—"

"Listen," I said. "You have some explaining to do. How? How was a fae, a member of a species that hates humans, raised by humans? Why was I pulled away from my family? And don't you dare try to escape this. I can clearly see that you aren't telling me the whole story." I glared at him. Frustration and curiosity vied within my mind, and a need for knowledge pulled the words out. "What are you hiding from me?"

A tense silence filled the room. Everyone avoided eye contact with me. Mrs. Kaylessa shuffled nervously. Mr. Taelin scratched his neck, and Mr. Lavadan grasped his head. The atmosphere grew heavy while my question hung in the air.

Unlike them, Shaeli looked around, put her hand on her hip, and rolled her eyes. "Yeah, I suddenly don't wanna be here. I'll be returning to trying to look for Onas…if you need me. But please, don't need me."

She left the awkward room, making me wish I was her.

"Well? I would like an answer," I said, letting out a sharp sigh.

Mrs. Kaylessa cleared her throat. "Okay, honey. You…You're special. Something you have to understand, sweetie, is that our world is in shambles. Things are falling apart quite rapidly, and—"

Mr. Lavadan stopped Mrs. Kaylessa. "No, I should be the one to tell her."

He looked at me with what seemed like the fatigue of a thousand lifetimes in his eyes. "My dear, you have been put into a very important role. You were raised with humans for a reason. This gives you a vantage point. Now, this arrangement certainly was not our idea or wish."

Mr. Taelin crossed his arms. "Leiwyn Zinshyre was a close friend of ours. She was young, only ninety-seven. Instead of looking ahead towards a prospective future, she tended to let things anger her very easily. Leiwyn decided that there was only one way to fix the problems Leorn was telling you about: by stealing a baby and having them raised by humans."

Mr. Lavadan gave a subtle nod. "She wanted you to grow up differently than all other fae. With the ability to shed a light on the evils being done. To show others the evils that are hiding amidst their gaze."

Mr. Taelin went on. "We never saw Leiwyn again after she took you. No one is expecting anything from you. It was her plan alone."

"But then why didn't my family come looking for me?" My hopes of still having a family to find were renewed, but I needed to know why they had let me grow up with humans. "If she was the only one who supported this, then why did they go along with it?"

The three of them glanced at each other.

Mrs. Kaylessa said, "We all looked but couldn't find you. The human world is vast." She chuckled and crossed her arms. "There are quite a lot of them."

"Once we found you, we were unsure if we should bring you back," Mr. Lavadan said. "You had a home and had grown up in a society so very different than our own. And...your family felt the same. They were in despair that they let this happen and weren't sure if you wanted to be with them."

I hugged my abdomen, beginning to understand. "Where are they? Do they know I'm finally back?"

Mr. Lavadan sighed. "Yes, they just...They want you to get adjusted to fae life first so they can figure out how to tell you."

I nodded solemnly. Disappointment sat at the pit of my gut. But *I* wasn't even ready to finally meet them. Too much was going on for me.

"But listen, my dear. There are some who oppose the idea of a fae brought up by humans. They will despise you, but that is all I will tell you for now. And before you protest: No, I'm not just hiding things from you for 'fun.' You will learn and grow, and we will help with that. However, that also means that some information will come with time. All you need to know right now is to trust us and listen when we say something is a bad idea. Like, for instance, admonishing our rulers."

Before agreeing to anything, I pointed out, "You guys *do* know that I have no reason to trust you at all, right?"

"Perhaps so," Mr. Taelin said. "But you know as well as we do that you're walking in the dark right now. Blind to everything around you, you have two decisions: keep marching on through, hoping that nothing attacks, or take the hand of a stranger. While we may not exactly know the way, sprout, we can at least assure you some safety. Some support is definitely better than none."

*Support…*I glanced at each of them. They were all there to do exactly that: support me. *I'll keep a safe distance, like normal, but I chose this path. I guess if I didn't want complications, I should've just stayed in the group home. Now, I have to rely on them to help me through it.*

I nodded, a bit more fortified. "So, what's first?"

Everyone's smiles grew, and Mr. Taelin laughed.

"Well, that's great, but let's not get ahead of ourselves here. I'm sure you're still trying to soak in everything from today. So, instead of pushing ourselves too far, let me get my daughter to update her. Let's just hope she was only looking for Onas with her Matrix gloves."

Mr. Taelin left to find Shaeli.

"Mr. Lavadan, what are Matrix gloves?" I asked.

"Oh, these are," he said, holding up his leather-gloved hands. "They're akin to humans' phones. Most don't look like gloves, though. They can look like bracelets, human watches, or the like. They allow us to communicate across long distances, tell time, show our location, and do various other tasks. We'll get you some after you learn Voliun, since the languages used on them do not include English. They're not quite made for humans, and that is a human language."

"Dang. I was kinda hoping for some Neo-type twist," I said with a giggle.

Everyone fell quiet, confused.

Mrs. Kaylessa asked, "What's a 'Neo'?"

I squinted at her. "Are you kidding me? Neo…from *The Matrix*?" I couldn't believe what I was hearing.

"Is this a human thing?" Mr. Lavadan asked.

Dang, these people don't know any movies. Oh, this will be a hard time for me.

The sound of someone softly sobbing came from the open door.

We all got up to see who was crying. Not too far from the room was Mr. Taelin trying to comfort a weeping Shaeli. Mrs. Kaylessa clicked her tongue and rushed to her daughter's side.

"Oh, *baalih*. Let me guess…No positive updates?" Mrs. Kaylessa tucked a piece of Shaeli's hair behind her ear.

The girl sniffed and shook her head. "They're saying that Onas could be *dead*."

I tapped Mr. Lavadan's arm, catching his attention. "Who's Onas?" I whispered.

"Onas is Shaeli's betrothed—err, *fiancé*," he said in a hushed voice. "He went missing a couple of months ago. We've been assigned a few Guardians to help, and together, we have been trying to find him. However, we have had no such luck. The poor girl has been taking it harder than any of us. It's sad that you would have to walk in on this, twice now. This is what she was upset about earlier, before you met our village."

Shaeli was very irritating to me. I thought she was an obnoxious and annoying girl. However, seeing her vulnerable and hurting like this, I felt bad. Her fiancé was missing and now presumed dead. Shaeli had to be going through a lot. She was obviously buried in fear and frustration. I stepped forward, touching her hand, looking at her with a little more empathy.

"I'm so sorry. You must be so worried about him."

She immediately pulled away.

"You have no idea what I'm going through, girlie," Shaeli growled through her tears.

"No, I don't…I've never even had a crush or anything, let alone this." I softened my look and stretched a sympathetic smile. "What's he like? Onas? Can you tell me about him?"

Shaeli stood there a second, confused by my questions.

Mr. Taelin chimed in. "Elena, what you are trying to

do is really sweet, but this is a raw topic. I don't think that Shaeli—"

"No," his daughter said, interrupting him. She wiped her eyes, took in a deep breath, and steadied herself. "Onas…is the kindest fae I've ever met. He's loyal and super flexible, not bothered by little things, but he isn't as sly as he thinks about it." She giggled to herself, grinning. "The funny thing is that everyone thinks that he's so strict and stern because, well, he's so stoic. I swear, the fae only has one expression, but sometimes, if you show him something really funny or do something sweet for him, he'll smile. That smile is stronger than any Gift."

Only one expression? I wondered, searching for the root of the description's familiarity. The thought only lingered for a second, though.

Her tears stopped, and her face lit up. Shaeli seemed much more relaxed now that she was talking about Onas.

"What does he look like?" I asked.

"Well…he has soft black hair, but if I don't stop him, he likes to gel it. He has pale skin and almond eyes. Often, you can't tell what he is feeling or thinking, but just by glancing into those eyes, you'll know everything going on inside him…"

A shiver shot through my gut. The portrait she was painting of this guy grew eerily close to someone I had seen before. A pale man with a constant stoic expression and gelled black hair? My mind instantly went to the captain from the boat.

No…it couldn't be him. Pale skin, black hair, and almond eyes could describe almost any Asian man!

Shaeli caught sight of my change of demeanor. "What's wrong?"

I stammered, "I, uh, just thought of something. Please, continue."

She began jumping to assumptions and grew excited. "Wait, did that description sound familiar? Have you seen him before?"

"I—I…No. It's just…" I failed at finding an excuse.

"My dear, if you know something, *anything*, then we need to know," Mr. Lavdan said.

"Elena, have you seen him before?" Mrs. Kaylessa asked.

The pressure surrounded me. "Listen, I thought I did, but there's a lot of people that could go by that description. I-I don't think I've seen him before. Sorry."

Shaeli rushed to me and grabbed my hand. "But we could see! If you let me use my Gift, we can see if who you're thinking of is Onas!"

"What?" I asked.

Dang it! Is there some freaky fae way around this?

Mr. Taelin explained, "Shaeli is a Reminiscent Telepath. She can project memories, allowing us to see another's past. It's completely harmless and simple. Kiddo, we've gotten nowhere with our investigation. Anything, even just a faint memory, would be helpful."

Stupid magic. I sighed. *I can't get out of this, can I?*

If I insisted on my denials and got defensive, then things would get suspicious. I was screwed, so I nodded.

"What needs to be done?"

Shaeli took my other hand. "All I need to do is hold on to your wrists, like this. And if I focus, then whatever memory is on your mind will appear, like so…"

She closed her eyes, and a slight rush of warmth went through me. A purple beam of light, like that of a projector, shot from my forehead. To our left, my memory played like a hologram. Everything was a bit blurry, with only certain things in focus.

"Don't worry. Memories usually aren't very clear," Mrs. Kaylessa said. "It's rare to have eidetic memory."

Before us was the wheelhouse, but everything the memory wasn't focusing on was bleary, as if it had been splashed and drenched with water. The cloaked person was there again, whispering once more in the captain's ear.

"Wha—What's this?" Shaeli asked, watching the memory play out. Her grip on my wrists grew a bit tighter.

"Speak up. There is no one here. Plus, take off that hood. You are making me sweat just looking at you," the captain spat.

A collective gasp from the ladies was heard when he turned to face the viewer's direction.

Mr. Lavadan placed his hand on my shoulder. "What is this memory of?"

The image played on. I tensed when the pain of the explosion again ricocheted throughout my body.

"This was right before the cruise blew up."

Mr. Taelin shook his head. "No…Onas wouldn't do that."

I looked back at Shaeli. Her teardrops fell, one at a time, in disbelief.

"Th—There's another memory here."

Instantly, the projection changed to the attack in the alley. The fight between the two hooded people played in front of us.

"Wait…Is this…" Confusion riddled Mr. Lavadan's face. "Why would you think of this?"

I sighed, regretting my decision to let them see my memories. "He had spoken to me before you joined. His voice was exactly the same as that man you fought. I had made this connection earlier, but I didn't know who he was before."

Shaeli staggered backward, trembling. She let go of my wrists. "No…No! Onas is sweet and kind, not harsh or malicious, like how he is in those memories! That couldn't be him…He would never join the Ambition. He wouldn't…"

The introduction of a new topic caught my attention. "The Ambition? What is that? Does it have something to do with the explosion?"

"My dear…" Mr. Lavadan said, stopping me. "Do you remember when I said that there are people that would oppose you?"

I bobbed my head in affirmation.

"They are very dangerous, and it would be prudent of you to stay as far away as possible from them. And thanks to your memories, we now know what has truly happened to Onas. For one reason or another, he has joined them."

Disbelief clouded the room. Shaeli wasn't the only one distraught.

Mr. Lavadan turned once more toward me. "It's time to go home. Now."

Tongue of Nightmares

"**I'm** so sorry," I repeated, stepping off his cycle. "I didn't know —"

Mr. Lavadan put his hand on my shoulder. "My dear, you did not do anything wrong. Do not ever apologize when you are not in the wrong." He looked down at me, concern lingering in his eyes. "Another note…If you, at any point, experience anything odd or unusual, always come to us. Never hold back information like that for any reason, even if you think it will hurt us. Got it?"

Without hesitation, I nodded, but the action was done in partial deceit. Gratitude had begun making personal connections between Mr. Lavadan and me, but this also led to a bit of guilt pulling at my chest.

I had not wanted to make everyone upset nor kill their only hopes pertaining to Onas. These were the first people to genuinely care for me, and all I had done for them was complicate things.

It won't happen again.

We went into his house, and I headed for my new room, assuming that Mr. Lavadan wouldn't want to deal with me any longer.

"Oh really?" Mr. Lavadan said.

I stopped in my tracks and turned around. There he stood, with his arms crossed.

"You leave my whole village speechless, show me and my family hard truths that we didn't even think was possible, then think that you can hide away in your room?"

I chuckled, placed a hand on my neck, and looked away. "Well, I just didn't think…" I mumbled.

"Oh…no, no. You do not get to escape responsibility. What we are going to do is make the most of this day, despite its rough beginnings." He waved his hand, gesturing for me to come over. Mr. Lavadan strode across the living room to his bookshelf. "First things first. We start with the basics."

I sighed, but this time, it was with a slight smile. *He's not angry with me.* I dragged myself to where he was.

"What does 'basics' mean to you?"

He pulled out a book and examined it. "Why, learning our language, my dear. Partially. We will start with learning Voliun. It is critical that you do not become dependent on your translator. Others will see you as weak or unintelligent if you do not learn our tongue." He turned his head to me, and the corners of his mouth lifted. "Let us begin, shall we?"

Mr. Lavadan and I sat down on the couch. Beside us were stacks of books, pieces of paper, and a quill, which seemed to be the same as a pen, complete with internal ink, just fancier. He wrote out the Voliun alphabet. Instead of letters, he called them runes. They were elaborate in comparison to English letters.

After showing me the alphabet, he took another piece of paper and wrote out a bunch of the runes in a row.

"To help you understand the alphabet, let me show you rather than tell you." Then he exclaimed, "Oh! Before I forget, let's turn off your translator for now. The more you hear without a device helping you, the better you will learn how to produce the same sounds with your mouth."

"Okay. How do I do that?" I asked.

"Just hold your fingers on the patch for a few seconds."

I did as he instructed, and a beep sounded through the earbuds. Taking them out felt odd, but *good*—like when I undid a ponytail after a long day. Everything was clearer than it had been with the earbuds in.

"Good. Now we will go over my name," he said in English.

I turned my attention to the paper. On it, he had written his name in his native language: ꝲ ✳ ⊂ ⋌ |

Ⴤψ∧∪ℓ∪. I examined it for a second, not knowing what I was looking for.

"So, is your name pronounced differently in Voliun, or…?" I asked.

He tapped the pen. "No. Well, I mean…I suppose. Technically, my first name is pronounced lih-WOH-ERRN."

"Huh?"

"Well, in Voliun, none of our basic characters make the sound of 'or.' The same thing happens for the sounds of your letters M, P, B, and J."

"Wait, so your first name is pronounced…"

"Lih-WOH-ERRN. But, you see, that could be hard to say if your language naturally breaks up those sounds to somewhat simpler ones. The W-sound you hear goes away, and the separate 'oh' and 'err' combine in your language to 'or.'"

The gears ground away while I tried to comprehend what he was saying. Mr. Lavadan caught sight of the confusion I surely must have been displaying in my face and laughed.

"I know it might be hard to understand at first, but I will show you more examples as we move on. And hey," he said with a dismissive smile, "your language is much more perplexing than mine."

"What? No way!"

He shook his head. "English has letters that make different sounds depending on what they are next to, never fully retaining one single pronunciation. You have *multitudes* of silent letters, different tenses for the exact same word…And do not even get me started on contractions!"

The two of us laughed for a bit, and I relented in my argument.

We talked for a while, trying to get through what each character in the Voliun alphabet sounded like. Most of the basic pronunciations were like vowels with very few consonants or in-betweens.

Of course, then he taught me that vowels and consonants in Voliun were torn between the tone of each sound. Vowels were fluid and mostly consisted of variations "ah", "ch", and "sh". Consonants, on the other hand, were sharp and abrupt, like that of T.

Yeah, it was pretty different from English, making it hard to wrap my mind around.

Additionally, Mr. Lavadan would put a line between every word when he wrote sentences out. Apparently, this was equivalent to spaces between words. He wanted me to focus on pronunciation and reading first, since this would be most apparent to onlookers.

My head was spinning with the amount of information being pumped into it. I was constantly asking questions, trying to soak it all in. He kept on suggesting for me to take a break, but I wanted to fully understand a certain topic before I stopped. I hated leaving something incomplete. Of course, finishing one topic would only bleed into another.

We went for hours like this.

When lunch came around, Mr. Lavadan disappeared and reappeared with food. I had been concentrating so hard that I didn't notice him leave or how hungry I was until I smelled what he had made. The same thing happened when dinner came around. In a blink of an eye, the day was gone. I had even missed the sunset.

"My dear, I believe that it is time to go to bed. If you tire yourself, then you will not learn nearly as much as you want to," Mr. Lavadan said.

My eyes were dry, and my back ached from sitting all day. "Yeah, maybe you're right."

Together, we began collecting the papers, stacking books, and putting things away.

"I applaud your want to learn. Do not worry. Each day, we will be working on Voliun, but tomorrow, we will also cover a new subject. Now, if you wish to practice in your free time, there are papers and a quill in your desk. Ah, one more thing."

He proceeded to hand me the papers we had been writing on. On them was the whole Voliun alphabet, example sentences of various kinds, and more.

"Keep this with you. It has some pretty good information on it."

I took it from him and stood up with a long stretch. Nearly every bone in my back cracked. "I don't quite get it yet, but I think I made some progress."

"I am glad you are so ecstatic about this. Just try to retain that excitement as I continue to teach you."

I grasped the papers in my hands. "It all depends on the subject taught. Goodnight, Mr. Lavadan."

"Good night, my dear."

Before I left the room, I took one more look at him. He appeared tired and exhausted, just like me, but somehow, he also seemed so cheerful and content. I had a lot of fun that day and felt happy too.

Once I opened the door of my room, I put the papers on my desk, along with my translator, and plopped on the bed.

The big cushy mattress nearly engulfed me. Every muscle in my body began to relax…That is, until I looked down at my dirty boots on the blanket.

With a sigh, I bent down to take them off and was stopped by my stupid corset. Frustration accumulating, I groaned the entire way as I fought with the leather straight-jacket, throwing it off, and kicking my boots to the other side of the room.

If I wasn't achy before, I sure was now. I tossed myself once more onto my bed, not bothering to reposition. Not wanting to move a muscle. I let my eyelids drop closed and the tension in my bones melt away.

Of course, I was not lucky enough to get peaceful dreams.

I was chained up, just sitting on the couch in the Cruz family's old living room. Someone came from behind me and tied a blindfold over my eyes.

They whispered, "Come on. Prove you're more than a rat and rescue them before it's too late."

I thrashed and thrashed, trying to get loose of my bindings. Even though I was blindfolded and could not see who was in the room with me, I could still hear the screams of panicked people. A ticking filled the air around me. Everyone around me was running, trying to find sanctuary before the explosion. I felt useless, just trapped there and unable to do anything, helpless.

A cold hand pulled me backward, interrupting my nightmare. I fell to the floor, and my head hit the ground hard. A familiar pitch-black place. I rubbed the back of my head.

"I see how this is gonna go. You just won't listen to my advice, huh?" an eerie voice said softly.

I looked up, and sure enough, Umbra stood in front of me. She wore the same goth outfit I had last seen her in, and she held her arms tightly crossed.

Umbra clicked her tongue. "Did I not tell you to just come to Afautiya when you go to sleep?"

I mumbled, "Oh, great…This dream again…" I tried standing up, struggling once more in a place where light would not aid my balance.

Her laugh was sharp and the harshest sound I had ever heard come from her mouth, especially contrasting with how soft her accent made her words. "Oh, child…Must I remind you that this is *not* a dream? Or will you just ignore me more if I tell you that?"

Right, she doesn't think this is a dream. Before, she seemed to know a lot more than she let on. Perhaps I could get her to explain.

I pretended she was right. "Well, how would I know how to get here? The only other time I've gotten here was through you."

Umbra seemed genuinely confused by my question. She scratched her chin. "Huh. I mean, I assumed that you would just know how to get here."

I scoffed. "What kind of reasoning is that? Why would I *know* that?"

She began to rub her temples and murmured, "Wow, so now we have to *teach* her?"

"We?"

Umbra stopped, glared, and began walking toward me. "Little girl, are you telling me that you know nothing of your Blessing or how to control it?"

"Blessing? What are you talking about?" I looked up at her and made eye contact. "Are you referring to my Gift? If that's the case, then I hate to break it to you, but I have no Gift."

"Oh, look at the genius go!" she said, glancing around and waving her arms, as if presenting me to some unknown person. "Of course, you don't have a Gift! Don't you know by now? You are 'special.' Too good for the rest of us, apparently."

Her sarcasm and what seemed like envy made me realize I was hated both in reality *and* in my dreams. I took offense at whatever she was implying and grimaced at her.

"Listen, I don't know anything, so stop making accusations of me about things I know nothing about."

She clicked her tongue and turned away. "Must I have to *work* for this?" Umbra glowered at me. "You know, I'm kinda ticked off at this new information. Just return to your body. Go wake up. You'll survive with what Essence you've made in this time."

"Excuse me?" Not only did I not understand a word she said, but I was upset that I had gotten no answers from her. Only more questions. "You can't just tell me to wake up. This is my dream, whether you believe it or not! I've only been here a few minutes!"

She groaned and rolled her head. "Wow, you're already trying to boss me around, huh? Now" — she put her cold, pale hand on my forehead — "wake up."

Umbra pushed me backward, somehow making my whole body glow.

With a burst of light, I jumped up from bed. *Dang it! Why did I wake up?* I looked to my left and rolled my eyes when I noticed the moon was still out. There had to be something that would tell the time.

To my right was a clock on the bookshelf. I snatched it up quickly to try to read the time. However, the triumph was short-lived. It was all in Voliun runes. In defeat and increased frustration, I hurled the clock halfway across the room.

I laid back down, hoping sleep would return to me.

And there I remained for what felt like an hour. I watched the moon drift across the sky ever so slowly. Like an annoying snail. Even though I felt tired, I just couldn't seem to fall back asleep. The suffering restlessness I felt kept me tossing and turning, flopping like a fish out of water. After a while, I gave up trying. I was bored out of my mind and needed a distraction.

*Ugh…All right, let's see. Well, I can't read any of these stupid books because they're in an entirely different language. Oh, how I wish I had my phone…*My eyes floated to my desk. An idea had popped in my head. *Mr. Lavadan did say that I had papers and a quill, and I have those notes from before.*

I sat down at the desk, took out the writing supplies and notes, and began. The quill felt odd in my hand — since I wasn't used to writing with a literal feather — and it was kind of hard to make out the pages because I had very little light. Despite this, I found myself soon relaxing while I started to memorize the Voliun alphabet.

I knew I wouldn't get far without a teacher, but I figured out how to write each character, forced to draw the unfamiliar runes over and over until it became easy.

First, I taught myself to write Mr. Lavadan's name in Voliun. Beside each character was a pronunciation written in English. Any progress I made would be beneficial in the long run, so I carefully practiced pronouncing each rune. Although I didn't know a single word in Voliun, I was determined to make sure I knew how to say the alphabet.

With the moon as my only light, I worked the night away.

***

"This feels ridiculous," I grumbled under my breath.

"Why, it only feels that way because you are not taking it seriously!" Mr. Lavadan exclaimed.

Instead of continuing with language lessons, once we ate and the day had gotten started, Mr. Lavadan thought it a wonderful idea to try to figure out what my Gift was. While I was a little disappointed in the change of direction, I was kind of curious to figure out what kind of magic-like power I had.

Unfortunately, I did not think it would entail this.

"How can I take this seriously? This is stupid! What good can flicking the light do?"

I had been there for at least half an hour, just standing, with only the task of switching the light on. Then—plot twist—a second later, I would switch it off.

Oh. My. Gosh. Why could we not just work on Voliun?

"We are trying to figure out what Gift you have, if you have any. By the change in light and darkness, we can see whether you have a Gift in either of those Elements. Just focus. Try to feel if either the submission to the darkness or the light feels different." He leaned on the wall and crossed his arms, making himself comfortable.

I rolled my eyes and tried to follow his instructions, staring at the light in the middle of the room.

When the room was dark, I imagined the shadows seeping into my skin, briefly crawling through my veins. Once the light turned on, I imagined the rays of photons shining their way across my mind, clearing it of all worries. I fantasized, hoping to find something abnormal with me.

Deep down, I truly wanted a Gift. Not only would I feel like a superhero with it, but I would also find a way to fit in better with other fae.

I sighed, disappointed in my results. "I don't know

what to tell you. Nothing feels out of the ordinary."

"That is okay!" He stood up straight and smoothed out his clothes, ridding them of wrinkles. Mr. Lavadan began to lead me out of the room. "These are but two of the possible Elements you could have a Gift from. We will move on to the next—Water."

We went downstairs, and I soon found myself having to hold my hands in a bowl of water.

"What am I supposed to be doing now?" I asked, with a slight groan.

"Now, I want you to focus on the water. See if you can connect to it in a deep way." He pulled up a chair and stared at me, waiting for some spectacular thing to happen.

"'Focus on the water'? 'Connect to it in a deep way'? Do you even hear yourself?" I cocked my head, giving him a frustrated glare.

He dropped his head. His laughter was jovial and genuine. Mr. Lavadan looked up at me with a hand on his neck. "You really are something. You know, if you question every method we take—"

The ring of the doorbell cut him off.

"Who's that?" I asked, trying to see the door from a room away.

"Well, let me find out..."

Mr. Lavadan went to the door, opened it, and began talking to the other person, but I couldn't understand any of it.

Voliun.

I instantly remembered I had not put the translator on yet, so I pulled it out of my pocket, inserted the earbuds into my ears, and placed the patch on my neck. Surprisingly, it was still sticky! I quickly put my hands back in the bowl, though, not wanting him to scold me for having taken them out.

Meanwhile, Mr. Lavadan led the visitor into the house.

Darunia greeted me. Her curls bounced while she walked. She was wearing a type of corset. Fortunately, she didn't seem to care that I wasn't wearing one. I was *not* going to voluntarily put on that thing again.

"Elena! It's so nice to see you! What are you doing?" she asked.

I chuckled awkwardly. "Oh, this is a stupid experiment Mr. Lavadan wanted me to do." She must have thought I looked ridiculous.

Darunia giggled. "*Ngahn* Lavadan, why are you having her do this?"

"Miss Qikian, I've told you time and time again, you don't need to call me that. Just 'mister' is fine."

"What is that? *'Ngahn'*?" I asked. "I've heard it used before with that ruler of yours, but my translator isn't, well, translating."

"Oh, well, you know how in English you say 'Mr.,' 'Ms.,' and 'Miss'? This is an honorific, like those," he said. "Now, even though we have honorifics like them, this is a different one. This is used for males with the utmost respect. Much too fancy to use for someone like me, but we use this mostly for the male Ancients." Mr. Lavadan turned back to Darunia. "And to answer your question, we are trying to figure out what her Gift is. We're testing every Element to see if something sticks out to her."

Darunia placed a hand on her hip. "What? Why doesn't she know — Oh, wait! That's right. You said she didn't do the Ritual, huh? What if she just doesn't have a Gift yet, *Jeerei* Lavadan?"

Great. What's "Jeerei"?

He took in a sharp breath and looked at me. "She may not, but I don't know. Something feels off with saying that. Without Gifts, fae are incredibly energetic, like how we used to be. You understand more than most. Often constantly moving — fidgeting, really — and without long attention spans. She has displayed none of that."

"*Hehe*, that kinda sounds like ADHD," I said.

They both ignored me.

Darunia played with a coil of her hair, as if it would

help her think. "True, true. But if she does have a Gift, just putting her in contact with different Elements and hoping she feels differently in a certain one isn't exactly a foolproof method. I mean, what if she *does* feel a difference in a certain Gift but has gotten used to that by now? Then we would never be able to figure out what her Gift is!"

Mr. Lavadan crossed his arms. "If you don't like my methods, then what do you suggest we do instead?"

She only had to ponder for a second before her head shot up. "That's it! We need to put her in extremes!" Darunia turned to me, beaming with excitement. "You see, when put in intense situations of the Element of what our Gift is, our Gift naturally shines through! It's perfect!"

Mr. Lavadan absently combed his hair with his hand. "I have already considered it. Don't you think that she would be apprehensive about doing this? Things could go *very* wrong. All it takes is one wrong move…"

She didn't seem swayed and still turned to me. "Elena, are you willing to take these tests? I just don't see how *Jeerei* Lavadan's method will be helpful. Unless you feel you've made progress—"

"No!" I said immediately.

Mr. Lavadan grinned and raised an eyebrow.

I stammered, "Well, uh, I mean…It might be *more* helpful to try a new go at this. Something different, y'know?"

I rubbed my arm with my wet hand and smiled, nervous. All I wanted at that point was to do *anything* besides what he was making me do.

"My dear, we have barely started. Perhaps if we try this method a bit longer—"

Darunia cut him off in her excitement. "Yes! You won't regret this, Elena!" The girl grabbed my wrist before I could even blink. "We're gonna find out what your Gift is!"

I was whisked away without another word.

Tenacious Trial After Trial

My expectations of what was to come were quickly ushered aside, and apprehension took root instead.

"Let's begin with something a little less risky. I think we should start with Light," Darunia said, pushing me into a room.

"Wait, but Mr. Lavadan and I just did that. He had me…well, flip the light switch on and off."

She stopped in her tracks and looked at me. Darunia stifled laughter. "*What?*" She turned to Mr. Lavadan. "*Jeerei,* tell me she's kidding."

He began rubbing the back of his neck. "I didn't want to push her too far, and the process still let her be exposed to the Element, so…"

The girl returned to closing the door and covering the windows, giggling all the while. "It's no wonder she's doubting our methods when you begin with *that.*"

The room became progressively darker until my vision was limited to faint outlines of the people and things around me.

I muttered, "What exactly is she doing?"

Before Mr. Lavadan could respond, Darunia grabbed his wrist. "Oh, no. It's the surprise of it all that makes it fun!"

She pulled Mr. Lavadan over, reached up to his pointed ear, and whispered into it. Even in the darkness, I could see his eyes widen.

"Are you sure, Miss Qikian? She—"

"*Yes*. This will be fiiine! Now, let 'er rip!" Darunia announced.

A familiar sigh came from Mr. Lavadan when he flicked his wrist. A blinding light overtook me, flooding my vision. I shut and covered my eyes with my hands, but nothing could stop the light. A powerful sting seared into me.

I held back my screams, attempting to fight it. My eyeballs felt like they were on fire. Soon, amidst the light, I could vaguely see the outline of a man. However, the figure was hard to distinguish, making me think it was just a trick. Or, if it was really there, then maybe it was Mr. Lavadan.

I suffered for what seemed like an eternity. Faintly in the background, Mr. Lavadan and Darunia argued about how long I should be in this state.

Hot tears rolled down my cheeks involuntarily, trying to wash out whatever was hurting my eyes. My head bumped a wall behind me while I vied against the light.

A whisper floated to me amongst my pain. *Just don't fight it. Will it gone. Release it.*

It was very soft and echoed gently, but it was odd in a way I hadn't experienced before. Like I had heard it without my ears.

I didn't know what else to do, so I obeyed the instructions relayed to me, calming myself down, stopping the thrashing and screaming. My eyes opened slowly, and I focused on one thought: *Release.*

The pain eased when I lessened my resistance. The light flashed. Mr. Lavadan and Darunia shielded their eyes during the brief second the light brightened the room. I could now see.

They both stared at me with wonder.

"Welp, that settles it!" Darunia showed a toothy smile. "She's either an Illusionist or a Luminary! My bet's on a Luminary."

Mr. Lavadan gazed at me in wonder. "I don't know…It feels wrong to say that." He looked deep into my eyes, searching for something.

I shared the mysterious unease he expressed.

When I commanded the light, it had been like finding

a puzzle piece I had been seeking for days. The thing was, I knew it wasn't the last piece. For the first time in my life, I felt an underlying potential ready to be exposed.

I matched his stare. "Let's try the other Elements, just to see."

"What?" Darunia looked back and forth between the two of us. "This is pretty absolute! I mean, only Luminaries and Illusionists can do what you just did!"

I shot her a determined glare and repeated my statement. "Let's try the other Elements."

Meanwhile, Mr. Lavadan opened the window and the door, letting natural light into the room. He and I shared a nod.

I'm ready.

Within a second, he stretched his hand. I was engulfed in darkness.

Unlike with the light, this wasn't painful. I looked around, unable to tell the difference if my eyes were open or closed, almost like Afautiya. But at least there I had an aura, which let me see the ground.

No, at that moment, nothing was distinguishable. Confused, I glanced around, waiting for something. A minute passed. Two minutes…

"Is anything happening? I can't make your vision any darker," Mr. Lavadan said, seemingly from nowhere. "I'm not a Tenebral. I can only get rid of light, not create more darkness."

"I don't know. The light before was horrible, but nothing's happening now," I said to the void.

Bored, I tried looking for something—*anything*—amidst the endless shadows. As my frustration grew, everything somehow gradually grew darker. I noticed a face in the distance, but it was gone as soon as it was there.

Surprised, I squinted, trying to see it once more.

Was that just my imagination?

And then came the whispers.

A din of indiscernible dialogue came from all around. In front of me, a cloaked man appeared, with his hands held out for my neck. He jumped in my direction.

I gasped and stepped back. My stumbling feet tripped on some unseen object, sending me directly to the ground. Phantoms of this man kept on reappearing, attacking me. He lunged at me with a dagger.

I squirmed and backed away, trying to avoid him, shouting for him to stop. My head bumped against an obscured wall. I covered my ears and shut my eyes.

"It's—It's not real…It's not real," I repeated.

The more I tried convincing myself, the louder the

whispers grew. Every part of me trembled. My skin perspired. Hands touched my shoulders. I violently shook, trying to get away. My heartbeat echoed all around me.

An annoyed voice broke through the whispers.

Ughhhh, fine! I can't stand this!

A cold hand pulled me to my feet. When I looked, all the darkness had left, my vision returned, and a figure I had thought was restricted to only my dreams stood before me.

Umbra yelled, wearing a deep frown. "You gotta be a lost cause! Do you know *anything*? You don't succumb to fear when surrounded in shadows! That's practically just asking for death, or *worse*."

Behind her stood a speechless Darunia and Mr. Lavadan, both gawking at the woman. I couldn't blame them, though. Likewise, I was left wide-eyed at her presence.

Umbra placed her hands on her hips. "Got something to say?" she asked.

My eyes darted from her to them to her. I looked at the two over her shoulder and pointed to Umbra. "Can you guys see her too?"

The corpse-like woman rolled her eyes while Mr. Lavadan and Darunia both nodded.

"This…This can't be…" Mr. Lavadan mumbled.

Darunia quickly found her voice as well. Hers just

came in the form of an interrogation. "Who *are* you? What kind of accent is that? It is so odd. And how did you appear out of thin air? I never saw any rift."

Umbra glared at Darunia, barely turning her head toward her. "It's wonderful how much this generation knows. I feel *so* respected."

"So, you *are* real? Not just a dream?" I chuckled, ignoring Darunia. "I guess you weren't lying to me after all."

Umbra scoffed. "Listen, if I could, I'd lie to you every second, just to mess with you. But lucky for you, I can't."

"You know her?" Mr. Lavadan asked, slowly walking toward us.

"Well, the past couple of nights, I've been having dreams with her in them. So…kinda? It's weird," I said, attempting to explain. "Do *you* know her?"

He laughed, seemingly amazed. "Of course, I do! I mean, almost no one would nowadays, but I took advanced loric studies in my 70s. My whole job focuses on the times when she was more well-known. You…You are Umbra, yes?"

She raised an eyebrow and smirked. "At least one person here knows who I am."

Darunia tapped his arm. "Mr. Lavadan, how do you know her?"

"Dear Darunia, you must pay more attention in your history classes," he said, turning to Umbra. "I have only read descriptions about you before, *Milah*."

I whispered to Darunia. "*Milah?*"

"It's like *Ngahn*, but the female version," she said.

Mr. Lavadan continued. "I can't believe that you…I thought that all our old beliefs were just superstitions!"

"Who *is* she?" I pushed.

"This is no other than the Element of Tenebrosity! Darkness incarnate!"

What? The Element of Darkness? Like, the Elements that the fae worship?

A wide smile grew on her pale face. "I'm impressed you actually know me. And you're a kid too. How old are you? Couple centuries?"

He stammered, "I, um, I am around one hundred and twenty-four."

"Woah. Maybe there is hope for fae after all." She chuckled.

"What?" I shouted at the two of them. "How on earth is that considered young? I don't want to know how old is 'old' for fae!"

Umbra turned to me. "Hah! You think a century is old? Try being around for…What's the word?" She stared blankly for a second and then crossed her arms. "Well, however long I have been around. A long time. Okay?"

"I think the word you are thinking of is *eons*," Mr. Lavadan said, grinning.

My jaw nearly dropped to the floor. "*Eons*?"

Darunia jumped in. "Wait, wait, wait. 'The Element of Tenebrosity'? You're kidding me, right? Darkness isn't a person. Shadows are inanimate."

A growl rumbled from Umbra. With a snap of her fingers, shadows crawled up the young fae, turning her eyes as black as tar. Darunia began freaking out, shaking and pleading for it to stop.

Umbra sneered. "Does that feel 'inanimate?'" Subtly, Umbra licked her lips. She flicked her stringy black hair over her shoulder, and the shadows left Darunia.

The girl panted, trying to catch her breath. Her eyes returned to normal. Mr. Lavadan rushed to Darunia's side and helped steady her.

"Wait...I don't quite understand. If you really are an Element, then why are you here?" His eyes turned to me. "And why is she showing up in your dreams?"

I raised my hands in submission. "Don't ask me."

Everyone turned to Umbra, awaiting an answer.

She chuckled. "I—"

A little ping of light flashed beside her head. Once more, she growled. Her attention was directed to the light.

"Hey! How stupid do you think I am? Of course, I won't!" Umbra sighed and turned back to us. "I am just here to help. That is *all*. No questioning my methods unless you want to live in nightmares for the rest of your life. And trust me, I wouldn't be totally against you choosing that."

"Help with what?" I raised an eyebrow, already tired of her demeanor.

A thin smile pulled across her face. "You don't really think that you'll be able to learn anything by just plunging yourself into complete darkness, do you? I gotta say, the only thing that could come of that is insanity. Literally. No, no. While I am here, you will be *learning*. You will figure out how to control shadows."

She strolled downstairs to the couch. We followed Mr. Lavadan walking to the lounging Element.

"*Milah*," he said, "would you like us to leave you? I do not dare question why this is all happening—something I will instead do with Elena later—but if you want privacy with her—"

"Yes! That would be amazing. I hate being around fae more than I need to. For way too many reasons. Goodbye, peasants!" Umbra waved them off.

Mr. Lavadan led Darunia out of the room and up the stairs. I glanced at the lady on the couch, disgusted.

Controlling Darkness (For Dummies)

"**Now**, to start off, here's a fun fact about me: I thrive on fear," she said, not even bothering to sit up on the couch. "Since I'm chained in Afuatiya, I need to gain energy so that I can interact with mortals and do my stupid duties. I do this by—well—*eating* fear. It's weird to explain, but if anyone is in complete and utter darkness, then anxiety will be amplified. Fears will fill the person. This emotion is so raw and powerful that I eat it and gain Essence. You and your friend here felt this not too long ago." She shrugged. "When you're in this situation, next time, just redirect the shadows."

"Oh, yes, that makes sense," I said sarcastically.

"Of course, it does. That's because it is so simple. Now, we start with a few shadows. It takes a lot of experience to deal with the amount you faced, and that is something you don't have. So, for the little baby, we have to take small steps first."

"Mhmm…Pushing aside the fact that you just called me an infant, what does that mean?" I tapped my foot, growing impatient.

"Well, the easiest thing to start with is your own shadow. Try moving it."

Pft, really? I raised my hand and waved it. My shadow followed suit. "Done," I said, grinning.

For the first time since I had met her, the Element giggled. "Okay, that was actually funny. Come on, though. Actually put effort into it. Starting with your own shadow is the simplest path because you already have a sort of a connection to it. Try making it disappear. Tell it to go into the shadows of the couch."

I glanced at my shadow but hesitated. My somewhat sane self still had a tough time accepting the idea I could even *do* anything like what she suggested. Elemental immortals and fae were one thing, but me actually doing something akin to magic just seemed too…personal.

My life since the cruise had been almost a nonstop dream. Everything was so outlandish and mystifying, but I followed it to the best of my ability.

I wasn't really given a choice.

But once it came to something that relied on my own ability, that was when I felt trapped behind a fourth wall. It seemed so ridiculous and arbitrary.

I can't actually move shadows. That's just stupid. This isn't —

She sang, "You're overthinking it."

I looked to her, watching Umbra stretching and making herself more comfortable.

"You can read my mind?" I asked, slightly scared.

"Nope. Not like I'm Jeongsin. It was pretty obvious since you were just standing there for a couple minutes, staring at the floor. Like you're crazy. Whatever you are asking yourself or doubting, stop it. Controlling darkness needs little to no thought."

A light flashed beside her.

"*Oh my Ether*, would you leave me alone, you little pest?" She swatted the light away. "Listen, *Hasha*, all you need is to formulate a simple want. Feel the connection. Want it to obey. Oh, and most importantly" — Umbra looked over her shoulder, curling her black lips to a smile — "take your time. I got nothing going on. I am not impatient, like Brazen."

I arched my eyebrow. "Okay, who's Jeongsin, and who's Brazen?"

She waved her hand at me dismissively, much like she had done to the others. I silently vowed that if she called me a peasant, I would kick her out of the house.

She said, "Just try again. You have to will it to work. No thinking. Got it?"

Will it to work… Defeated, I nodded. I examined the shadow once more. After closing my eyes and taking a deep breath to clear my mind, I focused on my feelings. On what I wanted. I knelt onto one knee and softly touched the darkened floor.

Obey.

A subtle shutter spread through my bones. I gradually opened my eyes. The shadow had seemingly attached itself to my fingertips, like tar. Where it touched, my skin seemed to tingle. Even though it stretched when I moved my hand around, I didn't feel any resistance. I gawked in wonder.

With a gentle sway, I lifted my hand. The darkness pulled itself from the floor, following my hand and collecting in my palm. My body no longer cast a shadow.

No, now that it was in my hands, it was tangible. Curiosity enthralled me. The shadow felt like a puppet, submitting to my every wish.

This isn't possible…

When disbelief snuck its way back into my mind, the shadow began to fight. It became malformed, writhing and threatening to return to the floor.

My grip on the darkness grew tenuous. *I can't doubt. I can't doubt.* The oddity in my hands calmed down. The longer

I controlled it, the more I began to feel a bit of exhaustion weighing me down, but it didn't matter. It felt right. Another puzzle piece found.

"That's a bit more like it," a soft voice fluttered in my ear.

I flinched, surprised by Umbra's presence.

My focus on the shadow waivered. It stretched in chaos, pouring out of my hands and back onto the floor. It returned to its original shape, once more depicting my silhouette.

Umbra tittered, which was an interesting sound, with her breathy voice. "Oop. Well, at least you got pretty far. All I actually expected you to do was to move the shadow or something. Congrats. You slightly impressed me."

Adrenaline rushed through my veins. Like I had succeeded in completing a marathon. Exhilarated, I turned back to her. "What else can you teach me? I want to learn."

She placed her hands behind her head. "Hah. Fine. Instead of detaching the darkness, like what you just did, try making it melt away. Y'know, what I told you to do *before*?"

More confident in my abilities, I bent down and touched my shadow, willing it. The connection instantly formed again, with the same internal shiver, but I knew I should probably start listening to Umbra before a blood vessel burst. This time, I tried pushing the shadow away from me with my hand.

Unfortunately, it didn't obey.

"Wow, that was sad," Umbra said. "No, physically controlling it requires detaching the shadow. But you aren't detaching. You're supposed to be moving it. So instead, use just the connection you feel to control it. Tell that connection what you want. It will respond much better to that. But you gotta get better at this. I can't be giving favors out left and right."

Wow. How vague.

I stopped my train of thought, knowing I needed to focus on the task at hand. Not entirely sure of what to do, I pretended the shiver had come through me again. Sure enough, the shiver did reappear, following the memo.

Curious, I imagined it flowing into my command: *Move away.*

My imagination became reality. The invisible force surged through my limbs and, one by one, to my fingers.

Once it reached the floor, it left me, chasing the darkness away into the couch's shadow. For a second time, I was left without a silhouette beneath me. As if I were a ghost. However, it didn't last for long.

When I pushed aside the shadow, my stamina depleted. I quickly found myself perspiring and drawing bigger breaths. While my exhaustion increased, the shadow came back from where it had been hiding. I shakily stood up.

Umbra tsked. "Can barely even do that, huh? Well, I

guess that's my cue to leave."

"What?" I asked. "But…I thought you said you would help me."

The Element walked toward the wall, hiding from light. "Yes, and I helped you."

I scoffed. "Are you kidding me?"

She shrugged. "This won't be the last time you see me. I will help when I feel you need it. I will *not* work more than I have to. Plus, you're already tired after only two tries! Before I come back, you have to find a way to forget that disbelief you got and find a way to last longer."

Umbra raised her arms and gestured around her.

"This is real. It's time for you to accept it." A small ghostly grin appeared on her face. "I'll see you tonight."

Within an instant, she melted into the darkness, disappearing before my eyes. Left by myself, I began to contemplate what had just happened.

It had occurred in front of me—*I* was even the one to control it—but it was unsettling. Somewhere in the depths of my mind, it didn't register as reality. My fourth wall reemerged.

Although I was physically tired, it was my mental fatigue that burdened me. With how things were moving, I wished I could just accept what had been presented to me at face value. I wished I could forget all I had known for this new world. It would have made everything so much easier.

So that's what I'll do.

I vowed to force myself to have an open mind. At that point, I would have done anything.

Audience of Ten

I found Mr. Lavadan and Darunia talking in an upper room of his house.

Mr. Lavadan jumped up, frantic. "My dear! How did it go? Did—did she further explain her being here? Are you done with your lesson already? Where did—Is *Milah Umbra*—"

"Whoa, whoa," I said, laughing a bit. "She…left but I haven't seen you this riled up before. What gives?"

The man seemed as enthusiastic as a nerd at Comic Con. He had always appeared so much more knowledgeable than his age, but maybe that had only been my perspective. He really looked like a new kid in college to me. However, this moment made him feel more relatable. I enjoyed seeing him geeking out.

Mr. Lavadan combed his hair with his fingers, ridding it of any strays. "It's just…It's my job to study and learn about our past, figuring out how to keep the good parts alive and learn from the mistakes. To find out that our lores were actual events is just…You of all people should understand! Hidden truths and all that." Mr. Lavadan smiled, awaiting an agreement.

I hesitated. "Well...It's—It's a bit different for me. The stories that I've heard were all old fairy tales and such. I never believed any of it. Isn't this 'lore' related to your religion? Because it seems like it is more personal for you than what I've felt."

He shook his head. "My dear, it is like I said. The fact of the matter is that we have no religion. When it came to worship, most of it was out of obligation and wanting favor with them, but none of it was very zealous. No one *believes* in them. In fact, if I remember correctly, many of our tales include how mortals would secretly despise them, although I don't know why." Mr. Lavadan's gaze wandered away. "I should brush up on my Elemental studies."

"Well, to answer your previous question, apparently, she just wanted to show me a single trick, then leave. I think she's the kind of person that likes to weasel their way out of as much work as possible. She's kinda shallow." I shrugged. "Who knows, though? Maybe she'll help me more in the future."

Darunia stood up with slight trepidation. "I need to go home, Mr. Lavadan. My mom will be back soon for lunch, and she will freak out if I'm not there to say hi. And I mean, *really* worried." She turned to me with a smirk. "This was...*interesting*, to say the least. I hope we can meet up again soon!"

"Me too," I said. Her cordiality was touching, truly leaving me hoping the same.

Mr. Lavadan led her to the front door. I watched out the window while she walked to a cycle she had left by the porch and rode off into an eventual portal. It still perplexed me how they were able to travel this way.

Another question for another time.

He returned upstairs, closing the door behind him. "Okay," Mr. Lavadan began, a little indignant. "So are you planning on telling me what that was all about?"

"Oh, well, she just, err, *guided* me, showing me how to touch and move my own shadow. Mind you, I use the word 'guided' in the loosest term possible."

He sighed. "No, I mean *how in Rishi's name an Element personally knows you.* Or maybe the fact that she has taken an interest in *teaching you.*"

"What?" I asked. "I already told you…I. Don't. Know. I didn't even know she was the Element of Darkness until you told me! All I know is that she's been showing up in my dreams."

He rubbed the arch of his nose. "And all of this on top of the fact that you seem to have multiple Gifts…"

I remembered what Umbra had explained to me the night before. It was difficult to refrain from kicking myself for forgetting. In my defence, I didn't exactly think that any of that was real.

"Well, it may be too late to tell you this, but Umbra told me that I don't actually have a Gift."

His eyes bored into me. "What?"

"Yeah, in fact, she said that I have a 'Blessing,' although I have no idea what that means."

Mr. Lavadan crossed his arms. "I haven't heard that terminology before. I will make sure to look into it." He knelt to my eye level. "But, my dear, is there anything else you would like to tell me? *Anything*?"

"I-I don't know. I don't think so."

He murmured something inaudible under his breath and stood up. "Okay. Thank you for telling me what you know. Now, I would like to continue exploring this, but I assume…"

Mr. Lavadan turned his wrist. Voliun runes projected in the air over his hand. I gazed at the display in wonder. It reminded me of those futuristic movies I used to watch.

"That's what I thought. Well, my dear, I'm afraid we must go to an event I planned for us. We will continue this another time." He put down his hand, turning off the hologram.

I crossed my arms in defiance. "An event?" I groaned.

Yes, I was pouting, and I believed I had every reason to. Since I had arrived, it seemed to be a nonstop roller coaster to Crazy Town.

I need a break. And a distraction. Maybe sit back on the couch and just watch TV for the rest of the day…I quickly abandoned that idea, remembering I was in a fae's house. *Dang it. He doesn't even* have *a TV, does he? Is there anything else —*

He cleared his throat, grabbing my attention. "Did you hear anything that I just said?"

Like an idiot, I stood there, trying to recall something, anything.

Mr. Lavadan pursed his lips in disappointment. "Okay. Can you please pay attention this time?"

I nodded.

"Good. Now, what I was saying before was that the Ancients wanted an audience with you. You are the first fae to be raised purely by humans, and they are wary about your integration into our society" — he shrugged his shoulders — "which is fair."

"Hey!" I scoffed.

"Well, my dear, take it this way. Say you know a particular group of people who are notorious for getting into trouble and making bad decisions. One day, a girl comes to you from that group, saying she wants to now join your community. Would you not be skeptical of what she actually values or how she behaves?"

I rolled my eyes, hiding the fact I would have, indeed, been very suspicious in that scenario.

"Anyways, they want to meet you and ask you some questions. That's all."

"Uh huh. Aren't the Ancients your *rulers*? You make this sound like a simple meet-and-greet, although even the last meet-and-greet wasn't exactly 'simple.' Actually, thinking about yesterday, doesn't one of them hate me now?"

With a gentle hand, he held my shoulder. "We might have had a rough start, but *Ngahn* Sarkis was only one of our ten Ancients. We can gain their approval yet." He gestured his head to my room. "Why don't you go get ready? We both need to present ourselves professionally to help create a good image."

Quite quickly, a new worry sparked within me. "What exactly am I going to wear? Because I *know* you won't have me putting on that organ displacer again. And this is my only outfit, which is pretty sad, by the way."

Mr. Lavadan smiled, a bit amused. "Well…not wearing that 'organ displacer,' as you so eloquently put it, would only make your upbringing more apparent. The kids today love leather, and the girls seem to wear these corsets the most. It's odd that you complain about it. I haven't heard anyone call them uncomfortable. Plus, I know I didn't do a good job preparing for your stay. We'll get right on fixing that with Kaylessa as soon as we can."

"Mr. Lavadan, you do know that humans used to wear corsets all the time in, like, the medieval age, right?"

"*Ha!* Of course I do, and the new generation has made

it a fad. Although its popularity and appearance varies on the tribe. Humans had made them rather constricting, but we have—"

"Replicated it exactly!" I threw my hands up. "Because whenever I'm wearing that *thing*, I can't breathe!"

He looked off into the distance, as if in deep thought. "Yes, yes...so you say. Although I do not know why it inconveniences you so." With a slight grin, he pushed me off toward my room. "How about you put it on, and we'll see what I can do?"

I gave in and went to my room, searching for the horrid corset. Upon finding it, I muttered some curses to myself and slipped it on. I went to Mr. Lavadan, needing him to tie it for me.

He was in the middle of putting on a vest atop his tunic. Mr. Lavadon had fixed his hair and put on a golden pin bearing the symbol of a shimmering eye.

I waved my strings at him. "Well? I need you to put these on. I can't."

He walked behind me and grabbed them. While he tied the strings, the corset compressed my ribs, and my lungs threatened to pop.

"Dude. You can't loosen it in the slightest?" I asked.

"My dear, I'm tying it *as loose as possible*," he said, growing impatient. "Any looser and I wouldn't have enough ribbon to actually tie it!"

Vexed, he threw his hands up and let them fall to his sides. I wasn't sure whether it was me or the strings he was annoyed with. It was most likely me. As a kid, I liked pushing issues until I couldn't anymore.

Mr. Lavadan crossed his arms. "Okay, well…It's not getting any better. I'm sorry, but we need to leave and not fiddle with this any longer." He straightened his clothes. "Come on now. Tardiness will not help your social image."

He took a bag from his pocket and threw its contents into the air. Crystals formed an oval, creating a rift. With a soft touch, he grabbed my wrist. For the first time in a long time, I felt like a kid again.

His dark hair brought out his pensive eyes. His gaze gave me comfort, although I didn't know why. In my gut, I knew I could rely on him.

"Okay, I'm ready," I said.

I walked with him through the portal.

Coming out the other side wasn't very pleasant. The air was crisp, chilling my skin. My fingers became icicles.

Before me stood a towering building, wide-set and incredibly detailed. The silver structure reminded me of trees and vines stretching up and around the opalescent glass ceiling. Clamor filled the air all around me. Hordes of people were heading in the same direction as us.

I was grateful Mr. Lavadan held onto my hand; otherwise, I would have been swept away by the masses.

We all herded inside, but the crowd made it near impossible for me to even make out the interior. I was an insignificant child amidst hundreds of adult fae. Never had I felt so small.

As soon as we stepped in the building, Mr. Lavadan fought the flow of traffic, trying to break the two of us free. After some pushing and him pulling on my hand as if it were a leash, he led me to another room.

Now free from the chaos of the crowd, I was able to take in my surroundings.

Practically everything was made of glass. The ceiling was nothing but layers of transparent-colored sheets, creating a tunnel effect upward. Light from both the torch-like lamps and outside bounced everywhere, making every surface look pristine. The walls were all lined in silver, clean-cut and beautiful.

In front of us was a desk similar to the one back at the village center. Behind it was a man, who was frantically switching back and forth between a dozen golden holograms. The poor guy had such bags under his eyes that I could have packed for a weekend away with them. Amidst his multitasking, he was constantly talking to people as if he were on five different calls simultaneously. Yet, I never once saw a phone.

"No, I'm sorry. We don't do that. Try calling another department. Hi, uh, yes. They are full for the next two wanings, but perhaps we can work something out. Hello, how may I help you…" he rambled on.

Mr. Lavadan waved at him and tried speaking, but the man didn't notice us. With a *tsk* and a bit of grumbling, Mr. Lavadan walked up to the desk and put his fingers to his mouth. A sharp whistle pierced through the man's talking, calling his attention.

He wearily smiled at us, his hands still working on the holograms. "Hello. How may I help you? Do you have an appointment?"

Mr. Lavadan leaned on the desk. "Yes, we do. It's at ten."

Instantly, the man's face flushed. He ceased his multitasking. "You're...You're at the tenth phase?" His gaze turned to me. "Does that mean she's—"

"Yes, she is," Mr. Lavadan replied with the tiniest bit of an eye roll. "We're going to get enough of this today, so can we skip past the shock and deterrence?"

The man blinked and shook his head, trying to get out of his trance. "Um, yes. Okay." He handed us two metal circles the size of dimes. When he touched a hologram, a door opened to our left. "Go on through. It'll lead you to the attendant's section of the Pantheon."

"Thank you," Mr. Lavadan said.

Pale and concerned, the man stared at me while we walked out. As we left, I thought to say something, but the look the man behind the desk gave me left me mute.

Mr. Lavadan handed me one of the dimes. "This will

project your voice. Put yours here," he said, touching a spot right above the middle of his collarbone.

He placed his first, and I did likewise, although I was slowly beginning to feel more like a cyborg than anything, thanks to all the gadgets on my neck. The dime stuck to my skin rather comfortably, much like the translator I had equipped above it.

We walked down a hallway where the wall to our left was made entirely of windows. Outside, a constant flow of people were going to the side of the building. We turned into a right corridor, away from any more windows.

We walked for what felt like an eternity. I wanted to break the apprehensive silence.

Small talk time.

"So, Mr. Lavadan, what's the Pantheon? Did they mean like the Greek gods' Pantheon, or…?"

"I don't know anything about Greek gods, but the Pantheon is where all the big councils — that include a majority or more of the Ancients — convene."

Anxiety tensed my muscles. Breathing became laborious. I squeezed my hand. Obviously, I had not had a great experience with the first Ancient I met. Fear left me worried about my next encounter with them.

I tried shaking myself out of nervousness. *It…It will be fine. They're just people, right? It'll be fine. I'll probably just tell them my name, age, and whatever, then we'll go. It'll be —*

Upon our arrival, the doors opened, revealing a room about half the size of a football stadium. The space was a circle with a vaulting ceiling. The seats for us were situated in the very center. In front of us were ten thrones arranged in levels, like stairs, filled with who I knew could only be the sovereigns of fae.

The wall to my right opened to outside, where the crowds all peered in. Above the opening and lining the back and left walls were hundreds of seats akin to bleachers, each one filled with murmuring fae.

Oh hell.

"Come now," Mr. Lavadan gently urged. "It's best to get this over with."

Once we took our seats in the center, the Ancients all stood. Each one of them had different markings on their face, and I don't mean like freckles or moles. Sharp and soft embellishments lay precariously on each of them. The Ancients either sneered at me or seemed unimpressed.

It wasn't until Mr. Lavadan cleared his throat that I realized everyone but me was kneeling. Again.

Dang it!

Embarrassed, I dropped to my knees. The Ancients sat down. Those of us with seats did likewise, while the audience outside just stood, peering in.

"Please state your name," one of them told me. Her braids were tied back and woven meticulously, putting every rope I had ever seen to shame. Her cold stare seemed intensified by the golden markings around her eyes.

Mr. Lavadan bent over to my ear and whispered, "That's *Milah* Yuneasa Rosandoral. She's the spokesperson for the Ancients as a whole, being the only one with a Luminous Gift. She is the person to have on your side, more than anyone else."

I straightened my posture, attempting to look confident to impress her. "I'm…Elena Cruz," I said, surprised at how my voice boomed with little effort, thanks to the device I had put on.

Another Ancient groaned. "No, child. Your *fae name*. No one cares about your human name."

What part of growing up with humans don't they understand?

"Uhh, I don't quite—" I mumbled.

"Syndra," Mr. Lavadan said. "Her fae name is Syndra."

I stood there, speechless. Confused, I tugged on his arm to get his attention, but Mr. Lavadan answered my question before I could ask it.

He touched the dime-sized technology on his throat. "If you admitted that you had no fae name, that would only further separate you from us," he said, his voice now quiet. He darted his eyes back to the Ancients. "I had to pick something spur of the moment. Hope you don't mind."

I copied him, temporarily turning off the vocal magnifier. "Oh. No...No, I don't, but—"

"Mind including us in on your conversation?" one of the rulers asked. Even though he wore a gilded tunic, he had a messy cut of hair and slightly wrinkled clothes. His markings were around his mouth and on his hands. He was resting his head on his fist, looking as bored as a child in math class. "Might be nice to know what you're talking about."

Mr. Lavadan took his hand off his device. "Nothing, *Ngahn* Thenelis. She just had a trivial question that I answered."

Ms. Rosandoral chimed back in. "No side conversations, Lavadan *Gee*." She turned to me. "Now, because of your upbringing, I assume that you have no surname. Where are you staying, young child?"

"I'm staying with Mr. Lavadan right now," I said.

"Ah. That's why he's speaking for you. If that's the case, then I assume he will be your acting guardian for the time being?" She raised her eyebrow, curving the markings on her face.

"Yes, *Milah*. That's right." Mr. Lavadan nodded.

"Good. You'll need to fill out documentation, though. To transfer into an Independent village, Miss Syndra will need to go through some paperwork."

"Listen," another Ancient said.

Just my luck, Nylian Sarkis had decided to chime in. I stood, praying he had forgotten about our previous encounter. He hadn't.

Sarkis spoke, "These questions are minutia. Let's not waste our valuable time with a disrespectful child." He looked at me and crossed his arms. "Let's get to real issues. What is your Gift, and what school are you attending?"

I rubbed my arm. "I don't...really *have* a Gift. Nor am I—"

The crowd went into an uproar, as did the Ancients.

"What? What kind of a fae are you?" one of the rulers shouted at me, jolting upright.

My will crumpled like a can under the shoe of expectation. I felt isolated and afraid, as if they were going to stone me or something just because I had no Gift.

They are *fae. Maybe stoning isn't an absurd conclusion for them.*

Mr. Lavadan shot up out of his seat. "Please!" His voice echoed, turning everyone's attention to him. "Is it Gifts that separate us from the other species? Last I checked, they were just a bonus. Are we really defined by our Gifts?"

The audience simmered down in response, not quite disagreeing. His voice became stern and strong.

"She is a fae. She just hasn't done the Ritual yet." His gaze shifted to the Ancients. "Additionally, I don't think it's

172

correct to say that she has no Gift. From what we've observed, she *does* have some sort of ability or something akin, but we don't know what it is yet."

A pause followed. Each of the Ancients began tapping their fingers in the air. They glanced at each other, some sighing and others gently nodding.

"Well, then. Such ambiguity can only be dealt with by equally tenacious plans," Ms. Rosandoral said. "Our schools are very strict on the kinds of Gifts allowed in. As such, your education will be taught by Mr. Lavadan until you complete your Ritual. Additionally, there is apprehension and skepticism when it comes to matters with your morals relating to your upbringing. As such, an emissary will be periodically visiting, making sure we are updated on each matter of yours."

What am I? A criminal?

I wanted to say something to address the "probation officer" they were going to send to me and how ridiculous that was, but Mr. Lavadan spoke up before I could.

"Thank you. We will make progress and have her ready for school soon enough." He bowed before them.

I tried to protest. "What? I—"

"Good. Your mentor will visit within the week. Council adjourned."

The Ancients all stood up and left. The crowds followed their lead, only with a bit more commotion.

When Mr. Lavadan and I walked out, I could feel the gossip about me spreading, even though I only caught a few words here and there. The two of us returned the vocal magnifiers and headed outside.

Not only will I have someone watching over me like a warden, but I also have to do a Ritual. I hope it'll be nothing too troublesome.

Before Mr. Lavadan could create a rift, a familiar face rushed over.

"Hey…That didn't go so bad," Akkar said between panting. His draped clothing was obviously disheveled. He pulled his slipped ruby cuff up his arm so it wouldn't fall off.

I chuckled. "Not very in shape, are you?"

Akkar straightened himself and flipped his hair rather dramatically, attempting to not look tired. "Nah. I'm perfect. Plus, I ran all the way around the building to catch you! *You're welcome.*"

"Dear boy, are you here alone?" Mr. Lavadan asked.

Akkar's smile lessened a bit. "Yeah. My parents were…*busy*, but hey! You got someone better."

I put my hand to my forehead and scanned the crowd. "Really? Haven't seen 'em yet."

Akkar laughed and put his hand to his chest. "Ouch. You might be more fun than I thought." He looked at Mr. Lavadan, squinting. "You know, Lavadan, you look pretty dead. She's been a pain, I assume?"

"Uh…No, it's not—" Mr. Lavadan stammered, subtly trying to fix his clothes.

Akkar ignored him. "Yeahhh, don't actually care. Anyway, I'm getting bored, so how about we get Ms. Human here home?"

"What do you mean '*we*'?" I asked.

"It's your lucky day! I'm interested in helping you, so you'll see me around quite a lot from here on out!"

I scoffed, starting to get very tired of people "helping" me.

"Who do you think you are? It's not *your* house! Mr. Lavadan, are you going to let him be so bossy?" I asked.

Mr. Lavadan peered at me sheepishly. "Cainaris *Gee* knows very well that he is welcome in my home at any time."

"*Ha*! And you thought you knew better." Akkar wagged a finger at me. He began to walk off.

Mortified, I looked back at Mr. Lavadan. In return, he shrugged and followed Akkar.

Are you kidding me? What's with this kid?

Almost as if he could hear my thoughts, Akkar glanced back at me and proudly grinned. Annoyed, I succumbed and dragged myself over there.

In Deeper Truth

I had never been homeschooled before, but sometimes, I had wished I was because of how my classmates treated me. My foster parents never cared enough to do that.

Homeschooling was no easy feat, though. Since Mr. Lavadan had a job being a historian, I was often advised by others. Every day, at least one person was helping me along.

At times, Kaylessa would explain fae physiology. One would think a species so akin to humans would have similar anatomy. Nope, completely different functions.

Taelin would do his fair share too, showing me the kinds of technology fae used. Being a Speech Hacker — a fae with the Gift to control programs with a word — he demonstrated the different capabilities fae technology had in contrast to what I was familiar with. It was quite difficult to follow him at times since I wasn't very tech savvy.

Lucky me, the couple hated to be called by their last name, so I avoid learning how to pronounce it.

They were super helpful, but the more I worked with

Mr. Lavadan, the more I appreciated and preferred how he taught. He should've been a teacher. Mr. Lavadan explained subjects thoroughly, making sure I was taking notes when he would talk. Although the constant, forced note-taking was tedious when we began, I soon found myself fervently jotting down every new thing he taught me.

Of course, I bet I would have learned faster had Akkar not been interrupting my progress every other second.

"You're only teaching her the formal stuff. She's never gonna use any of that!" Akkar complained, throwing my papers on the couch.

Mr. Lavadan meekly helped me pick them up.

Annoyed, I asked Akkar, "Then what would *you* teach me?"

"Well, you gotta take your translator off first to learn any pronunciation." The boy grinned.

Reluctant, I unequipped the translator from my ears and neck. "There," I said in English. "Now take your best shot."

He cleared his throat. In Voliun, he said, "*Shou n'tai koni. Draash —*"

"Dude." I shook my head. "I can't understand you. Can you try explaining in English?"

Akkar squinted his eyes. "*Laui?*"

"*En — glish*," I over-enunciated.

Mr. Lavadan stifled laughter beside us. He put his hand on Akkar's shoulder. "*Veich, Gee.*"

Akkar nodded and waved his hands as if to try again.

"Okay," he attempted in English. "This…Here — *esh*, need…"

Mr. Lavadan began cracking up. His laughter was boisterous and made it hard for me not to join him. The man shook his head. "This is *not* going to work. Akkar *Gee* knows no English." He turned to Akkar. "*Taa draan. Ain thereiss uh.*"

"*Kin shiv n'saw eh ain! W'kaan liun eh Veich,*" Akkar shouted, trying to defend himself. The boy flopped on the couch, pouting. "*Oith. Ain chosh wain. Ain kov wain seeaan.*" He held up his hands.

"What did he say?" I asked through my giggling.

"He said that he is going to shut up now," Mr. Lavadan said with a big smile. "But it is okay. Maybe he will be more helpful later as you learn Voliun. I am sure he can be more of aid once we have your Ritual."

Mr. Lavadan began covering simple words, trying to get me to produce the same sounds. Akkar was no help with this, as expected. He was constantly getting bored and wasn't afraid to let us know. Although I had no clue what he was saying since it was all in Voliun, his contempt was clear.

After a few hours, a knock came at the door. Before

Mr. Lavadan let them in, I quickly equipped my translator.

"About time you put that back on," Akkar said rather indignantly.

Mr. Lavadan walked in, distracting me from responding. Behind him followed a towering man, scanning the living room.

Mr. Lavadan said, "This is Mr. Vruiyn. He—"

"I will be your emissary, Miss Syndra." The visitor gave me a cold, hard stare, but that lessened once he caught sight of Akkar. "Greetings, Cainaris *Gee*. I…didn't realize you'd be here."

"Pft. And why not? I mean sure, Lavadan is a hermit and awkward, but Elena here is pretty entertaining!" Akkar said.

A hermit? I looked at Mr. Lavadan, who seemed humiliated but wasn't going to protest.

Akkar put a hand to the side of his mouth, as if to exclude me. "Between you and me, it's incredibly fun to taunt her. And she makes it so easy!"

"Yes, *Gee*," Mr. Vruiyn absently said, looking a bit nervous. "I'm just gonna ask her a couple of questions and I'll be out of your hair."

What is with this kid? How does everybody know him? Confused by the interaction, I scanned them, trying to search for answers.

Akkar waved him on, slightly reminding me of how Umbra had treated Mr. Lavadan and Darunia. The boy slumped backward, getting comfortable. "Yeah yeah. Go on with your policies and useless questions."

Clearly miffed at the boy's attitude, Mr. Vruiyn cleared his throat. "Let's begin. Miss Syndra, how fluently can you speak Voliun?"

"Can't speak a word. Next!" Akkar replied for me.

"Excuse me. I don't think that's your place to say," I spat.

He giggled. "Aw, *Juruh*. I was here while Lavadan was teaching you. You know *nothing*. Next!"

Mr. Vruiyn nodded. "Miss Syndra, I need to know what the extent of your education is thus far. I will give you a test—"

"Come on! You know the answer is 'human education.' Next!" Akkar said.

Although Akkar had given him the vaguest and most confusing answer possible, Mr. Vruiyn didn't seem like he wanted to correct the kid. He searched for words, unsure how to respond. The kid clearly made this guy uncomfortable. My frustration with Akkar was slowly transforming into amusement.

It was more fun to be in the spectating end of his arrogance than the receiving end.

Mr. Vruiyn continued. "Moving on…In order to help further figure out housing and your Gift, we can do a blood test. With your permission, we can figure out who your biological family is. There will be a highly likely chance that if we can't find your parents, we will be able to find more distant relatives, but this has to be done with your permission."

I clenched my hands and shifted uneasily in my seat. Everything had been too much for me to take in as it was. I didn't want to add parents into the equation.

Unable to tell him any of this, I just sat there, contemplating what to say.

Akkar put his hand on my shoulder and leaned against me. My heartbeat pounded against the skin of my face. His hair felt like feathers brushing against my cheek. His breath was warm, and he smelled good, but I couldn't quite place the scent. There was no right word to describe it. *What is it…?* And then I caught myself. *Wait, why am I smelling him?*

Akkar said, "Ooookay…Well, I think your visit is done here. She obviously doesn't want to donate blood for freaky tests, and your questions have been all answered. Goodbye now."

Mr. Vruiyn obviously wanted to put this boy in his place. But he didn't. He stumbled with his words, not ready to leave.

Akkar simply cocked his head. "I said: goodbye

now."

Furious, the fae gritted his teeth and stormed out, slamming the front door behind him.

"Hah! Who's the child now?" Akkar laughed.

He stood up for me, I thought, dumbfounded. Against my wishes, a bit of blood rushed to my face. I internally reprimanded myself. *The dude's awful. Just because he did one nice thing doesn't make him a nice person.* It didn't help that I began realizing how handsome he really was…objectively, of course. Not that I cared.

Mr. Lavadan, shaking his head, sat down beside us. "I'm not sure that was the best idea. He'll just be back later."

"Meh. Not that big a deal. Then maybe I'll just be back to ward off evil. My presence is powerful like that." Akkar got close to me and whispered in my ear. Blood flowed through my veins, heating my neck, while he proceeded to speak. "Be open minded, though, okay? And patient."

"What?" I asked him, but he headed to the door.

Akkar ignored me and stretched. "Well, I guess that's my cue to leave. See ya later." With a wink at Mr. Lavadan, he added, "Maybe next time we can make some nummies. 'Kay?"

As soon as he left, I turned to Mr. Lavadan. "Did you understand any of that?"

Mr. Lavadan shook his head with a smile and then came and plopped down beside me. "Cainaris *Gee* has an interest in baking. Since I've had to provide food for myself for a while now, he thinks I have skills. The boy likes coming over to prepare food with me from time to time."

Well, you're certainly not giving yourself as much credit as you deserve for your cooking.

"That wasn't what I was talking about. He said stuff about being 'patient' and 'open-minded' or something. What was that about?"

He shrugged. "I've yet to meet a soul that truly understands that boy. Maybe he just meant about learning about our ways. Who knows?" Mr. Lavadan grinned. "With the distractions gone now, would you like to continue?"

***

I threw my head into the pillow in defeat.

"We have to focus. I need to understand this and I am no closer to learning this than I was when Mr. Lavadan left!" My voice was muffled, struggling its way out of the pillow.

Akkar crossed his arms. "Oh, I'm *so sorry* that I was helping you understand why your clothes deserve to be incinerated."

Kaylessa had gone shopping for me to help make up for my lacking wardrobe. Apparently, the corset was so horrible because Mr. Lavadan had gotten one too small.

Despite Kaylessa getting me new clothes, I had insisted on wearing Kylie's whenever I could. They would help remind me of less confusing times. Akkar didn't care, though. According to him, they were, and I quote, "the tackiest and most uncomfortable-looking clothes to have ever been made."

"Ughh. Yeah. I'm trying to learn Voliun so I don't have to rely on this stupid translator. I'm *not* trying to enter a beauty contest!" I screamed at him through the pillow.

I pulled my face out and brushed my now messed up hair out of my eyes with a scoff. "A little help here, Darunia?"

Darunia, in turn, was sitting at the end of the couch, trying very hard to not stare at Akkar. Her complexion glowed as red as Rudolph's nose and she incessantly fidgeted with her clothes. "H-Help? I— Uh, *Nim* Cainaris was just helping you, right?"

I glared at her. "*No*. He was *not*."

I was so annoyed with her. But, in her defense, she *was* a great aid, teaching me different pronunciations of words and such.

In fact, in the week I had lived with Mr. Lavadan, she had helped with most everything I was learning. Mr. Lavadan had a job and, much to his chagrin, was unable to be with me twenty-four-seven. Darunia, however, joined me after she got back from "Magical Training School" or wherever she went. She was able to aptly walk me through certain concepts.

Alas, it all came to a halt whenever Akkar joined us.

Darunia explained that the Cainaris family was very famous and powerful, like celebrities. But they liked to use the word "Descendent" rather than "celebrity." Reputations were everything to fae, and to have a longstanding lineage meant the world to them. Akkar's family name went back ten generations. But the Cainaris's popularity meant that Darunia had never spent much time with Akkar before, and it was clear to me how she felt about being around him.

Akkar chuckled. "Why, I think I was helpful! Even 'Runa agrees! And look how she dresses!"

"It's—ah…Darunia…" she mumbled.

I groaned. "Akkar, it is getting late. Mr. Lavadan will be home soon. Please, just help me understand these…Uh, what are they called?" I turned to Darunia, giving her a chance to say something.

Of course, it took a second for her to hear me past her distracted thoughts. "Oh! They're called honorifics!" she stated proudly.

"Pft, I don't know why you need help with them. You just used one! 'Mr. Lavadan'?"

I clenched my pillow, ready to chuck it at his head.

"I'm using a *translator*! Everything I say normally in English just naturally translates for you! That doesn't mean I know what I am saying!"

He rubbed his ears. "Geesh. Simmer your Essence. Don't have to be so loud."

"Simmer *what*?" I snarled.

Darunia peeked around Akkar's shoulder. "It's a phrase. It just means to calm down." She came over and sat between us, attempting to separate Akkar and me.

"Wow. Rude," Akkar said.

I whispered into Darunia's ear, "I can't even begin to understand why you have a crush on this guy. I don't care if he's popular or not. He's a nuisance."

She pretended to not hear me, but her ears defied her, turning bright pink through her thick hair.

Darunia cleared her throat and moved on. "Now, there are a few specific honorifics. The main ones you need to know are the respect based ones. These—" she wrote two runes on a paper, "are respectful honorifics used for those younger than you."

The paper read: 𝓖ᴏ | 𝓑ᴏ

"The first is pronounced *'Gee'* and is used for guys. The second one is pronounced *'Bee'* and is for girls. Oh, and both are put after the name rather than before it. And then there's *'Nim'* for older males, and *'Mei'* for older females. Both go before the name."

She wrote two more words, separated by a line:

I asked, "What about *'Ngahn'* and *'Milah'*? Aren't those honorifics?"

"Oh, that's right!" Darunia wrote two more words on the page. "Sorry. We rarely use them. They mean the most respect and honor given to the person you are talking to. Like for Ancients."

Akkar leaned over Darunia's shoulder, causing her to freeze like stone. "But you should mainly focus on the other ones. People use them the most. For example: every adult fae calls me either 'Akkar *Gee*' or 'Cainaris *Gee*'. You can feel free to call me *Goni,* though," he said with a wink.

"'*Goni*'?"

"W-well, there are also honorifics that are more sweet or, uhh, endearing." Darunia wore a nervous smile. "*Goni* kinda means older brother, but it can be used for any guy that's close to you and older. '*Chee*' is the same, but for older girls. '*Tain*' and '*Jurah*' are for guys and girls who are equal to you. They are also endearing."

"Ohh, so Mr. Popular here is old, huh? Since you want me to use an older honorific for you?" I grinned at him.

"Ugh, don't tempt me. I wish I was old." He sighed. "Sadly, I'm only sixteen."

I stared at him for a second, mildly confused at how he had taken my joke. "So you want to be old? Or-Or do you mean *older*, like young adult? Around twenty-three?"

"Twenty-three is super young. What's wrong with being old?" Darunia cocked her head. "Wisdom comes from experience. Imagine being able to see the centuries go by. To see everything change. Now, *those* would be some good memories."

Akkar walked around Darunia and sat on the edge of the couch beside me. He tried using my shoulder as an armrest, but I pushed him off. I didn't understand how he could make himself at home so easily. Nothing bothered the dude. No, he was too far above it all for it to affect him.

He clicked his tongue, ignoring me. "Every kid wants to be old. Mental and body functions only get better with age! Plus, you get to try so many different things! By the time you get past your early hundreds, then you really know what you like doing and where your place is. It's the best."

All I could think of was what the two of them would look like if they were old: their hair gray and their skin all wrinkled. *Wait, fae don't age like humans. Mr. Lavadan and Kaylessa both are over a century old, and they still look super young.*

I played with my pillow. "So, are those all of the honorifics?" I asked. I didn't share that common yearning for intensely old age like they did.

"No. The last few are '*Baalih*', '*Var*', '*Chouh*', '*Jeerei*', '*Appi*', and '*Meia*'." Darunia wrote each one out. "I know it's a lot. The last few are used for older fae. '*Jeerei*' and '*Appi*' for males and '*Chouh*' and '*Meia*' for females."

"So, I could use '*Appi*' for Mr. Lavadan?"

Akkar writhed in laughter, almost falling off of the armrest.

Darunia smiled nervously once more. "Yeahhh, I don't think you should. It's endearing, sure, but it's for…It, uh, means something similar to…well, 'Daddy.'"

My face flushed. "Oh."

She stammered, "Well, I-I mean, it also means 'Father' but—"

"No, *please*. Call him that! See his reaction!" Akkar said.

Fed up, I whacked him with my pillow, causing him to fall backward. There we sat, laughing at the boy on the floor.

Akkar rolled the pillow off his face. "Ha ha. Laugh it up. Real funny." He sat up. "I wasn't entirely fooling around, though. You know, it isn't the worst idea to start using one of those personal honorifics with him."

I wiped a tear from my eye and took deep breaths to calm myself. "What? What do you mean?"

"The guy does a lot. Feeds you, teaches you…He even acts as your emissary so Mr. Vruiyn won't come back! Calling him 'mister' is nice and all, but it's really, like, for strangers."

I looked at Akkar for a second, unable to think of a time Mr. Lavadan had ever treated me like a stranger. He had welcomed me openly into his home and had been providing for me since.

Darunia cleared her throat. "You also have to keep in mind that *Jeerei* Lavadan lives a quiet life. He's been through...*interesting* things."

That's right. Akkar called him a hermit.

"Are you talking about his wife's death?"

Darunia became squeamish. Even Akkar's arrogance had turned to solemn silence.

She softly replied, "Death...Death is a hard topic for fae. Usually, if a fae dies, it's because of humans. And even that is usually after centuries. His wife died only around a decade after turning her first century...for some unusual reason years ago. All I know is that it wasn't caused by humans. I've known him my whole life, and I was never able to see her before she died."

It was odd to me. He was a gentle guy, but I couldn't imagine why he was so introverted. Mr. Lavadan truly seemed to enjoy being with others. I remembered how he conversed with Taelin and Kaylessa. In fact, the whole ordeal with his late wife intrigued me. I just didn't know how to bring it up with him.

"I don't mean to sound insensitive, but what does that have to do with me?"

"You're not listening are you?" Akkar asked. "This guy has mostly been holed up in this house since she died. Then, a couple years later, a friend of his disappeared and has been gone since. Yet he has taken on the responsibility of taking care of the girl raised by humans. Sure, it was his friend that placed you with humans, but I would say that deserves a little recognition, huh?"

"That's right! I keep forgetting about her. Her name was Leiwyn, right?" Darunia pondered.

The name choked me, and resentment rose to my throat. *All of this is her fault.* I needed a subject change.

"Okay, how are you so connected in all this?" I asked Akkar. "I thought you were from this super important family. Not from this village."

"What are you talking about?" He shoved the pillow into my arms. "We're a part of this village just as much as Darunia! Village events and meets are just ridiculous, so we don't attend them."

Darunia, sounding rather disappointed, whispered, "The Cainaris family doesn't attend *anything* unless it piques their aloof interests." She smiled and spoke louder. "The point is, maybe just show him you appreciate what he does. Just by calling him *Jeerei* would show that. It's an endearing title, but not weird for a non-relative. Like what you would call your parent's brother."

I think she means it's like "uncle."

It made sense. I could be a thorn in one's side. Snarky comments and incessant questioning probably didn't make for a good roommate. Plus, he was doing all this despite going through all he had?

Maybe Mr. Lavadan was a stranger. Maybe I hadn't known him all my life, like how Darunia had. Maybe we had met under unique circumstances. But he was helping me much more than I was giving him credit for. He was my teacher and provider. I made a quiet resolution to respect him a bit more.

***

Mr. Lavadan came home late that night.

I waited for him hours after Darunia and Akkar had left. Often, if I did something good or if I showed progress in anything, he would shine that proud smile of his. I had never made anyone proud before my new life began. And even after a long day, I wanted to see if he would give me that same smile after I called him *Jeerei*: an example of my learning.

After a while, I grew impatient and just hung around in my room, practicing Voliun. I refused to fall asleep, wanting to see him. Even the night sky outside my window seemed still in anticipation — or at least it did to this twelve-year-old.

When the sound of the front door echoed through the house, I immediately jumped up to go see him. However, I caught myself when I got to the stairs. I didn't want to appear overly enthusiastic.

I slowly walked down the stairs, like any normal kid would in the dead of night when their guardian had finally come home. Perfectly normal.

But when I got closer to the living room, I heard him. Mr. Lavadan was talking with someone else. I crept down each step, trying to see.

It was Kaylessa.

He stuttered, "I can't—I'm not—"

"You can't keep evading it forever," she said.

Mr. Lavadan had his head in his hands. "Don't you think I know that? It's just…She's finally getting comfortable. I see how she connects with her friends. With you as well. I don't want to throw another obstacle in her path. She is *learning*."

"Leorn, what you are doing…it's not right." Kaylessa placed her hand on his shoulder. "She is her own person. You can't—"

"Please keep your voice down. I don't want to wake her."

She sighed. "If you cared about her well-being at all, you would tell her."

I furrowed my brow. *Great. What is he keeping from me now?*

"How? How would I tell her?"He chuckled nervously. "How would I tell her that her mother died when she was born? *We* don't even know how she died. All I knew is that one moment, my wife was giving birth and the next, she was gone."

I took a sharp breath. My eyes widened, and I clenched my hands. *His wife? My mother?*

He continued. "Then, in a blink of an eye, my little girl was taken from me. She—"

"What?"

They both shot their heads toward me. I stood at the staircase, unable to blink or move, unable to get enough breath in. Tears stung.

Mr. Lavadan shook his head. He took a second, trying to figure out what to say. "My dear…I can explain…"

"You lied to me. You lied to me! Even after you found me!"

I ran to my room, practically tripping on the stairs along the way.

My door slammed shut behind me.

Swallowing Stone Cold Pills

When I was younger, I used to wonder who my parents were. I had wanted to be with my biological family since neither my home life nor school life was the best. But after that night, I wished to return to my former life.

Anything to get me away from this.

I hid in my room for as long as I could. Almost an entire day passed without Mr. Lavadan coming in. After a while, he attempted to explain things. I didn't remember much of what he said because I blocked him out.

His once welcoming voice became grating. "My dear" this and "my dear" that. I never wanted to be called "my dear" again.

The only time I would venture out of my room would be when he gave up and went to work. Then, either Akkar, Darunia, Kaylessa, or Taelin would come to keep me company.

The couple—or rather, my *aunt* and *uncle*—attempted comforting me. They told stories about my parents. My mother had been Taelin's sister. She had cared about me greatly, even though I hadn't been born yet.

But it all fell on deaf ears. After all, they had been in on it. They *chose* to not tell me anything.

Darunia came around as much as she could. With all her might, she tried to help me ignore my problems and believe that I lived a normal life. That things weren't so bad or confusing. She hadn't known about it, but she was intent on making me feel better.

Somehow, she found ways to make it not seem as overwhelming as it felt. But a part of me wanted to linger in dismalness, so I ignored the points she made. I divulged almost nothing to her, knowing she might take a different stance on things since she had known Mr. Lavadan for her whole life.

Darunia spoke a lot to distract me. Sometimes, she talked about how school went that day, making fun of boys.

She got me to chuckle at one point, but I could mostly only fake smiles.

Speaking of ridiculous boys…Akkar would always come to me with a different tale. This guy was gossip central and believed that other people's woes would make mine look seem nothing. One guy tripped and hit his head on a table during class. A girl was exposed for having six different suitors at once—apparently, that was what they would call "boyfriends." Of course, Akkar's stories didn't work. I nodded and grinned every now and then—all of it empty gestures.

But, unlike the others, he recognized his failure. One day, he decided to take another approach. A better approach.

A heavenly aroma floated into my room.

Sweet and warming, something surely flavorful and filling at the same time. Almost like…biscuits? *Wait, it could be Mr. Lavadan making something.*

I disregarded it, not wanting anything *he* was making. I went back to trying to read my fae book. And let me just say, reading Voliun was no easy feat.

I held out as long as I could. The smell only grew stronger. My stomach growled, angry at me for not having lunch. Or breakfast for that matter. Focusing on reading the book became impossible. All I could think of was what might be producing that smell.

It wasn't biscuits. Too sugary for that. It wasn't buttery enough for croissants. *I've waited a while. Maybe he's left. I can probably just grab some and leave without him noticing…*

I snuck my way down to the kitchen, being as quiet as I could. Although, I probably would have been quieter had I not missed a step and tripped down the stairs. Thankfully it was only the last couple steps I fell down. The tumble echoed through the house.

"There you are! I was ready to eat all this myself!" a voice shouted from the kitchen.

"Akkar?" Then, upon hearing his footsteps, I realized I was disheveled. I shot up, pretending like nothing had happened.

He flung himself around the corner. "Who else? Lavadan left for work before you even got up. Now, come on. They're getting cold!"

"Exactly *what* have you been up to?" I asked.

I wanted to avoid him, even though my hunger betrayed me. My social battery was at an all time low. Especially for being in *his* company…Conversing and pretending sounded like a chore. Yet, it was my empty, growling stomach that pulled me to follow him. It was more powerful than my depression.

Coming into the kitchen, atop the counter was a tray with pastries in the shapes of flowers.

They were golden brown, with a coating of what looked like frosting. Fresh-cut strawberries were placed on each petal, creating patterns. My mouth instantly watered.

"Yup, looking pretty!" he said proudly, hovering above his creations. He squinted his eyes. "The puffs, I mean. Not quite you."

My face went blank. "Wow. Thanks. Just what I needed."

He rolled his eyes. "You're welcome. Now, these are baked blooms. Made by yours truly! Try one." Akkar handed me a plate.

A grin appeared on my face. I took the plate and peeled off one of the petals so that it was bite-sized.

Steam arose. The layers pulled apart. It was a little sticky because of the frosting. Something melted out of the center where the petal had been attached. I ate it. Whatever it was filled with tasted like a salty-sweet combination—almost like chocolate and a bit of butter. The strawberry contrasted, breaking through with tang.

Of course, I wasn't going to tell him how much I loved them. He had a big enough head as it was.

"So, what are these?" I ate another petal and avoided giving him any complements.

"I just told you. They're baked blooms. You need to work on your listening skills." Akkar shrugged. "They're nothing special, just practice! Good, aren't they?"

I leaned on the counter, finishing off the pastry. "Okay. Try explaining what it is to me again. Pretend like I know nothing because I know nothing."

Akkar picked one up and took a bite. "Mmm, okay. So, they're made with calendulas, cacao, strawberries, and… uhh, a few other things that I can't quite remember." He laughed. "But that's what you're mainly tasting. Cacao and calendula."

I sighed, but he groaned before I could say anything.

"*Esh!*" He threw his head back in frustration. "Before you start complaining about not knowing things again, calendula is a flower and cacao is a bean. There. Because you know *nothing*, I must educate you in every little thing. These aren't just fae things, you know? Humans use them too, I think."

I couldn't help but giggle. Pulling out a chair, I sat at the counter and took another bloom. "Yeah, I know what a cacao bean is."

"Wow. So you *do* still know how to laugh?" he asked, sitting beside me.

I looked away. He had almost gotten me. But I knew. He had known about it all and just hadn't told me. Akkar had even warned me about it before. Plus, he had an opinion about everything. Didn't quite make me want to talk about it.

Akkar flopped his head on the counter. "Okay, *Juruh*. But I'm gonna get you sooner or later. You can't stay like this. Poison withers from the inside out."

"Poison?"

With his head still sideways, he smiled. "It's just a saying. Just means it's not good to keep it in."

His smiles seemed to make him even more handsome. Usually, they radiated confidence or self esteem, always making me feel a little uncomfortable. Not this one. This one felt sincere.

I couldn't match it though.

The afternoon stretched on. We talked about surface stuff while munching on the blooms. Often, he pushed for me to confide. Like he wanted to be the hero. But I never let him.

A part of me was grateful that he tried. But it wasn't what I needed. I didn't need a strong, judgey opinion to comfort me. Hours painstakingly passed by. The sun traveled across the sky when we talked about absolutely nothing. I just wanted him to leave. Of course, I didn't get a break once he did.

"You know I'm just going to be back he—re, right? You make for a good taste-tester," Akkar said, heading to the door.

"Thanks for the food."

When I opened the door, Mr. Lavadan rode up on his cycle. *I don't get to have a second of rest, do I?*

Akkar nodded to Mr. Lavadan when he passed him by. "Seems like we're just switching out, huh?" the boy asked.

"Seems so," Mr. Lavadan said, staring at me solemnly.

This was the first time I had paid Mr. Lavadan any actual attention since I found out about everything. Similarities became abundantly obvious. He had gray eyes, like me. His light skin had a pink undertone. His lips were subtle but full. I winced with each matching aspect I found.

Then I noticed it. Dusk was coloring the sky orange. The setting sun's rays stretched through the branches of the surrounding trees. *I used to love this time of day.* My eyes drifted over to Mr. Lavadan. *There's no reason why I can't now.*

I scowled and rolled my eyes in disdain, then pushed past him and headed to the forest.

"What? Where — where are you going?" Mr. Lavadan stumbled after me. "It's getting dark, my dear."

I scoffed at those two words. My teeth gritted against each other. "Good. Maybe then I won't have to see your face."

Bushes brushed against me when I traversed deeper into the woods. The wind gradually nipped at my bare arms. I hugged my torso, trying to keep warm. *Why'd I have to wear short sleeves?* I was yearning for a jacket or whatever the fae equivalent was.

A minute passed. Five minutes. Ten.

I wanted to enjoy the sunset before it left, but I hadn't quite thought through my plan very well. The trees obscured the sky. I could barely see anything. At this point, I was just searching for a clearing. However, endless towering timbers were all I could find. *Tree, tree…Oh look, another tree…*

When I was about to give up, I found myself stumbling upon a cliff. I strolled over to the edge, cautious, astonished at the sight. Below was a sea of green. Foliage and plants stretched for miles. The waning sunlight made the forest below glow.

I sat down and leaned against a nearby tree. *I guess the trees are much less annoying from further away.*

Footsteps crunched against the ground behind me. My shoulders slumped. "I want to be alone. Leave. Me. Be."

Someone giggled. "Nice to meet you too," the person said with a soft accent. A familiar accent.

I turned around in confusion. Before me stood a girl, young but almost an adult. Her red hair fell in soft waves to her shoulders. She wore pastel green chiton with gold chains elegantly draped across her pink cheeks, resting on her nose. Like a Greek goddess. She had a strong aura about her.

"Uhh, hi?" I stared at her, bewildered.

She smiled. Her chains swayed when she placed a hand on her chest. "I'm Aithalis. I shouldn't be talking to you, but I couldn't let Umbra keep you all to herself."

It clicked. Her accent resembled Umbra's, wispy and fluid. Like she was talking in thin cursive. Her aura was similar, as well, but it wasn't as harsh as Umbra's.

"Are you an Element?"

Aithalis nodded, jingling her jewelry. "Element of Nature. She said that you don't know much about your Blessing or how to use it. Is that true?"

I groaned silently. I was going through enough and

didn't want to add Element stuff on top of it. Yet, I didn't know when I would be able to talk to an Element again.

They were very erratic.

Although weary, I began my string of questions, "Yeah, what exactly is that? I've asked, but no one I've talked to knows what that is. Is it like a Gift?"

She played with her hair. "Of course, no fae would know. There's only one person who has a Blessing. You, *Hasha*."

I rubbed my temples. *Of course*. "Okay. Now what does *that* mean? '*Hasha*'?"

"It means Fated." A vine grew up up around her arm like a snake. She played with it. "We call it a Blessing because it is something powerful that was set in place for you to receive. Something we don't know much about, for we didn't gift it to you."

Thinking about it became burdensome — a mountain of questions with no energy to be doing any of this. I pushed through, head on my hand.

I asked, "If you didn't give it to me, then who or what did?"

She stared at the ground. "The only mortal that I called my friend." Aithalis glanced at me. "I'm sorry I can't tell you more about him. You'll find that this fae is a painful subject for us to talk about. Maybe one day we'll tell the story. But it was him that foretold you. He said: 'She will be one of you, yet have the innocence of a mortal. She will be your moderator.'"

I raised a brow. "One of you?"

"Yeahhh." She nervously pulled her hair behind her. "He kinda said that you would be an Element. A new one."

There's no way I'm going from human to fae to Element. "But I'm not. I don't know what it's like to be a god, but it sure isn't this."

Her vine grew and gathered her hair into a low ponytail. She snapped it so it didn't connect her wrist to her head. "No, we are Elements. Not gods. Immortal but not omniscient. Omnipresent but with only one physical form. We have more limitations than mortals know about."

Aithalis locked eyes with me with a soft illumination in her eyes. I knew right then that this would be the gentlest person I would ever meet. Kaylessa was sweet, but she was sharp enough to stop others from taking advantage. I couldn't see Aithalis doing that.

"You are not an Element. But there's something there. Something none of us can place our finger on."

I put my hands down in my lap. "So you're taking a gamble? You don't even know if I have a Blessing?"

Aithalis winced and held her head briefly. "No, you most certainly do. I apologize. This is one of the reasons why I shouldn't be talking to you."

I scoffed. All I wanted was a straight up answer. I hated being left in the dark. But Aithalis gave me the most innocent smile I had ever seen.

"You're struggling with something. That's why you're out here. That's okay. Unlike Umbra, I'm not looking for a teaching session yet. I'm not supposed to be talking to you, remember?"

"Uh huh. You keep saying that."

The vine in her hand grew a flower. An azalea. She placed it in my hands. "I just wanted to tell you that if you ever need a safe space, my trees hold no judgement. And if you ever want to talk to me, you can call for me here."

I nodded, cradling the flower so as not to crush it. While I didn't understand, I needed a break. She crumbled into soil, falling to the ground and scattering about.

Immortals have the oddest exits.

I watched the sky drift from the warmth of dusk to the cold of night. Although I was freezing, I didn't want to leave or go back. I felt a calm that I didn't have in Mr. Lavadan home. Confinement didn't hinder me anymore.

Finally relaxed, I was overcome by my emotions.

Abandonment welled within. Confusion stung. Frustrations turned to apprehension, tensing every muscle. I embraced it all. That night, I fell asleep to the warmth of my tears.

Rest wasn't something that came naturally to me. So, I couldn't begin to describe how relieved I felt when it enveloped me through the cold night and into the morning. Of course, sleeping against a tree didn't make it very easy to retain that.

My leg cramped. It writhed, as if I had pulled it out of its socket.

I awoke with a start, trying to undo whatever I had done to my poor limb. It passed after a minute or so.

Annoyed, I panted, regaining my breath from being scared out of deep sleep.

I tried looking around, but my eyes fought back. Everything was blurry, and my eyelids refused to open all the way. I rubbed them groggily, quickly realizing how crusty they were.

Ugh, must've been the tears.

I regained my sight and scanned my surroundings. The sky was bright, and the sun was right above me. *Dang, I must've been asleep for a while.* All I heard was the tranquil rustle of leaves. *I could live here, alone, amidst the bushes.* But that couldn't happen. After all, I had a sneaky feeling Mr. Lavadan would try to find me after too long.

I stretched, attempting to relieve my back from the aches it had gained from sleeping on a root.

Something felt unnerving, as if I wasn't alone. I scanned my area. Nothing seemed out of place. No Elements as far as I could tell. I shrugged. *Probably just me —*

"Hey."

Acquaintance

I just met her, and she had already almost died. This girl must have been addicted to that state of being or something.

She squealed and jumped backward at the sound of my voice, right toward the cliff. I lunged to grab her before she fell. The girl yelped when I pulled. Of course, I accidentally flung her into a nearby bush. *Oops. Didn't mean that...* I hesitantly approached her. *Should I help her up?*

I stood over the bush. "Oh my Ether. S-sorry."

The girl struggled with the plant, stumbling out of the now dead pile of branches. "Well, a little help wouldn't have hurt."

Esh. Probably not a good impression.

She brushed the leaves off herself. "Who are you?"

I examined her now that I had a chance. She had a messy head of hair. Cut short and rather frizzy. But maybe that was just because she had slept outside and then fallen into a bush. I hadn't quite caught her at her best.

Her eyes were a shade of gray, with an opalescent shine. *It's been a while since I've seen a fae with gray eyes.* Her skin was tinted pink, although it was hard to tell beneath the smears of dirt.

Her voice sounded odd. Rather nasally. And the way she pronounced words felt off. I understood once I spotted the translator on her neck. *Oh. That's right. She doesn't know Voliun. She has an accent.* The translator was surrounded by a ring of grime and oils. I cringed. *Does she sleep in that thing?*

"Well?"

I snapped out of my head. "Oh. Sorry." *Okay. Gotta be welcoming.* "I-I'm Onvyr. But...I should be the one asking questions." I tried my hardest to sound curious. "Who are you? Why are you here?"

She squinted at me. "And why should *you* be the one asking questions? You're the one on... *my father's* land." She strained her words, like it hurt her to say it.

Leorn, right? Leorn Lavadan.

I arched my brow. "I didn't know that. I've been coming here every other revolution for the past orbit and never seen you." I tried at a scoff. "If this is your family's land, then why haven't I seen you before?"

The girl bit her lip and stared at the ground. "Oh. Yeah, I just...moved in." She cleared her throat. "But how could you not know this was someone else's land? Especially since you've been coming here for an orbit? My father lives right over there." She pointed behind her, deep into the woods.

I shrugged. "I just hang out around here. Never been that far into the forest."

She put her hands on her hips. *Oh, she's a sassy one,* I thought. *That's gonna make things easy.*

"And what exactly *do* you do here?"

"Just climb the trees and enjoy the silence." I looked up at the canopies above us. "I like the peace."

When I glanced back at her, she seemed disappointed. In what or who, I didn't know.

"Yeah, the peace is nice..." she said under her breath, drawing in the dirt with her shoe.

Every instinct in me wanted to stay quiet. To wait until she said something else. My Essence was building up, making me anxious. *I should've had a training session or something before I left. Something to have kept my Essence in check...*My emotions left me not wanting to make things more awkward, but I couldn't just stick to my comforts. That wasn't the point of this. *Welcoming. Be* *welcoming.*

I fidgeted with my tunic. "You...never said your name."

She peered at me.

I pushed myself to carry on, forcing a grin, "That's pretty rude. Not answering my question."

The girl giggled. "Oh, is that so? Well, I think flinging a stranger into a bush is pretty rude."

"I saved your life. 'Less you're an expert Astrokinetic or something, you would've died." I crossed my arms.

"Well, maybe, but...uh." She searched for a retort. "You could've at least helped me up! I lived just to be crashed into a pokey bush!" She pointed a finger at me.

I stared at the little finger and couldn't help but crack a laugh. The girl copied me, breaking out in giggles.

I rubbed my arm. "Yeah."

She tilted her head. "Onvyr, right? How old are you?"

"How old? I'm young."

"Wow. No kidding?" She shook her head. "I meant your *age*, weirdo."

Why does she want to know my age? Probably just wants to know if she's older than me...

I shifted my weight, playing with my glove. "Tell me your name, and I'll tell you my age."

She must have been nervous. The girl began looking around again, softly nodding. "Syndra. My name is Syndra."

Syndra? But, I thought it was...

I felt extremely uncomfortable and desperately wanted to leave. The whole name thing made matters just a bit more weird. And my Essence wasn't exactly making anything any easier either. But I couldn't just walk away. *Talk about her name, idiot.*

"That's an awesome name, you know?" I said.

"What? Why?"

I tried smiling. "I mean, 'devoted servant' is pretty cool."

She blinked. "Thanks. I, uh, came up with it by myself." The girl attempted to seem proud.

I bet she did. I rolled my eyes. "I'm fifteen. You?"

"I'm twelve orbits old."

Her gaze began drifting behind her, as if she was

apprehensive about something.

I need to wrap this up. "How long 'til your father comes?"

Her eyes widened, like I had caught her defacing the Pantheon. "What? How did you—"

I shrugged. "You look nervous. Bet you came out here to avoid him." My grin lessened. *I know a thing or two about trying to avoid people.*

She nodded. "There's just been things going on. I needed to get away, but I should probably head back before he gets too worried. That's his favorite pastime."

"I get that."

No, I didn't. I couldn't remember when someone had worried about me. Or at least, about my well-being.

She turned around to leave. *Please...just take the bait...*

The girl stopped abruptly. She looked at me with a small smile. "You come here every other revolution, right?"

Success. "Yup," I said, trying to disguise my triumph.

Relief flashed across her face. "See you in a couple revolutions, then?"

I nodded. "See you soon, Syndra."

There I was, left alone while I watched her find her way back home.

I began wondering what it would be like if I had someone constantly worrying about me. Choa Zentha took pride in me when I did good and Goni Wyn took care of me when it mattered.

But what if I was in danger?

Wyn would encourage me to overcome it if he knew. He would shout from the sidelines. "Come on! You're better than that, naak!"

Zentha would probably toss me a weapon in excitement, to see what I would do. She loved watching my progress and would boast to others about me whenever she could.

Neither of them would exactly worry for me. I shook my head, hardening myself once more.

They wouldn't worry. They would be helpful. Worrying is useless. Yet, something didn't feel right. Something from the back of my mind bothered me.

Like a memory that wasn't there.

It was probably just my Essence causing me to doubt myself. If it collected too much, it seemed to like to play with my emotions.

I stood there for an eternity, lost in thoughts.

Quiet. It's been a while since I've been in quiet.

Hesitation stopped me from returning. I loved what I did. I mean, I was *dedicated* to what I did. But this was the first time in wanings I'd had time to myself. *Linger just a little longer. Please.*

A rift opened beside me.

"Naak, we were getting restless. What's taking you so long?"

I looked up. Wyn stood in front of me, arms crossed.

"Come on," he said. "You know you're my buffer! Zentha's getting on my case again, and I need you to calm her down."

Wyn, the guy with a bunch of responsibilities, came to get me. I grinned. *Maybe he does worry about me sometimes.*

"Maybe you deserve her on your case. What'd you

do this time, Goni?"

He scoffed. "She's just being picky about my dorm."

I shook my head. "You left it a wreck again didn't you? Aren't you older than me? I feel like you should be more responsible."

"Oh, disperse you! It's not like they'll kick me out because of a little mess. My family has been with them—"

"For generations," I finished for him. "Yeah. I've heard that before."

He yanked my arm, dragging me through the rift. "You don't know anything," he mumbled, clearly annoyed.

Zentha was training in the sparring ring, waiting for me.

***

It was like she couldn't decide what to say. After the first meeting with Syndra, I had thought it would all be easy from there. Of course, she was much higher maintenance than that.

"How...was your day?" she asked.

The girl plopped on the ground before me with a strained smile. The way Syndra sat confused me. Her legs were folded inward and intertwined like a knot. *Her legs have to fall asleep like that at some point.*

"Good. Yours?"

She mumbled, "Ok, I guess..."

There was a dullness to her words. Like something was pressing on her, making it so she couldn't talk, but I could tell she wanted to talk. *I* wanted her to talk. But she wouldn't, and I needed to fix that. Me, the kid whose nickname behind my back had been literally "Mute" for orbits. *Why did they choose me for this again?*

I focused on her, looking for literally anything to talk about. My gaze couldn't move much further away from the disgusting translator.

"So, you learning a language or something?" I asked.

Her eyes shot to mine. "What? Why?"

I fiddled with my Mat gloves. "Just thought that was why you're wearing a translator. Don't see them often outside of human jobs..."

"Oh, um, yeah. I am." She tugged at a piece of hair.

I cleared my throat. "You okay?" I needed to be playing dumb. "Is something—"

"Iwasraisedbyhumans," she blurted. Syndra held

her breath, as if awaiting some grand reaction.

I hadn't been expecting her to say anything like that. *What should I do? What should I say?* I wanted to make sure I didn't offend her. That would break anything I had built with her. But how could I do so with how I felt about humans?

"Um, okay."

I decided to just leave it at that and see where she went with it.

Syndra, on the other hand, scoffed. She was as baffled as I was. Only for a different reason. "What? No disgust or...or anything?"

I shrugged. "Your translator makes sense now. And it's not like you're a human."

But it was. And I knew it. We all did.

Every muscle in her body relaxed. She let out a shaky sigh of relief. "I guess...I guess I'm just used to a different response."

Elements favor me, I don't even know how that all worked out.

"But tell me something," she went on, peering at me. "why do you all hate humans? What if I *was* a human?"

I hid my contempt behind a dry grin. "It's not that we-we *hate* them. They just tend to be rather...*violent.* Y'know? They got a lot of intraspecies crimes, like..." My voice waivered while I searched for a delicate explanation. "It wasn't like they had long lives to begin with. But then they just, uh..."

Shut up. Shut up. Shut up.

"Not all humans are like that." Her stare turned from nervous to trepidatious. Like if I said one word out of place, she would become distant from me.

I brought my knee to my chest, squeezing it to distract me from my accumulating Essence. "Yeah, I know. I just...haven't been with humans a lot before, so I can only go off of what I've heard."

An emptiness rang through my words, and a memory tried to flash in my mind. *The last time I was with them didn't exactly end nicely.* Thankfully, only I could hear the difference in my tone. She didn't seem to notice it.

"It's not as common as you think. I've...been with nice people before." She looked down, searching for a memory. "Oh, Juan! One of my foster fathers...He was really sweet. A bit of a pushover, sure, but sweet." Her eyes dimmed. "He's gone now, of course. We were on a cruise that exploded. I was the only survivor."

The only survivor. An unfortunate outcome.

Uncomfortable, I decided to stay away from the topic and move to something a little safer. "*Foster* father?"

"Yeah, I was in the foster system. Although I've probably been marked as a missing kid since I left." She picked at the grass.

I shook my head. "I don't understand. What's the foster system?"

Syndra looked confused by my question. *I don't know every little fact there is about humans, and I don't exactly want to. Give me some slack.*

"It's something that gives kids temporary homes. They get fostered by different families until they get adopted or can go back to their real family."

She chuckled wryly and pulled her hair back with her hands.

"Or they just cycle endlessly through families because no one wants them, waiting to at least become an adult so they can live on their own."

That sounds right for a species of selfishness. I have no idea why anyone would just give up their only child.

There was no way she wasn't talking about herself,

but I didn't want to find my way into a cry fest, and I had no idea how she would react to me pushing it. Yet I needed more from her. *I need to take this carefully.*

"Must've felt special being with them. Humans." Energy simmered beneath my chest. "Did you hide your Gift from them? Doing so would've been hard."

"My Gift?" She tucked her legs tighter into the knot. "I...don't have one."

I wanted to laugh. My Essence riled within me, almost spilling out. "Well, that's not true," I said, clearing my throat to restrain myself.

She crossed her arms. "Oh, yeah. That's what I'm doing. I'm just lying to you for fun."

I scoffed and copied her. "Without a Gift, pure Essence piles up in you. Acts weirdly, 'specially when it comes to emotions. Waves of different feelings can make it hard for you to do simple things. Can't say I've seen anything like that with you."

Her look of indignation softened. "What? But, that's not what others told me. They said it would make you hyper and it would be hard to focus on things. It's like ADHD."

ADHD? Must be some weird human thing. I lowered my arms to my lap. "I mean, crazy mood swings would make it kinda hard to focus."

"Well, I guess," she said, "But they said it gave fae short attention spans."

No, that doesn't seem right. I've never had a hard time paying attention and I've certainly never been hyper. Except when I would use my Gift. But even then, I wasn't hyper as much as excited.

I needed to not lead her on. "Interesting. Well, fae don't know much about it since everyone has a Gift. It was more common around an eon ago, before we got Gifts."

Syndra stared at me for a beat, lost in her thoughts. Like she was uncertain of something. Quickly, she blinked out of it. "I just realized, I need to get back. I was out here for a bit before you came. Mr. Lavadan might kill me if he gets too suspicious." She stood up, walking backward. "Thank you for hearing me out. See you in a couple!"

I let her leave, waving as she went. *Is there someone else that knows about how it works?* A sigh slipped through my lips. I didn't need someone else because I had Choa Zentha. *But it'd be nice to have more voices.*

With a sharp breath, I remembered. I had completely forgotten about pushing for what her Gift was. I slapped my forehead. *By Rishi's wrath! Ugh, maybe I do have a problem with paying attention.* Even though I couldn't see her, I shot a glare her way. *At least, when it comes to her. She just baffles me. So annoying.*

I brushed the dirt off my clothes and stood up. "I'll need to go slowly with her. She's just too unpredictable," I muttered to myself.

I remembered her explanation of the cruise incident. *Such an unfortunate outcome.*

Fault in the System

Everything seemed to become a little easier. I regained my excitement for my studies. And talking to Mr. Lavadan wasn't as hard anymore.

Akkar was right.

Once I started talking to Onvyr, it was like the weight of the world was lifted off my shoulders. Of course, Onvyr didn't get the reference. Fae knew nothing.

At first, I wasn't sure if I could tell him personal things. A strange kid with a big scar on his face and completely slicked back hair wasn't the friendliest sight. And yet, I found him more helpful than all my friends combined.

He was quiet and observant. I didn't get any judgment from him, even though I could tell he had some preset views on certain topics. Onvyr was complacent with just lending an ear. He wasn't trying to fix me, like how the others were. Onvyr just stayed with me.

I found out quickly that he hated talking. Perhaps that was why he would just let me rant on—because he didn't want to say anything. But he *did* ask questions when he talked.

He wanted to listen. And it turned out I just needed someone to vent to.

I looked forward to sneaking out to talk to him every other day—or, I mean *revolution*. Took me a while to get used to that, along with years being called "orbits."

Darunia was more than ecstatic that I was doing better. In fact, she wanted to take me out to celebrate.

Of course, it involved being in a crowd.

"You're gonna love Essence Erupting!" she told me over the side conversations around us.

We were in the room I had been in when I was first introduced to the village. Apparently, that was their social center. This time, it was only filled with kids around my age. A bunch of teens with their cliques. Even Akkar wasn't with us. I subtly stayed as close as I could to Darunia without invading her personal space.

"Essence Erupting…What is that again?" I asked, scanning the crowd.

Darunia was great, but I wanted to be with Akkar too. *Maybe his jokes could distract me from the crowd.* Despite his failed attempts at helping me earlier, I liked being around him.

Darunia tucked a dread behind her ear. "Okay. So, Essence Erupting is a competition to see who can express the most Essence in a single burst. Adults tend to make it a bigger deal, making bets and stuff like that. But it's really fun, and anyone can participate!"

I shook my head. "Sounds like it's for anyone who knows how to control that stuff. I hope you don't think I can—"

"You always worry too much." She chuckled, shaking her head. "Yes, practice can make you better, but it's a skill. Some people can do really well without much experience. I've never been to one of our village's competitions before, but I've done it a good amount at school. Just give it a shot. Okay?"

Her smile was wide and practically shone in the light. I had a feeling she wouldn't let me be embarrassed. She wouldn't allow it.

I grinned. "Okay. I'll try."

A guy pushed passed, knocking me into Darunia. "Hey!" I shouted to him.

He glared at me over his shoulder. "Hey yourself. Go back where you came from, *naak*."

I scoffed, ready to pass him off as any other bully I had met. Darunia wasn't.

She scowled and mumbled under her breath. Purple strings of light ran down her face, collecting at her lips.

Seeing her angry made me more uncomfortable than having the guy bump into me. He turned around.

"I-I'm so sorry. I'm sorry…" he told me over and over. But despite his pleas, it didn't sound like he meant it. It was like he was empty inside.

What is this?

Darunia quivered and shook her head, as if trying to fight off a headache. The purple disappeared. The guy blinked and rubbed his temples.

He growled at Darunia, causing a few people to look our way. "Underprivileged *wik*! You had no consent to do that!" He looked at me. "Of course, these are the people you associate with. She's probably Underprivileged too for all we know."

He stormed off. I made sure Darunia didn't accidentally stumble into someone. She giggled and regained her balance.

"It's okay. He won't bother you while I'm around." She smiled once more, although it was smaller.

"Are you okay? What just happened?"

She nodded. "I'm a Manipulative Telepath. I changed his thoughts and forced him to think about what I wanted him to do. It's kinda like puppeteering for the mind. It's a scary Gift—and one I'm not fully in control of yet." She clicked her tongue. "But it's the jerks like him that give me people to practice on."

I realized something. "Wait, so I could have a Gift like that?" It was a frightening yet exciting thought.

Darunia laughed. "You're better off without it. Or else you will be disgusting in the eyes of everyone around you." She seemed sad behind her smile. "You'll be *Underprivileged*."

I squinted, still not understanding that word. "I don't get it. What does that mean?"

"Are you ready!" a voice shouted from the middle of the crowd.

"I'll tell you later," she said, barely over the increased din around us. Her attention was no longer on me. Darunia seemed practically shaking with enthusiasm, like a chihuahua.

Everyone moved out of the way of a person standing in the middle of the room. Beside him was a column sticking up from the floor. It was intricate, with subtle platings of silver and a teardrop crystal at the top. The boy, not much older than Akkar, leaned against it.

"It's the start of the night! Are you ready to see who is the most powerful fae in the room?"

An uproar of excitement erupted around us.

Darunia, of course, seemed to be the one making half of the noise. She cheered so loud and was so animated that I had to duck to avoid getting hit by her.

"Sorry!" she told me. "Don't worry. You'll understand

how it works after a couple rounds!"

The guy put a finger to his mouth. "Shhh…"

Everyone quieted immediately. Although some seemed rather miffed to be silenced.

"As always, we will compete in pairs until there is one fae remaining! Competitors, circle up! Spectators, make sure to stay to the walls. Don't want to get hurt!" the announcer instructed.

"Get hurt?" I whispered to Darunia. Panic pricked my neck. "People get hurt at these things?"

She went right along and dragged me into the inner circle. Either she didn't hear me or she had chosen not to.

He shouted, strolling away from the column, "First pair is up!"

Anxiety constricted my limbs. My eyes darted to and fro. I began to realize I *really* did not want to participate in this.

Even being with the other competitors made me uneasy. Luckily for me, I caught sight of a friend amidst my internal panicking.

Akkar stood outside the circle, conversing with a few kids around his age. Honestly, he stood out like a sore thumb. Everyone in the room was wearing medieval clothes, reminding me of a Renaissance fair. Akkar, instead, wore his usual variation of chlamys, complete with draping clothes, a long tunic, and accompanying golden rope belt and cuffs.

The people he was talking with also had various notable items on, with a girl wearing a Victorian dress and a guy with embroidered textiles. But it was Akkar who seemed especially from a different place and time period.

Of course, it only made him look more striking. Not that I cared…

I ran to him, pushing through the crowd. "And why are *you* isolating yourself from this supposedly 'fun' game?" I asked him, interrupting their conversation.

"Why, *Juruh*! I'm surprised to see you out of that hole you made for yourself." He chuckled, combing through his hair. "I know you are doing better, but I didn't think you were *that* better!"

Akkar played with his cuffs, laughing to himself. "Essence Erupting is super fun to watch. People get crazy competitive and if you get good players, you even get to see some sparks of Essence. Parents really get into it. I mean, if you got a knack for it, you could go to the big leagues!"

The guy beside Akkar rolled his eyes. "Yeah right. Every fae gets into it at some point in their youth. So few actually go *that* far."

"Shh!" the Victorian girl teased. "Quit your yapping! The first pair is going at it!"

I turned around. The crowd in the middle of the room was even more rambunctious than when I had left them.

Two kids each had a hand on the column. Water had accumulated into droplets suspended in the air around one of them. The other kid's hand was glowing like a neon sign. Both seemed to be concentrating deeply on the crystal. Whenever the water kid had another surge of energy, the droplets grew bigger.

However, it was clear who was doing much better. The glow in the other's hand only grew brighter until it became hard to look in that direction. In one last flash of light, all the water fell to the floor, and the boy with a still faintly glowing hand began jumping up and down in triumph.

The announcer stepped back in. "Winner! Do we have a volunteer to go up against him?"

"Hey, I was thinking…I haven't seen you around here before," the girl said, distracting me from the competition. She leaned against Akkar. "When'd you join our humble village?"

I want to be with him, not you.

"A month or so ago," I mumbled. "I just haven't been coming to events like these. Darunia was the one who brought me."

She scanned me. "A month ago? But…the only person that joined us then was—"

"Oh, there's no way I'm letting Elena skip out on this," Akkar said, pushing her off his shoulder. "Talk to you later!"

He grabbed my hand and led me to the crowd. His hands were soft and his grip was light. Not that I cared.

"Sorry, are you being called Syndra now? Wasn't sure if you wanted to be called by your fae name," he said.

I rubbed my neck. "Oh, uh, yeah. I'm not quite ready for that."

He shrugged. "Thought so."

Introducing myself by that name to a stranger was much easier than transitioning fully to "Syndra." Even then, I had only told Onvyr my name because I felt a little embarrassed confiding in him my human name, since so many fae hated humans. He obviously held at least a little contempt for them.

"So, you said Darunia brought you?" Akkar asked.

He grinned, trying to change the topic.

That's right! I had left her all alone. "Yeah, she's over here." I tried to move my way through the packed people.

Another round had begun and everyone was shouting again. I found Darunia closer to the middle of the room.

"There you are! I wondered where you went," Darunia said. "*Nim* Akkar! I thought—Are you, uh, gonna compete?"

"Nah, but I'm not gonna let Elena slip her way out of a game." He smiled, placing his hand on my shoulder.

All I could focus on was that hand. His comforting hand. But Darunia was the one who cared. Not me.

Another round ended with a roar of cheering. The same glowing hand guy had won again.

The announcer shouted from the corner of the room, "The Luminary triumphs! Time for the next match!"

"Don't worry! You got this. I know this guy. He's awesome at first but tires out after a bit." Akkar gently shoved me toward the middle of it all.

I started panicking. "What? But—but—" He chuckled. "But nothing. You'll be fine!"

Darunia came up to me. "He's a little pushy. Sorry. All you need to do is put your hand on the Conflux gem and focus as much Essence as you can. If you feel tingling going up your arm, that means he's winning. Remember, this isn't just about skill or practice." She backed up into the crowd with a nod and mouthed, *You got this.*

I shook my head. "Listen, I know I said I'd try, but—"

"Great, we got our next volunteer!" the announcer exclaimed, leading me over to the column.

My opponent already had his hand on the gem, impatiently waiting for me. He had slight perspiration on his face. The glowing hand guy was getting tired. I got a glimmer of hope that I could best him, so I placed my hand on the smooth jewel and sighed. *What am I doing?*

I remembered the feeling of playing around with shadows. The energy I had used and the shiver it had given me. I quieted my thoughts and searched for it.

It came to me, but it was different. This was full of life and seemed so very immemorial. It dazzled and enthralled me. This wasn't Essence. At least, not what I had felt before.

"Ready? Start!"

I tried using this new energy but was stopped by another mysterious voice.

Don't. You don't know what it's capable of. You're not ready.

I recognized that accent quickly. It was an Element. One I hadn't met yet, rougher and deeper than the others.

Tingling flew up my arm from the gem. Instinctively, the familiar shiver came and stopped it from traveling further. I struggled with my Essence, fighting back my opponent's rush.

This thing seems much more powerful than normal Essence. I'm going to lose. Why can't I use it? I thought, hoping the Element who had spoken to me was still listening.

No. We don't even know what it is capable of. It's not worth it to risk it all for a silly mortal game. Knowing this kind of stuff, you could very easily accidently kill everyone in this room if you use it without training.

I took in a sharp breath. *Kill?*

With me thoroughly distracted, my opponent's Essence took control and shot through my body, making me stumble backward and onto the floor. He began cheering. Akkar was wrong. This boy had more than enough Essence left.

The announcer rushed past me, ignoring me on the floor. "Unstoppable! Do we have a challenger to take down the reigning champion?"

I crawled my way back to Darunia and Akkar.

"Well, now we know." Akkar crossed his arms. "There are just some kids that don't have a chance at these games. Don't worry. You're fine. But maybe you should just keep your distance."

"You're the one who pushed me into that!" I hissed.

He started walking away. "Can't learn if you don't fail. Now, I'd suggest you just hang in the back with me. Come—"

"All right! New fighter! Give it your best shot," the announcer shouted behind me.

Akkar looked in that direction. "This oughta be fun."

"What?"

There was Darunia, with her hand on the gem. She

caught my gaze and gave me a determined look of confidence. *There's no way she'll beat that guy. He still looks like he has a lot more to offer.*

"Ready? Start!"

The boy's hand glowed brightly once more. It shone hard and strong, hindering every spectator's vision of the competition. He seemed incredibly happy with himself, as if his victory was within his reach. Darunia just stood there with a thin grin. We were able to watch the Essence take the form of light travelling through the gem and up her arm.

She stared while it moved through her. I thought she was going to be done and out within seconds. But something was odd. I knew what it felt like when he was winning, and it went by much faster than that.

Is she purposefully waiting him out?

Then she breathed.

With a single exhalation, a rush of what seemed like Essence poured out from her. Yet it appeared different than the Essence I had witnessed her use before. It moved in sharp motions, like a crystal growing in the air.

Almost instantly, it flew through the gem and launched the boy into the crowd behind him.

Everyone was shocked silent. Not even the announcer approached her.

Darunia giggled, completely unfazed by any Essence

expenditure. She glanced back at me. "I told you that you can still win without years of prac—"

"Underprivileged!" one angry fae shouted.

A ripple of complaints rushed across the room.

"Cheater!"

"You manipulated him!"

"You're not allowed to use your Gift like that!"

"You don't deserve to win!"

She stared at the floor, brought down by the interjections. I couldn't understand. *Everyone had cheered so loudly when the glow boy was winning. What makes this any different?*

The announcer rushed in, shakily chuckling. "Okay. Okay." He waved his hands, trying to calm the crowd. "Quiet, please. Quiet!" His eyes narrowed when no one listened. "I said, *quiet!*"

A wisp of orange light briefly played around his mouth. The noise stopped abruptly. Although everyone was still shouting, no voices ever left their lips. The kids all scowled.

The orange went away, and the announcer combed back his hair.

Akkar explained in my ear, "He's a Vocal Orator. Can control voices. Mighty bold of him to use his Gift, given the situation at hand."

I asked, "Why?"

One girl walked out from the group. She snarled at the announcer "Who are you to intervene? Or have you forgotten that you are Underprivileged scum too?"

The announcer gave a hard response. "You all know me well. I have been spearheading our local Essence Erupting for years."

"Thank you," Darunia whispered to him, barely loud enough for me to hear.

The announcer addressed the crowd of children. "Obviously, something greater was in play. Plus, the previous champion is currently unable to continue. Because of this foul play, we will start with a new couple of competitors. Qikan will be disqualified."

Darunia was shook. "What? I-I did nothing wrong—"

He ignored her. "One match will not ruin the rest of the night. Next two, come step up."

Everyone was a little hesitant, but a couple of eager kids had no quarrels with anything that had occurred. Darunia, defeated and hurt, came back to us. Upon reaching us, she tried shaking it off and faked a smile.

"I'm so sorry. You totally won that," I said.

She shrugged. "It's okay. That's…That's just how it

goes."

The games continued like normal, and the announcer came toward us to get out of the way of the new match. He stood—a bit more solemnly—by Darunia with his arms crossed.

Her smile faltered. She stared at the match. "If we don't defend each other, no one will," she told him under her breath.

"If I had defended you, they would have eaten me alive. There's only a handful of Underprivileged in our village. And some fae don't make that easy for us." He glared at Akkar.

Akkar raised his hands, as if to claim innocence. The announcer only rolled his eyes.

He continued, "And it's not like you can deny something wasn't different. When you used your Essence, it didn't even come out like your Gift. By Rishi's wrath, that was sketchy."

Darunia rubbed her arm. "I know. It's complicated. It's why I've never played here before. Wasn't sure how they would react."

He shook his head and stared at her. "Well, until you can uncomplicate it, stay out of the circle." He glanced at me. "You too. Don't think I didn't notice those peculiar particles. Don't stir up trouble in my arena."

The announcer walked off, as enthusiastic about the

new victor as ever before. The crowd of children and adolescents cheered with the end of the match, as if nothing had happened.

Akkar scoffed. "Weirdo."

"What particles?" I asked the two of them.

Darunia grinned. "Didn't you see? They were gray but refracted different colors. Almost opalescent. It didn't last too long, though. What *was* that?"

"I don't know," I said.

I could think of no actual answers, but a warmth prickled at my bones, as if it knew she was talking about it. This *thing* concerned me as much as it made me curious. *Something that could kill.*

And it seemed to like Darunia, a friend I could never imagine hurting. I grew a fear of myself. Of what I was capable of. Of what this was. I needed advice.

***

"Why the Ether would I know?" Onvyr mused from the tree branch above me.

"Sounds weird and freaky. Kinda like you." I smirked.

He chuckled. "How so?"

I put my hands on my hips. "You never talk about you or your family. You got this scar across your face. And

241

could you get down from there? You know I can't climb."

Onvyr swung and landed like a gymnast. His blond hair started to fall out of place, but he left it like that.

"This coming from the girl raised by humans. Brave of you to bluntly bring up my scar. Most avoid it."

My face flushed slightly. "Oh, I'm sorry. I-I didn't mean—"

He shook his head. "It's fine. Been through a lot, that's all. As for my family…" His eyes wandered. "Feels weird to talk about my mother and brother. They're two very separate people. Wyn is awesome at everything."

I played with the bush nearby. "Is that your brother? Sounds like you really look up to him."

"He has so much on his shoulders, yet he is so dedicated to what he does. Never seen him fail at any task given to him."

Onvyr was a puzzle to me. I couldn't wrap my head around anything he truly meant.

He sounded like he was yearning for so much, but for the life of me, I couldn't figure out what. Yet, I trusted him. The one thing I knew was that he wasn't nearly as impartial or apathetic as he was trying to seem. He would show a cringe in slight disgust when we talked about humans, a distant glaze in his amber eyes whenever I would finally convince him to talk about himself, or a squint in his right eye when he tried to avoid smiling at a joke or comment.

Something about him just felt intriguing to me.

"I was wondering about something," I said. "Fae seem to highly value Gifts. Yet, I've never thought to ask… What is yours?"

"Perspective Empathy." Even though his voice was undisturbed, pride flickered in his eyes. His emotions betrayed him. "And before you call me out about being Underprivileged, I'll have you know, my Gift is very rare and cool."

I cocked my head. "Okay…What even is that? I keep hearing that word. Darunia said she is Underprivileged. From what I saw, it doesn't sound like a good thing. But I don't know because she's also awesome."

His face fell flat. Onvyr wrung his wrists. "She's that girl you were talking about, right? That controlled that boy?"

I nodded. "She said she was a Manipulative Telepath."

He bit his lip. "You were right. Fae *highly* value Gifts. We got this weird thing determining what Gifts are better than others." He sighed, continuing, "Light, Dark, and Technology related Gifts are the best. The most highly respected. Fire, Water, Earth, and Air lie in the 'okay' range. Meanwhile, Gifts from the Elements of Flesh, Emotion, and Mind are at the bottom. The Underprivileged."

"What?" In the back of my head, I remembered similar discrimination between humans. "But why? I don't understand. Darunia was incredibly powerful! Shouldn't that deserve respect?"

He shook his head. "I don't know why. It's stupid, for sure." He gave me a cold glance. "You wanted to be one of us? Well, welcome to our world."

I crossed my arms. "What about me? I won't know if I'm 'Underprivileged' until I get my Gift?"

"Mhm."

Silence hung between us. Frustration pulled at me.

Although the Elements had said I had a Blessing, I hoped I would still get a Gift once I went through my Ritual. Even though I had no idea what this Blessing was, for certain it wasn't like Gifts. One more thing that would set me apart. I desperately needed a Gift, but now I wondered if it was better to have no Gift at all than to be Underprivileged.

Cold air tensed me.

I sighed. "I should head back before it gets too late."

He gave me a small grin, crinkling his numerous freckles. "Don't be worried. The Gift you get will be from the same Element as one of your parents. Your dad's an Illusionist. Unless he broke fae standards and married an Underprivileged rather than one of his own, you'll be just fine."

I lowered my head. "I guess so."

I still had a hard time accepting Mr. Lavadan as my father. It all was very uncomfortable for me. But I felt a little more relaxed about what Onvyr told me. *If I have a Gift high in that hierarchy he said, then things might turn around for the better.*

"Wait, that's it!" Onvyr snapped his fingers. "Don't know about the odd voice you heard, but maybe that weird Essence is just pure Essence ready to be formed into a Gift."

I chuckled. It didn't sound right, but I prayed it was. "See you soon, Onvyr."

He gathered his brows, distorting the scar. "May the Elements favor you, Syndra."

I headed back to the house and silently entered, trying to avoid Mr. Lavadan and knowing I should probably get to my studies. *I'll work more on pronunciation before he gets home.*

"I've had it." Mr. Lavadan stood in the kitchen entrance, arms crossed and eyes stern. His mouth sharply formed a scowl.

"What? Had it with what?" I asked, indignant, although it was rather fake. He kind of scared me.

"You're constantly leaving! Every revolution I watch you leave the house and come back phases later." His hands clenched tightly around his arms. He didn't seem to feel any pain, just anger.

"It's only every other day," I mumbled.

I was used to being yelled at, and I had done my fair share of shouting at him, but seeing him like this crumpled my will to fight back. He was a patient man. How horrible was my offense to him that he was heated beyond his limit?

Mr. Lavadan seethed. "I don't know where you go or when you'll be back. You are a *child*. And there are people who wish harm upon you! So, yes, I've had it. We may have a strained relationship, and I have not been able to raise you, but I'm here now. I've respected your space, thinking that you'll tell me at some point, but that point needs to come *now*. No excuses and no arguments. Where *were* you?"

I stared blankly at him. It was as if a completely different person was standing before me. I wanted to tell him off about trying to scold me when he had hidden so much from me. Wanted to scream about how he was never there for me but wanted to have that authority now.

But I couldn't. I had no resentment left for him. All of it had already been said.

Plus, how did one stay mad at a person who only gave? Who only offered support? Despite his mistakes, he still did for me. When he was strict, it was only to help me.

That didn't mean I would tell him everything.

Onvyr was the only friend I had ever made on my own. He was a quiet boy who I couldn't imagine speaking loud enough to even be heard through a mic. There was no way he was dangerous. However, if I told Mr. Lavadan, he would become overprotective again. I probably wouldn't be allowed to see Onvyr. I couldn't risk that.

"I go out for a walk around the house. I never leave here. It helps me wrap my head around everything."

His shoulders slumped, and he combed through his hair. "I'm even weary of that. But I know how hard this must be for you." Mr. Lavadan came to me, knelt on the ground, and put his hand on my shoulder. "My dear, please, stay close. And don't be out long. I can't protect you if you're out of my reach."

My hair brushed against my cheek when I nodded.

Onvyr would do me no harm. Of that I was certain. I had only known him a few weeks, and yet I felt like I had known him for years. For a boy who had no control over his emotions and just a whisper of a voice, I knew him entirely.

Distortion

Finally. It's done. I panted for air. A strand of hair fell free of the gel. A smile stretched my lips. This was one of the only times I could feel like I pushed my limit anymore. My Essence was drained, almost to the point of complete exhaustion. I loved using my Gift. Everyone was always proud of how well I did. Sometimes, it was harder than others, but that just made it all the better when I succeeded.

I strolled out of the room, leaving Zentha to do her part. When she passed by, she briefly tucked my strand of hair back into its gel casing.

She looked down at me, seemingly as satisfied with my performance as I felt. "You've never let me down, Prodigy."

Prodigy. I was her Prodigy. A nickname that had become a title. No one called me by my name, but by something greater. I was their Prodigy.

I grabbed some food from the cafeteria. *My favorite.* Although no one was in the room when I got my meal, surely enough, I wasn't allowed to stay alone. Wyn walked right in as soon as I got situated.

"Oo, elk rolls!" He snatched one up, practically eating it whole. "Good dinner. Heard you did well again today. Sounds right. I worked you hard enough this morning." Wyn fixed his hair, as if it needed fixing.

His red crew cut was too short to get messed up. Meanwhile, Zentha insisted that I slicked back my hair for "efficiency," but I was not allowed to touch it.

I raised an eyebrow. "Yeah, I don't think it was alchemy studies that helped me do well."

He licked his fingers. "Listen, if you hadn't gotten through as much work as you did this morning, then you wouldn't have had time to do anything now. And trust me, you wouldn't have been able to go through your work if I didn't teach you."

I rested my head on my hand. "You're my mentor. That's your job."

"You're welcome, naak." He stole a second roll.

I ignored him, smiling while I took in the passive compliment.

"Gonna go be with your betrothed?" he asked, putting his feet up on the table.

I winced at his joke. "Ew. That's not even funny."

Wyn shrugged. "Just because you didn't laugh doesn't mean it's not funny." He gave me a devious side-eye. "Gonna introduce us soon?"

I hardened. "She's in a tough spot right now. But yes. She asks about you now and then."

"Wow, no. I'm good. Definitely would rather stay away from her as much as I can. But once you persuade her..."

I stared at my now empty plate. I couldn't wait. *But something feels off.* I reminded myself of the pain they had gone through. Their lives ripped from my grasp. *This has to be done so no fae goes through that again. And it's not like I'm harming her. Just...showing her my Gift.* Yet still, I felt uncomfortable.

I decided to change the subject.

"Is that why you're bugging me about this? You gonna be lonely without someone to harass?"

A laugh cracked from Wyn's throat. "What? Do you think you're important to me? Woah, the Underprivileged got an inflated head. Nah, Zentha has a list of chores for me to do." He groaned. "And it's with humans again."

Wyn always kept himself busy, especially when it came to mentoring me. *You need to take a break every now and then, Goni.*

Someone cleared their throat behind us. "And what are you boys doing here?" Teidove asked, his voice as flat as his expression.

Nim Teidove was the walking definition of monotone. Nothing could make him happy or particularly angry. But if you annoyed him, well, he had no fear to hold him back from reprimanding you for doing so. And we certainly were never to use his first name. That was the most disrespectful thing we could do. Not like we knew it.

Wyn sat upright. "Nothing, Nim. Just eating."

While Wyn was scared of him, I had a strange connection with Teidove. My Gift. I was sure he didn't have a certain disposition toward me just because of what I did. *I* surely did, though. It scared me sometimes how starkly he changed, especially because he became our authority.

But we need more like him. It was a good thing. It was good.

He narrowed his eyes. "If I recall, both of you have places to be. You can eat later."

Wyn nodded with a slight sigh. "We were just leaving."

Teidove stared at me, waiting for a response.

I played with my Mat glove. "We're leaving, Nim." He noticed my fidgeting and turned to his own gloves.

Without another word, he left.

Wyn elbowed me. "Don't wanna keep little Miss Human waiting."

I grimaced. In any circumstance, I couldn't see us becoming friends. She was my polar opposite. So giddy. So everywhere. I wouldn't voluntarily just walk up and start chatting with anyone, let alone a mouthy girl. It was difficult finding conversation with her.

Thankfully, she found it helpful to just rant.

Plus, I had to be honest—her retellings of her day were quite entertaining. The most normal things seemed so perplexing to her, like Essence Erupting. *I can't think of a single fae that hasn't played that before.* And somehow, she found her way into a lot of drama and had gotten close to a Cainaris. *I just can't believe she made friends with a Descendent so quickly and easily.*

Not that I wanted to be friends with a Descendent.

I already had a "Descendent" of my own, and he

was much more capable and awesome than those privileged children.

After traveling to our meeting point, I found Elena—I mean, *Syndra*—mumbling to herself, focused intensely on the flower in front of her. *Is she trying to use Growth Manifestation?* I grinned. *It's not like she can ethereally gain a Gift. She must really be looking forward to her Ritual.*

I strolled by her. "Make any progress?"

She whipped around with a gasp. I snickered.

"No. Absolutely not," she said. "You do not get to scare me again! Last time almost ended *very* poorly."

"*Almost*," I enunciated.

Even though it was a joke, some dark part of me wondered if I should have just let her fall. Would've made everything easier.

She shook her head. "I gotta get a bell for you."

I smiled. "Anything happen yesterday?"

"Just some weird stuff. More of those voices." Syndra nervously played with her hair.

"You mean the 'Elements'? Have you talked to your father about it?"

She laughed. "Of course not! He's too concerned about me as it is."

"And you're too concerned about *this*. I'm certain it's just some Telepath playing a trick on you."

Syndra crossed her arms. "I don't even know any Telepaths, I think. It's just really freaky and uber confusing."

The whole topic was absurd to me. Elements weren't people. It was like saying that every color was a different god.

But I never doubted her. She never lied to me. How she explained things seemed too genuine for that. Plus, she didn't really understand how much Gifts could actually do. She was at a point where anything could be possible to her. It didn't matter, though. I needed her to tell me about it all. Whether it was ridiculous or not.

"Wanna talk about it?" I asked. "Maybe..."

A brief gleam sparkled in her eyes. It captivated me, but it disappeared all too quickly. Like the shine of her iris had doubled.

Was that Essence? No, I know the look of pure Essence too well. Was that the weird energy she was telling me about before? But what is it?

A wave of emotions jolted through me. Like a

palpitation. *Can she tamper with emotions? Maybe she will be an Empath...*

"Well?"

My thoughts faded. She had a lively smile and big eyes, awaiting my answer. I hadn't heard a word she was saying. *Esh! I need to pay more attention than this.*

"Well...Uhh, could—Could you repeat that?"

She rolled her eyes. "I said: I wanted a change of pace. I got an idea. There's somewhere I want to take you. Is that okay?"

I scanned our surroundings. "Um, sure? Doesn't seem like you have a cycle nearby."

"I can borrow my father's." Syndra began walking toward her house. "Just give me a sec."

I smiled. *That's way too much work.* "No, we can just use my rift shards." I pulled the bag out from my greaves.

She stopped in her tracks. "Rift shards? What's that?"

Her confusion amused me. *The most normal things...*

"They are pieces of a special crystal that creates

rifts from Essence. Often used in cycles for transportation. Rift Shards are just...well...*shards* of the crystal." I handed them to her.

"Oh, I think I've seen these before. Why are you giving them to me? I've had no experience with these." She took one out of the bag and examined it. "Looks like glass."

I hesitated. Zentha would kill me if I lost her shards. "They're sharp, so be careful. You have to be the one to use them. I don't know where we're going."

She nervously chuckled. "Yeah, I guess that's true...So, how do I use it?"

"Just put them all in your hand and think of where you want to go. You have to will it to work."

Her head shot up. She seemed shocked. *I didn't say anything weird, did I?*

I tilted my head. "Something wrong?"

Her eyes drifted away. "No. Sorry. Something you said just sounded familiar..." She carefully emptied the bag in her hand. "Just think of the place?"

She's not keeping anything from me, right?

"Mhm. They'll do the work for you. Just let me go through first or else I'll be stranded here."

She closed her eyes and thought hard. The last few brain cells of hers were working overtime. *She's so dramatic.* The shards flew out of her hands and created an oval in the air. The air around it cracked, and a rift opened in the middle.

Rift

I stepped through and the edges of the rift brushed against my skin like leaves. I set my foot in a bunch of wood chips. In fact, the whole ground was covered in them. *What is this place?* In front of me were colorful structures. Some looked like tiny houses. There was a dome of metal pipes, and off to the side were two plastic boards attached to the ends of chains hanging from a metal frame.

Syndra stumbled out of the rift behind me. "Well, at least that felt similar to going through portals on cycles."

The shards rushed to her.

"Hold it out!" I snatched the bag from her hand and held it open. The seam of the pouch glowed when the shards went back into the bag. I sighed, closing it up. "It's stitched with the core of the same crystal the shards are from. They're pulled back when you're done using them."

"Oop. Sorry." She tugged at her earlobe. "They

wouldn't have still come to the bag if I had kept it closed, though, right? I mean, I would be standing in the way."

Flatly, I told her, "Yes. They would."

Her face flushed. "Oh. They...they would've hurt, wouldn't they?"

I put the bag back in my greaves. "Incredibly."

The girl cringed. "Got it..." She looked around and smiled. "Sweet! Seems like the kids around here are still in school. We got the whole place to ourselves!"

Syndra ran to a wall with fake rocks screwed to it and climbed into one of the bright green houses.

She's such a hurricane. "And where *did* you take me? Pretty odd place."

"Have you never been to a playground before?" she shouted from a plastic house.

The wood below me scratched my boots. "Doesn't look familiar."

"I guess you wouldn't have. I wasn't sure if fae had places like this." Her smile lessened. "I mean, they certainly should! I've *definitely* missed this."

I stopped. "Is this a human place?"

"Yeah, the amount of plastic here definitely

screams human, I guess. I've yet to see a single speck of plastic since I moved in." She shrugged and ran to a bridge between the houses. "You know what I mean."

Slowly, I strolled over to her. *This place is tainted by them.* The chaos of the area made more sense. I approached the fake rock wall but hesitated in touching it. It was incredibly difficult for me to be anywhere human. *Hopefully, we can leave soon.*

Immediately after I touched the wall, Syndra shouted, "By the way, try to avoid touching your face and all that! This is definitely one of the most unsanitary places on planet Earth."

I climbed up. "You know that most diseases humans have aren't contagious for us, right?"

Of course, when I said it, I realized something about the rocks felt wrong. *Why in Rishi's name are these sticky?* I flung myself up into the structure so I wouldn't have to touch them anymore and tried to wipe my hands on my pants. They just stuck to the cloth. One of my feet peeled from the floor with each step. *Ugh, it touched the rocks.*

Syndra stood in the middle of the bridge, hands on her hips—perhaps her favorite position to stand in. "I wasn't just talking about illness. I meant unsanitary in general."

I stepped out onto the bridge and grabbed at the ropes to my sides. It squeaked and rattled, swaying with every movement I made.

Syndra laughed at me, grasping her stomach. "With all of your crazy moves and sense of balance, I didn't think you would be so startled!"

"Well, I didn't think it would be so unstable."

"It's made to be! Don't worry, you big baby. You won't fall." She grinned.

A slight cringe ran through me. It wasn't like I wasn't used to swearing. Wyn did it all too often. I just had never expected her to.

"Didn't think you were one for cussing," I said.

She cocked her head to the side. "What? I didn't cuss. I just called you a big baby."

Oh, is it not a curse for humans? "Yeah. That's a cuss."

"That's so stupid. What if I called you childish?" she asked.

"Mhm. It's just...worse," I regained my balance on the bridge. "Our species hates youth. Just try to avoid saying anything related to that."

"Uhh, okay?" Syndra sat down on the bridge, making it sway once more. It was much easier to keep my balance once I was aware that it moved.

I joined her in the middle of the bridge and sat down. She placed her hands on her knees...which stuck out. Like a butterfly. *Seriously, how is that pose comfortable?*

"You know, Mr. Lavadan freaked me out the other day. He went completely berserk. Apparently, he hated that I would constantly leave. I mean, I know he doesn't like it, but whoa." She rocked backward. "It was crazy."

My shoulders tensed. *Will this be a problem? Having a Sensory Illusionist against us isn't the best idea.*

"He's...generous for letting you continue to leave," I said.

She straightened herself and examined me. "What about you? Does anyone care that you constantly leave?"

I hesitated and shrugged.

Syndra groaned. "What about your brother? You seem to be close with him. How old is he?"

How old? Early fifties? Or maybe late thirties? Unsure, I shook my head.

"I've told you everything from my childhood to

current fae drama!" Her arms burst wide and fell back to her lap. "But what do I know about you? You got a brother and mother. Whoop-dee-doo. Oh, and you're a Perspective Empath. I don't even know what a Perspective Empath is!"

Quiet.

Her words echoed in my head, but I could only hear one thing: *Did I blow it?* My hand slowly wandered to my belt hidden beneath my tunic. To my pocket. Conflict grew within me. I found myself not wanting to do it, but I also couldn't have it all dispersing to the Ether.

Luckily, she fixed the situation for me.

"I'm sorry." Her head hung forward. "I—I just don't know much about you. It's weird to talk to a...well, a void."

A sigh of relief silently shook through my throat. *At least she's not suspicious.* I nodded, understanding her frustration. *Might as well tell her...*

"Neither of them are my actual family."

She glanced at me.

I stared at the ground. "We were in an accident when I was younger. Zentha has taken me in since then. We both have a similar...*quirk.*" My Essence pulsed, recognizing what I was talking about. "Wyn's family was closely involved with Zentha. Since he was the youngest around, he became my mentor. He's a Conducting Astrokinetic. Really powerful."

Syndra gave me a solemn gaze. "I'm sorry about your parents. Sounds like Zentha really helped you, though." She chuckled. "But come on, man. You gotta fill me in on these Gifts. Conducting Astrokinetic? Perspective Empath? Sounds like a bunch of random words. They're not super clear names."

I nodded. "Wyn can control the weather, but only what's around him. Like, he can play with the wind, but only if it's breezy out. He can't create weather, just redirect it. And as for my Gift..."

I breathed through my teeth. *I can't tell her. That could ruin things. How do I address her curiosity?* An idea clicked. I gave her a smug grin.

"Your Ritual is tomorrow, right?"

Syndra nodded. "Yeah. I'm finally gonna get a real Gift! Hopefully." She rubbed her arm. "Now I just gotta hope that it's an acceptable one..."

I waved my hand, as if brushing away her worry. "Like I said, I don't think you'll be Underprivileged. It's unlikely. But my point is, once you *do* get a Gift, I will show you mine, and you can flaunt your new one."

She brightened up immediately. "Really? I love it! I'll

be sure to come to you as soon as we're done!"

That odd glimmer shone in her eyes again. For some reason, a prick of guilt unsettled me. Yet I couldn't understand why I felt it. *There's something about you…It's fine. All that matters is your Gift.*

"So, what's it gonna be like?" she asked. "Everyone keeps avoiding my questions about my Ritual. They want me to be surprised or something."

"And I'll tell you instead because…?"

She put her hands together and shook them. "Pleasseeee?"

I didn't feel annoyed this time. A part of me grinned, amused, but I couldn't bring myself to show it. It was a feeling I needed to shake off immediately.

Instead, I scoffed at her. "You'll basically just offer your Essence to the Elements. At least, that's how we approach it. It doesn't really have much to do with Elements. But yeah."

Her shoulders slumped. "Wow. You're very helpful."

"Thanks. I try sometimes."

Syndra rolled her eyes and laughed. "I wish you could come." She stared at the ground. "I just know Mr. Lavadan would freak out once he found out that I've been meeting with you. As if a kid would be part of a group of assassins."

Intrigued, I asked, "A group of assassins? What do you mean?"

She shook her head. "I think that's who Mr. Lavadan is trying to protect me from. He said they're called 'The Ambition.'"

"And they're a group of assassins?"

"Yeah, well…He originally said that they would oppose me. Especially since I was raised by humans. And now, whenever I ask, he just says that their whole thing is killing humans." She giggled. "I don't know how much of that is true. I've never heard of a group of fae killing a bunch of people, back when I was living with humans. But yeah, it sounds like they're a bunch of murderers."

Concealing my emotions was my top priority. "I've never heard of them."

She looked at me with an innocent glow. "Seems like something he would overinflate. Especially since it looks like most, if not all, fae already hate humans. Makes sense there would be some that especially despise them. That's probably what it is." Syndra shrugged. "I don't see people mass murdering humans, though. They're probably just like a 'I hate humans' club."

"Your father seems a little..."

"Paranoid? Oh yeah. Big time." Syndra giggled. "But hey...What can you do? Is your mom like that?" She peered at me curiously.

I couldn't help but scoff. "Nope. Exact opposite."

Her head tilted. "What do you mean?"

"Zentha is...very confident. But not carefree." I paused, looking for the right word. "I don't know how to describe her."

"Proud? Reckless?"

I remembered how she would do her job. Zentha didn't seem to plan anything out. Using her brain was not her strong suit. Yet, everything always ended perfectly. "Deliberate. She's deliberate."

Syndra blankly stared at me. "Uh *huh*."

I shook my head. "Tomorrow. Since you're getting your Gift, I can introduce you to her tomorrow."

She straightened and gave me a wide smile. "Really? So tomorrow, I get to see your Gift *and* your family?"

"Mhm."

Syndra pumped her fists in the air. "Score! That's so

awesome! Wait…Why only after I get my Gift?"

"Like I said before, Gifts are important to us. It's usually the second thing to be discussed, after your name, when meeting someone." I squeezed my arm. "Wasn't sure how she would react to someone without a Gift. But that's all changing tomorrow."

Her eyes became distant, but her smile stayed. "Yeah, I can't wait." After a beat or so of being lost in her thoughts, she got up and headed to the boards on chains. "Come on! Let's enjoy this place before we leave!"

Although I didn't like being there and had a fear of touching anything else in the playground, I followed her. Had to keep her happy. *But it's all changing tomorrow. Just one more day.*

I joined her, keeping the distance between us non-existent. At least, to her. After all, she couldn't know the truth. Not yet.

The Edge of Becoming

I was finally going to get a Gift. Fae would finally see me as one of them. But I wasn't excited. No, that melted away as soon as my mind began overthinking it. In fact, I was far from it.

My Blessing concerned me. It had seemed so confusing whenever the Elements talked about it. I had become incredibly aware of the difference between it and pure Essence.

Essence would flow through my body, invigorating me. Using it was like finding you had an odd skill you have never even considered having before. It was new to me, surely making me feel a little like a wizard. I didn't really know how to do anything with it. It felt new.

But my Blessing was nothing like that. It was like an old friend I had been ignoring. Always lurking there, peering over my shoulder but never approaching. It was familiar but unknown. Well, not entirely unknown. What I did know was that it had the potential to kill. It was something even the Elements seemed hesitant about. Yet they were omitting more from me.

The past few days preceding my Ritual were filled with Umbra dodging my questions and Aithalis repeating "It's difficult to explain." I was getting sick and tired of people hiding stuff from me.

That was going to end today.

After struggling and strangling my clothes for an hour, I finally got on the new dress Kaylessa and Mr. Lavadan had gotten me. An off-the-shoulder long-sleeve. The skirt itself was a shark bite, at its highest point hanging at my knees. And by long sleeves, I mean Rapunzel's-hair-length sleeves. The shortest part of it reached my wrists, but it tapered further down to my knees.

Although they could be irritating, the sleeves turned out to be good to fidget with. My fingers tugged and squeezed them while I waited for my Ritual to start. Everyone was talking to each other while others came in. My mind exploded as I tried figuring out what to expect. Luckily, Darunia came to me before it became too much.

She ran up and hugged me. "Isn't this exciting?"

Her smile was as big as ever, calming me down. She wore a long, asymmetrical spliced dress adorned with a row of amethyst buttons. Her hair was in intricate braids lying gracefully on her shoulders. *Effortlessly beautiful.*

"I wish I could at least know what is happening," I mumbled.

She giggled. "Listen, it's nothing to worry about. You'll spill some Essence, quietly ask the Elements for favor, and then you're done!"

"Spill Essence? That sounds pretty dramatic. Is that like what I did at Essence Erupting?"

"Pshhh. I have no idea what *you* did, but no. It isn't just a massive burst of Essence. It's like—"

"Today's the day!" Akkar popped up behind me. "You ready, *Juruh?*"

I shoved him. "W*ow*, rude much? Can't you hear when someone else is talking?"

"You need to not take everything so personally." He walked between us, appraising me. "It wasn't even like you were the one talking."

"No, Darunia was telling me about the Ritual because I have no idea—"

"Much better fit, by the way. I assume Shaeli did the shopping for you this time?" A devious grin curled on his lips while he looked down on me.

I growled. "No. Kaylessa did." I turned back to Darunia. "So spilling Essence. Please, continue."

She pushed a couple of braids out of her face. "It's

difficult to explain." Darunia glanced at Akkar, hoping for some help.

He shook his head. "I don't know how it works. All I know is that I cut myself, bled, and did a killer move that would've won me a round of Essence Erupting."

"What? You *bled*?" I had never been fond of the idea of blood. Some people had called me hemophobic whenever I would get nauseous around an active cut.

Darunia blushed, unsure how to continue. "No, it's—it's not like that. Well, I mean, you *do* bleed, but…" She sighed and locked eyes with me. "It is hard to channel pure Essence without a Conflux gem. It's much easier through blood. You'll just prick your thumb and try to channel the pure Essence into a single drop of blood."

Akkar shrugged behind her. "You might not get it the first time. Especially if you do too much at once. I mean, I did it just fine on the first drop, but sadly, you're not me. Some kids take a bit—"

"Which is *fine*." Darunia nodded. "I couldn't do it on my first try. I only succeeded on my second drop. But don't worry. You don't need to do much."

Mr. Lavadan wandered over to us. "I see you've gotten to her before I could." He placed his hand on her shoulder. "You're a good friend, *Bee*."

Her eyes practically glowed with pride.

He stared at me with a familiar look of concern. "May I speak with her privately? Not everything can be explained by friends."

Akkar playfully groaned. "Aw, but—"

"Sure thing, *Jeerei*. We understand," Darunia said for him. She pulled the boy away, blushing when she found herself alone with him.

I yearned to be with them. Or anywhere, really, that didn't include being alone with Mr. Lavadan.

He gave me a small smile. "This is a big event. You'll earn your place with us."

I still hadn't figured out who he was to me, and I had no idea how to feel around him other than awkward.

On his velvet vest, Mr. Lavadan wore his golden pin depicting an eye. When he caught my gaze, he straightened it. "Soon, my dear, you'll get a pin like this. It is a symbol of the Gift you harness. A reminder of who you are."

Mr. Lavadan knelt to my height. "It doesn't matter what you've been through or who you were. You are a fae and my daughter. That doesn't change, no matter what. I don't know what this 'Blessing' is that *Milah* Umbra speaks of, but you are a fae like any of us. This Ritual will show that."

I avoided looking at him. Fear kept me from allowing him to get any closer. *He left me once. What's to stop him from doing it again?* I couldn't go through another abandonment.

"Will it take long?" I asked, just wanting him to leave.

A wash of sadness dampened his voice. "Depends on the Element. Some Rituals are more elaborate than others."

He pulled a dagger from his belt. The metal swirled with filigree ivy along the sides of the blade. *That's right. I have to bleed.*

"Not too deep. Just enough to drip. It's sharp, so you must be careful harnessing it before the time comes." He handed the knife to me by the hilt. I slowly slipped it out of his hands. Mr. Lavadan stood up, straightening his clothes. "My dear, look around. We're all here for you."

I glanced up and realized the amount of people present. It seemed as though everyone was there. Everyone except Onvyr.

I squeezed the hilt of the dagger. "What...What is it I have to say? To the Elements?"

"That's up to you. What you say to the Elements is between you and them. Of course, previously, we believed that it didn't matter what to recant since it was only for tradition, but I guess it's a bit different now that you and I have seen that the Elements are, indeed, living beings."

He chuckled.

"I asked Darunia to refrain from sharing what she knows, else it will be too confusing. I have yet to figure out how to tell anyone myself. I've alluded to it with Kaylessa and Taelin, but they didn't quite understand, and it's difficult to explain. But we can do it together, you and I."

Oh what fun. Before I could ask him any more, a familiar lady approached. Her white lace choker stood out against her dark skin—an elegance that was often hard to accomplish. The golden markings stretching from her eyeshadow shimmered while she gave me an inquisitive glare.

"I can see that nerves are besting you yet, Miss Syndra," *Milah* Rosandoral said. One of her eyebrows raised when she scanned my neck. "Are you still using a translator?"

"Good evening." I attempted to sound braver than I felt. "I'm close to getting rid of this thing, for sure. Don't worry. I will be speaking Voliun on my own soon."

Lies, lies. Voliun was turning out far more difficult than I had anticipated. Especially with the different tenses only being indicated by context. Plus, pronunciations were turning out to be a pain in the butt.

She stood with her head held high, holding her hands together. "Good, because if there are two things you need to have conquered to truly be considered one of us, it is speaking our language and gaining a Gift as soon as possible." She peered at me. "I am not on the same page as Nylian. But that does not mean I am particularly on yours. Things are not black and white. So here I sit, in the gray of it all."

"Thank you for attending her Ritual, *Milah*," Mr.

Lavadan said, gently pulling me a bit more toward him. "It's an honor to have an Ancient here."

Her Victorian dress swayed when she turned to him. "Leorn, the fae you changed into a decade ago left us all disappointed. Your absence was noticeable." Her fortified expression turned grieving. "You have been given a great opportunity. Raising a young one is a privilege."

"Do you have children?" I asked.

The Ancient knelt on the floor, careful not to pin down her dress.

"No, not anymore." *Milah* gave a subtle sigh. "While you may have had a rough start with your father, a decade apart is nothing compared to centuries. Millennias. Grow from this." She looked up to him. "Raising a young one is a privilege. Potential is greatly shapeable during these short years. Such formation can be done through harm or nurture. Nurture this spark."

Milah Rosandoral rose, returning to her stern expression. "Your Ritual should be starting soon. I will find my spot. I ask the Elements to give you a Gift akin to that of your father's rather than your mother's."

"What?" My anxiety grew with her last comment, but she walked away. Scared, I jerked my head toward Mr. Lavadan. "What was she talking about? What was my mother's Gift?"

He pinched the bridge of his nose. "Nothing bad, I

assure you. All of these immature opinions are growing out of hand."

"What was her Gift?" I asked, needing an answer.

"Your mother was an immensely skilled Object Telekinetic." He flashed a reassuring smile, but his words left me reeling.

I muttered, "She was Underprivileged."

Onvyr was wrong. He married an Underprivileged.

Although I should have been relieved that Mr. Lavadan didn't submit to this, my chance of being Underprivileged had risen exponentially. *Onvyr was wrong.*

Mr. Lavadan practically barked, "Hey."

I looked up to a cross fae.

"That disgusting title means nothing. Do you hear me? I don't ever want to hear you use that. I don't care what anyone says. My wife was one of the most talented fae I had ever met. Just like how you'll be." He looked ahead, seemingly at nothing at all. "You'll see, my dear. You will surpass us all."

Darunia rushed over to us. "I am *so* sorry to interrupt, but my mother wanted me to tell you that we're all here and ready and, well, waiting."

I felt a tinge of guilt. Darunia was Underprivileged, sure, but she was incredibly powerful. She was a wonderful person, optimistic, smart, and gorgeous. I had to remember that they had chosen me because I was a clean slate, not so I could conform simply because I was afraid of what others thought.

Mr. Lavadan said, "Thank you. Why don't you head back to Imra? I'll follow." Mr. Lavadan turned to me. "Just go to the middle and do as your friends instructed earlier. May the Elements favor you."

My hands shook, and the dagger in them grew heavy. Everyone had formed a circle. I took a deep breath.

May the Elements favor me.

I practically crawled my way into the middle of the empty spot. Murmmurings surrounded me briefly until I finally felt all attention pointed in my direction. My eyes focused on the dagger, avoiding the sea of stares around me. I froze, unsure of what to say to the Elements. My views of them were incredibly different than what fae had used to—and did—consider them to be. The Elements were annoying, troublesome, and incredibly cryptic.

I knew what to say.

I kept my eyes on the blade while I wielded it and said, under my breath, "Tell me the truth. I need to understand. Leave nothing out."

It was so sharp I didn't even feel the metal cut my finger.

First drop formed.

I tried focusing my energy to my finger. It was harder to find my Essence than at the Essence Erupting games. *It really is difficult without that crystal.*

Second drop.

Ashamed at missing the first bit of blood, I searched deeper for Essence, wondering if it was purposefully eluding me. I followed the streams of blood within me to find the source. Instead, I found something greater.

Third drop.

My Blessing stopped me in my tracks. Even though I shouldn't use it, the energy prevented me from looking any further. All I could feel was it filling me. Almost as if it had a will of its own, it traveled to my fingertip, waiting for me to utilize it. Its movement intrigued me. I would be the laughingstock of the village if I allowed another drop to fall without succeeding, so I channelled it to the blood.

Fourth —

The blood swirled in the air, and gray particles shone around it. Different colors refracted from the energy. A warmth of connection captivated me, and I was dazzled at the spectacle.

Everything began to vibrate. Not like an earthquake, but as if I was being enveloped in static. The blood before me froze mid-air, but the particles continued circling it.

I looked around for help, but everything had become fuzzy. Colors surrounded me, like bursts from spray paint cans exploding sporadically. *What —*

"I told you not to use it."

I whipped around, looking for who was speaking.
Eleven different people had surrounded me, a couple of them
familiar; Umbra and Aithalis stood amidst them. I was
overwhelmed by a powerful aura emanating from the group.

Softly, I asked, "Are you…the Elements?"

Made, Bound, Blessed

The gray particles I had created pulsed larger and brighter, pulling my attention.

"This *thing* is very unpredictable. Why did you ignore me?" one spat, scowling.

He crossed his tattooed arms. His straight hair fell in front of a sharp, orange eye. A girl beside him leaned against him.

"Oh, Uli. Can you blame her? It truly is interesting, is it not?" she asked me. Her magenta eyes sparkled with curiosity.

Another Element stepped forward, smoothing back his already immaculate blond hair.

"Forgive them. They are not the best at introductions. Although some have done worse." He glared at Umbra. "I am Svitlo, the Element of Light. The one carelessly leaning on Ulithiganda is Alegria. She, along with Sentir — the one at her side—are the Elements of Emotion." Svitlo gestured to Umbra. "This is the Element of Tenebrosity, Umbra, but I believe you already know her. Same for Aithalis over there."

The Element of Nature rubbed her arm. "After all she was going through, I thought she would like to know there was a place she could head to for comfort."

"Pft! Yeah, real cozy—creepy cold woods. Bet she just goes there 'cause she has nowhere else to go!" An Element with shaggy hair brushed a few strands out of his face. "I should set a wildfire to that forest just to free her of whatever obligation she might feel."

Svitlo sighed, rubbing one of his temples. "*That* would be Brazen, and he is not—I repeat—*not* setting any wildfires by *Hasha*'s house."

Another Element shoved Brazen aside. "Yeah, stupid. It's like what I said before. Annoyance should not be a motivation for altering your duties! Just because you are bored absolutely does *not* mean you can just set everything on fire!" Her marine-blue eyes narrowed at him while she flung her hair back.

"And that would be Jharana, Element of Water. I apologize," Svitlo said. "We try to avoid congregating all together superfluously. After living alongside ten other roommates for eons, unable to have any contact with anyone else, you tend to come to despise them." One of his medallion-gold eyes twitched.

I stuttered, "I-I don't understand. What happened?

Why is everything so…"

One with white hair, as young as anyone else there, put a hand on her hip.

"Oh—well—the Law will harm us if we show ourselves too much around mortals. To avoid making a big spectacle, we just brought you here, to the Ether, a realm existing just outside of the mortal world. Our home. Now we can still talk to you without it hurting too much."

"Riah," Jharana snapped. "Are you really going to tell her about the Law? Might as well discuss the Bedlamite too!"

Riah rolled her whitewashed eyes. "Just shut it. We'd have to tell her anyway. She said she wants to know the truth and to leave nothing out."

"I think what Jharana was getting at is that there might've been a neater way to tell *Hasha*," Aithalis said.

"Riah is right. She asked for everything to be said." Uli stepped in front of me. "So here's the truth. You have been the focus of half of my attention since you were born."

Uncomfortable with how close he was, I stepped back. "What—What is that supposed to mean?"

He headed over to the particles I had created, which were still zooming around the frozen bit of fuzzed-out blood. "A little over an eon ago, there was a fae who taught himself how to control pure Essence. Upset as to how we interacted with each other, he looked for a solution so we don't 'kill all of mortality' or whatever."

"Kill all of mortality? What, did he think that you guys were going to bring the apocalypse or something?" A bit of fear pricked.

Svitlo interrupted, "We work in equilibrium. If only one of us were to fall under, the balance would be disrupted and mortal life would greatly feel that, eventually — if not immediately — to the point of extinction. Or at least, that's the theory."

"Anyways, that fae found that there was an Element that existed only in the form of Essence. One we were completely unaware of," Uli said.

"So, there was — *is* — an Element that literally none of you knew about?" I asked.

With only a handful of immortals in existence, how could they not have ever noticed another Element?

Uli combed his hair, keeping his eyes on the particles. "Those days were different. It was before the Law, so we lived with mortals and we lived much more distracted lives. The point is, this Element didn't and doesn't have a sentience or anything like us. It just was there. The fae used pure Essence to concentrate a bit of this Element into a way that it could manifest in someone, so it could gain sentience. He said that a new Element created from a mortal would have a sense of 'humility' that we apparently lacked. Of course, we hated this idea, but he did it without us knowing." He cupped his hands around the energy before him.

Imma kill something if he says that my Blessing is that

Element.

"This Blessing is that Element," Uli said.

Crap.

One of the Elements chuckled. His fluorite eyes briefly shined. The guy next to him elbowed him.

"Jeongsin, were you invading *Hasha*'s privacy?"

Jeongsin shrugged. "At least she's got some kick in her." He glanced at me. "I won't do it again. Just don't kill me, okay?"

I stared at him, concerned. *He read my thoughts. Wonderful.*

I turned my attention back to Uli. "So…what? I'm an Element? Because Aithalis said I'm not."

Svitlo shook his head. "No, you are a fae. There's no denying that."

Uli further examined the particles. "That's where I've been observing. I am the Element of Flesh and Body, yet I can't seem to fully understand how this Element interacts with you. You see, fae all have an intense amount of pure Essence. A bit of this is channeled to functions like thinking, feeling, and living, but the rest just gathers. Gifts taint that Essence and converts it to an Elemental Essence, allowing fae to tamper that Element."

"Does this *thing* affect my ability to have a Gift?"

He shot me a cold look. "That concentration of this new Element, your Blessing, seems to reside within you, almost immediately sapping up whatever extra pure Essence you possess. Leaving no room for a Gift."

Whatever hope I had dimmed. The Element of Flesh touched a particle, causing the energy to rush back to me. When it returned, I felt a punch to my lungs and was forced into a gasp.

"I have no idea how much Essence it's taking from you, but I think its activity has picked up ever since you were brought to live with other fae. It's probably the feeling of being around others with an influx of Essence that perked it up." Uli crossed his arms. "I am completely unsure if it is gaining sentience, but it sure is using your pure Essence. Being concentrated without a sentience to keep it in control poses a great danger."

One Element came right up to me and held my shoulders. I cringed when his breath hit against my ear. "Listen, Uli's just saying that you already got a Gift!" he said brightly. "Well, sort of. Not one that we gave you. But, just since we don't know much about it, try not to use it. Never let it out, and it can't hurt others!"

Svitlo rested his head on his hand. He groaned. "Sentir, get off of her. In no way are you being helpful."

The Element of Emotion lifted his hands off with an innocent smile and a gleam in his deep magenta eyes.

"I don't-I don't think the safety of my Blessing will

get better by avoiding it. Plus, wouldn't we learn more about it if I explored it?" I looked around at each of them. "Can't you all just help me when I use it instead of just saying to not touch it? Or are you that afraid of the unknown?'

Umbra stared at her feet. "When you've seen all there is to be seen, lived since the beginning of it all, it becomes scary when something new appears." She locked eyes with me. "And trust me, I know fear."

Hesitantly, Svitlo agreed. "Our species is omnipotent. If you are harboring an Element, there is no telling what it can or will do. And although we might be able to help keep those around you safe during your explorations, we can only do so much. Restraining an Element is no small feat, even for another Element. We certainly are not omniscient, and not all the answers lay in our hands."

Aithalis placed her hand on Svitlo's shoulder to comfort him. She turned to me. "Are you ready for that? You are right about exploring it, but are you truly willing to risk yourself to understand this Element?"

My Blessing swirled within my body, eager for me to acknowledge it. I nodded. "Ignoring it isn't the answer. Help me. I'm certain we will get somewhere."

Each of their wrists briefly glowed.

I looked at Svitlo. "What was that?"

He held his wrist. "The Law. Listen, we will help. And don't worry, you won't be Gift-less. For a while now, we've been doing you favors, keeping you from drowning, allowing you to detect unseen people, and more. We can continue to do so. But we can't do that too much, thanks to the Law, and you must learn. We can show you how you can still mimic Gifts without having one, like what Umbra was showing you before."

"Please, what *is* the 'Law'?"

Uli looked at me, stern. "*Hasha*, do you really want to hear all of history all at once? Do you think you can truly absorb eons more information on top of what has already been explained?"

My shoulders slumped. The thought of that made me realize how mentally exhausted I already was. "No, not really."

Their wrists all shone once more.

Svitlo nodded. "Don't worry. We will tell you about it all. Just maybe not right now. Don't you think that your friends and family will be worried about you? From their perspective, you've just been standing here for a bit now, looking not too different from a cloud. I think it's time you get back to them."

"Wait...Can they see me? I thought you took me somewhere else..." I wondered what everyone else was seeing.

Riah shrugged. "Oh, for sure, they can see you. The Ether is a realm that lies right on top of the one you inhabit.

288

All the fae at your Ritual currently just see you as one big fuzzy blob. To come here mortally alive, you have to hold a mid-dispersed state of being. When people die and disperse, they come here and become Essence again."

She gestured around us.

"Take a look. The different Essences that you see are each of us. Helps you remember that we're omnipresent."

I peered around, finally understanding what the different colors were. The green dust below me matched the color of Aithalis 's eyes. The blurred-out crowd around me was a mostly orange sea, reminding me of Uli's stare.

"Say the word, and we will come running!" Jharana told me, determined. "*Hasha*, you won't go through this alone. And you can't have anyone more worthy than us to help you through it!"

The eleven of them stood in front of me.

While they obviously emanated a power labeling them immortals, they weren't great deities or anything. Something within me felt I could relate to them. They seemed as confused about my Blessing as I felt.

My eyes rested on the one Element who hadn't spoken up. He stood with a high chin, arms crossed, and a harsh glare. *Which Element is that?*

Svitlo distracted me, "We're at your beck and call. See you soon, *Hasha*."

He smiled while the environment around me vibrated. Everything returned to focus. The apparent clamor and panic I had left behind immediately came to a stop as soon as I returned from the Ether. But I wasn't the center of attention. The Elements were.

Before me, they still stood, soaking in the murmurs and astonishment of the fae around us.

"I missed this," Umbra said under her breath.

Silently, it was clear they all shared the vague sentiment.

After a second, Svitlo nodded to the others and they dispersed away. The crowd gasped with the Elements' departure.

Mr. Lavadan ran up to me. "My dear, are you okay? What just occurred?" He glanced where the Elements had stood. "Were they...?"

I nodded, trying to figure out how to explain when I was still processing it myself. "I'm fine. They took me to the Ether to talk to me. But...basically, because of my Blessing, I'm not going to get a Gift. Ever."

Milah Rosandoral came to us once they settled down. The Ancient stopped others from surrounding me, although I could make out Darunia's worried eyes amidst the people.

Milah cleared her throat. "An explanation. Now."

"I—uhh," I stuttered, searching for what to say. "The

Elements…" — Mr. Lavadan shot me a shake of his head, stopping me from continuing. I looked around, thinking of an alternative explanation — "I…don't have a Gift."

"What?" She narrowed her brows. "That's impossible. And if you didn't get a Gift, then what just happened?"

Mr. Lavadan stepped in. "I was worried for her. When she couldn't channel her Essence into the blood, I began to believe that because she waited too long, she wouldn't naturally get a Gift."

I looked up at him, wondering where he was going with this.

"I conjured illusions, hoping that the influx of my Gift could help ignite whatever part of her would manifest a Gift." Mr. Lavadan lowered his voice. "Unfortunately, it seems that didn't even help. It is as she said: She doesn't have a Gift."

He shared a stare with her. "I do not ask for you to conceal this from the other Ancients, but from public knowledge. You know this will create a scandal."

Milah Rosandoral rubbed her face with her hands, pulled on her cheek, and sighed. She glanced down at me. Pity clouded her otherwise cold eyes. "I will see what I can do." She turned her gaze back to him. "However, you must be the one responsible for damage control. She is an Independent and certainly not *my* ward."

He nodded. "By Rishi's wrath, I swear."

The Ancient pulled out her shards and left without another word.

Mr. Lavadan pulled the crowd's attention. "The Ritual is complete. Thank you all for taking time out of your day to attend. Have a good day."

"But, Leorn, what is her Gift?"

"What was she given?"

"What's her Gift?"

The questions faded out while Mr. Lavadan and I retreated to the house. Time passed, and we waited them out. Lights flashed from the windows when fae took off in their cycles and portals transported them away. Mr. Lavadan and I sat on the couch in silence. He put his hands together and leaned on his knees, lost in his own mind. After a minute or so, Kaylessa, Taelin, Shaeli, and Darunia followed us in.

Darunia immediately began inspecting me, rapid firing questions. "What the Ether happened to you? Did you disperse? We all thought you died or something!"

"That's pretty accurate. We all felt pretty panicked," Taelin shrugged.

Kaylessa glared at him.

"What? What'd I do?"

"Don't scare her," she muttered softly.

I chuckled. "No, it's okay. I'm fine, I think."

Darunia nodded. "Those were the Elements, weren't they? Did they do that to you?"

The Heiwys family shot a confused look at her.

"Uh, sweetie," Kaylessa said, "I didn't realize your mother did not tell you. The Elements…They're not real. They aren't actual people."

Mr. Lavadan rubbed his neck. "Well…that's not entirely true."

A knock came at the door. Darunia's mother stepped through. "Hi, I-I don't mean to interrupt. We just…have to get going."

Darunia sighed. "But, *Meia*, it's her Ritual day. Can I please stay? *Please*?"

Her mother shook her head, obviously nervous. "No. I—No."

"Imra," Mr. Lavadan said, "do you think I would let anything bad happen to your daughter? If it is fine with you, I'm certain that we can bring her back to your house later on."

Imra stared at me. "It's not you I'm worried about, Leorn…" She begrudgingly nodded. "Okay, just not too long."

"Thank you!" Darunia ran up and hugged her mother.

I tried to ensure there were no hard feelings. "Thank you, *Maliei* Qikan."

Concern tensed her face, and she left without acknowledging me.

Taelin turned to us. "So, Leorn, were you behind any of the antics we saw?"

"No. It was nothing that simple. Although I wish it was. " Mr. Lavadan groaned. "Please, listen to me. As Elena, Darunia, and I have seen, our lores, they're actually history. The Elements are certainly real beings…"

He went on to explain to them everything we knew. I chimed in here and there, adding a little bit more clarity, but for the most part, I just sat beside him, trying to think it all over.

Overwhelmed tears pricked the corners of my eyes, wanting to overflow. *I will never be one of them.*

I had never wanted a Blessing. Or any of this. It took all my energy to not break down. I absently leaned against Mr. Lavadan, seeking comfort and wondering just how I would tell Onvyr everything.

Loyalty

I paced for what felt like phases. *I'm getting tired of having to deal with her*, I tried telling myself. What I was actually getting tired of was the constant pretending. Pretending I hated her. That she was a monster. I shook my head, ridding myself of such idiotic thoughts.

This is what she does. She deceives. Like a human. If left alone, she will contaminate the world we live in. We worked so hard to be free from humans and their immorality. I can't let her give them power.

The girl finally arrived, out of breath from running. I faced her with a fake smile, only realizing it then: I did hate her. I hated the conflict she made me feel and the obliviousness she held.

"I'm so sorry. The Ritual—" She gasped for air. Syndra avoided eye contact with me. "Things just got complicated."

"Didn't get the Essence in the first drop?" I asked.

She shook her head. "Well, no...Well, yes...But...that

wasn't the problem."

I held onto my upper arm behind my back. *I know you aren't going to try to lie to me.* "So…?"

"So?" She tilted her head at me, confused.

I playfully rolled my eyes. "What Gift did you get? Or found out you had?"

With a held breath, she hesitated. "I…didn't get one." Her hair fell further out of place when she shook her head. "Okay, listen. It was *crazy*, but…"

Words spewed out of her like a broken fountain. Constant but hard to follow. Something about strange Essence again and the Ether and Elements and a *new* Element and a "Blessing" and *oh my Ether.* It seemed like she never took a breath between sentences.

My eyes narrowed while I tried to comprehend what she said. I didn't even notice that my grip on my arm had tightened until my arm had fallen asleep.

What in Rishi's name are you saying? Please, just get to the point…

"So, yeah…I had to tell Mr. Lavadan that I was going to try to talk to the Elements again to convince him to let me out of the house. It's just all so…*ugh*." She threw her head back, holding her neck. After a beat or so, she looked back at me. "Any thoughts? I really need as much help as I can get."

I searched her face, looking for any indications she was lying. *Anything.* It was so convoluted it couldn't have been true. I stammered, "I—uh—but...So you—you got controlling a new Element as a Gift?"

She rubbed her eyes and pulled them down in exhaustion. "No, no, I didn't *get* a Gift. I was born with a Blessing or something. My Blessing—"

"Hold on." I held up a hand. "Just...give me a sec."

Something's wrong about it all. My brain struggled, trying to figure out what to do next. Everything moving forward relied on her Gift, so I *needed* to know how to evaluate this. I nodded, an idea in mind.

"Okay, just to help me understand better, can you show me?" I asked.

"What? Show you what?"

"Your Blessing."

Syndra violently shook her head. "I can't do that! It's dangerous, I think. I need them to help me contain it so it's safe."

I crossed my arms and leaned against a nearby rock. "'Kay. If it gets out of hand, call them or whatever to get them to help. Visuals will just help me. You *do* see how insane this all is?"

"I know..."

"Hey," I said, "I'm your friend. Just need to understand so I can help. You trust me, right?"

Syndra peered at me, innocently chuckling. "Yeah, I do."

"Just try to do something little. Nothing big."

She took a deep breath. "Okay, but I've never done this before, so I don't know what to expect."

I nodded, subtly observing.

She cupped her hands and focused on them. Nothing.

I stood there for a bit, just waiting for something to happen. *Yup. She was lying. Probably is Underprivileged or has a lame Gift and was trying to—*

Opalescent Essence flowed from her palms, swirling. It began moving out of her hands. *This...this is alive.* It captivated me. *This is that glimmer in her eyes.* My Essence pulsed in me, intrigued by the substance. She seemed to struggle to keep it calm. With a jolt, it shot from her palms to me. I had to dodge it to avoid getting hit. She and I both stared in awe at what it had become.

A rift opened where I once stood. *How in Rishi's name...?*

"It...it felt like using a cycle...or shards. A little nauseating," she mumbled, heading toward it.

I glanced at her. *Using shards doesn't feel like that. At worst, it feels dizzying.*

"What does it lead to?"

She shrugged. "I have no idea."

I ran to stop Syndra from walking through it. "Wait!" I pulled her back. "You created this. If you go through it, it will close, and you will be stuck on the other side. I...I will look and come back."

She nodded in agreement.

It looked like any other rift. Only, this one had been made without shards or a cycle. No crystal involved. With shallow breaths, I slowly walked through the rift. A sense of comfort flew through me. A memory tried to flash from the depths of my mind.

When I stepped out, I saw a place I had thought I would never see again.

A near-completed treehouse to my right, roots of the plant stained with sorrow. In front of me, a simple but perfect house, once a home now filled with shadows of a past I had been rescued from.

Echoes of their useless screams still lived within me. No one had come. Not until it was too late.

Sometimes, I wondered why I couldn't seem to follow them. Why I was the one who had survived. But it was Zentha and Wyn who reminded me why. Motivation. It was on me to help act as justice on the evil of a sinful species.

I stood. Essence amplified inside me—the pain of reliving the moment. The harm they went through overshadowed any good times I'd had there. My mind protected me from fully remembering the moment, but the emotions I felt couldn't be hidden. I swallowed the lump in my throat.

Back at the rift, I didn't push away any emotions which had accumulated. Instead, I remembered the training I had. I was an Empath. This was my fuel.

I returned to Syndra. My fortitude for our plans for her was relit. No doubts hung around my mind any longer.

"What was it? You look like you lost a fistfight or something," she said.

She's worried. About me. One doubt. *Disperse it, she isn't worried about me. She's worried about taking responsibility if something had happened to me.*

"It's a rift. That's for sure," I muttered. "It kinda forced me to think of a place when I walked through. Brought me there."

"What? Why would it do that?"

"Well, you didn't think of a place, did you? When you created it?"

She shook her head.

I shrugged. "Had to be given a destination."

Fear clouded her eyes. Behind me, the rift snapped shut, making her yelp. Syndra stared at where it once was.

Her Gift is unlike anything I've seen before. "Come on," I urged her, pulling out my rift shards.

"Where are we going?"

I tried piecing together a smile, but it came out strained. "Made a promise. If I've learned anything from who I grew up with, it's to always keep a promise. That is, if you're still up to meeting Choa Zentha and seeing my Gift?"

The storm in her eyes eased. "That would be awesome." She laughed. "Sounds like a great distraction."

I held the shards and thought of the place, making them rush before us. Bowing, I said, "After you."

She elbowed me before going through the portal. "Weirdo."

I hesitated to follow her and I let out a sigh. *Just, make this easy. Please.*

I walked through. The shards flew back to the pouch. I led her inside the elaborate cabin standing before us.

"Is this where you live?" Syndra asked, examining the room.

"Sometimes."

Zentha stood at the entrance to the hallway, leaning against the wall. "We travel often, so where we live varies."

She walked up to us with a smile as sweet as honeysuckle. Internally, I scoffed. Although she wore a permanent grin, it never looked like this. *She's laying it on thick.*

"This is your friend? Nice to meet you." She bowed her head toward Syndra. "I am Zentha Iarsys. I've heard a lot about you." Choa whispered in the girl's ear, "Or whatever I can pull out of him."

Syndra laughed. "Oh my gosh, I know right? He's like a clam."

My face fell flat. *I'm not a clam.*

"I'm, uh, Syndra Lavadan," she said awkwardly.

Choa Zentha softly chuckled. "I'm an Oblivion Telepath, but what about you, young one?"

Syndra stammered, "I—uh..." She glanced at me for help.

"She has a powerful Gift," I said.

Zentha looked at me, curious, her smile a little stiffer. "How interestingly vague."

Syndra stared at the floor. "Yeah, we're still figuring out the details. Onvyr said he was a Perspective Empath, though." She looked back at me. "You said you would show me your Gift, right? I still don't know what that is."

Zentha and I shared a glance. *No time like the present.*

"Syndra, remember how I said my parents died in an accident?"

"Um, yeah. But what does that have to do with your Gift?"

Zentha stood behind me, her hands on my shoulders. "It was a grim day."

"That's not exactly how it went," I said. "It wasn't an

accident. When I was eight, humans ambushed our home. My parents hid me, but they…" The reminiscent fear echoed in my chest. "The memory of them dying is still too painful to remember."

Syndra went pale. "I-I am so sorry. That's why you're not fond of humans, huh?"

"I miss them every day," Zentha cooed behind me.

I explained. "She was a friend of theirs. They called for her, but she was unable to get there in time. Zentha could save only me. Since then, she took me in. Her community took me in. They taught me, fed me, raised me… They became my family. I brought you here, wondering if you could join us."

"What?" She scanned me. "What do you mean?"

"You were wrong. We aren't murderers," I said.

Zentha laughed behind me. "My Ether, we've been called that quite often. What we do isn't a crime. It is a reckoning. A justice that no one wants to enact. The real criminals go about their business, killing, harming, and intoxicating *everyone*, including themselves and our planet."

"What? Murderers? I don't—" Syndra's eyes widened. "You…You're part of the Ambition? I thought they were—"

"Please, hear me," I said. "You've been harmed by humans before. They've bullied you, hurt you. You never belonged with them, and they made sure you knew it."

She bit her lip and slowly peered away, unable to oppose.

"I will be honest with you. You don't belong with fae either."

Her head shot up. She was hurt by my words.

"That's not your fault, but it's still true. But your Gift is something I have never even heard of before. You hold an unknown power." I locked eyes with her, holding out my hand. "Elena, join us. The Ambition takes in the different, and together, we are whole. Together, we can get rid of evil. No one has to be hurt again."

She stared at my hand. "You said Elena. I never told you that was my name."

Esh. Come on, look past it...

"Please, don't you trust me?"

"Do—do you kill people?" She looked at me with glassy eyes. "Have you killed innocent people?"

Zentha drifted toward the girl. Her smile grew more devious. "When weeds grow in a garden, what can you do other than pull them out? Not a single person we have dealt with has been innocent. We—"

"Onvyr!" Syndra shed a fearful tear. "Do you kill people?"

I shot up my hand, stopping Zentha from continuing. "Yes. It has to be done."

Syndra shook her head in disbelief. "No, I-I...This is *wrong*. I can't—" She looked around. "I need to go. I'm sorry."

My heart sighed, knowing what needed to be done. I stared at the floor, grabbing her wrist when she tried walking past me. "That's not how this goes."

I remembered what my parents had gone through. My Essence increased in my arm, and I flung her to the ground.

"No isn't an answer."

The Breaking Point

Trying to run was useless. Zentha grabbed me immediately. Her beautiful features twisted into a smile. I was staring at something infinitely more terrifying than the monster under the bed.

She pulled my arms behind me. Kicking and attempting to fight only succeeded in satisfying her.

"Oh, no, no, little eel. You can't worm your way out," she whispered.

In a single movement, she twisted my arm back, and a snap echoed through the room. I shouted when pain jolted through my limb.

"Oops." Her pale blond hair fell in front of her face. "Shouldn't have moved."

She — she enjoys this.

"Let's move it," Onvyr said. "Don't make this take

longer than needed."

Zentha forced me onto my knees, her foot heavy on my back. She bound my wrists tightly, causing my broken arm to throb and my fractured bone to contort in a way it never had before. I stared at Onvyr through a veil of tears, only able to think one thing: *I never knew him.*

"Please, don't…" I begged. My Blessing riled within me. I could have used it, but panic shook me too much to focus on anything.

He walked behind me. His hand on my chin pulled my head back, forcing me to look at him upside down.

"Why didn't you just say yes?" His voice was cold, actually disappointed.

"Don't hurt me. *Please.*" Lead tears fell off the sides of my face.

Onvyr's eyes began to glow magenta. A strand of his gelled hair fell out of place. "But I promised I'd show you my Gift, didn't I?"

A rush of heat ran through his handprint to my chest, jabbing inside it, like daggers tearing me apart. I screamed in agony when I felt myself being dismantled piece by piece. My Blessing writhed in similar pain. The energy ran to my skin, seemingly trying to flee from it. I knew the need to escape all too well.

My heart was being gnawed at by whatever destructive force this Gift was. I felt like I was being eaten by rats from the inside out.

Right when I thought I was going to pass out from the suffering, his Gift fled when he pulled his hand away.

I bent over, gasping and coughing from the pressure he had put on my neck. My Blessing churned within my body, putting the bits of me back together. A slow healing.

Oddly, Onvyr seemed shocked. He stared at me, confused and sorrowful. I noticed the tears he desperately tried to rein back. He looked like a lost little boy, vastly different than from mere seconds ago.

"Prodigy," Zentha growled. "What in Rishi's name was that?"

He fought against his jaw while it trembled. "I… ran out of Essence." He cleared his throat, trying to seem stoic once more. "Have to finish later. Just take her back. Now."

He created a rift and waited beside it, his eyes laden in shadows.

Zentha grumbled something too low to hear. She pulled me up by my broken limb. I tasted blood while I bit my lip in pain.

"Sounds like you get a breather, little eel. Don't take it to heart. You'll just get to go through it all over again."

She pushed a piece of metal against my neck. It jutted itself into me, pumping something freezing cold into my veins. I shuddered while it spread. My Blessing came to a halt. My heart was pressed in a vise, forced to slow. My eyelids became as heavy as stone covers to tombs.

Crossroads

"Shaken" didn't begin to describe how I felt. I found myself hiding in my dorm room, incessantly twirling my dagger, trying to figure out what was real and what was fake.

I had known dealing with her would be difficult. Though I had used my Gift so many times before, but this time, I had to actually look past her in order to actually do it. But I had never expected her to fight back how she did.

In hindsight, I didn't think she even meant to do it. Once I began, a tender energy traveled through my arms. My consciousness followed a connection it had made to the back of my brain. Memories flashed through my mind, but I didn't recognize them. My mind replayed it in disbelief.

It was the sight of Zentha decapitating my father and bleeding out my mother.

No. She—She saved me. It was humans that killed them...

The words she spoke afterward rang hollow in my ears: "Sweet boy, you're gonna be a little prodigy aren't you? Well, I got a pretty nifty Gift too."

Frustration burned. Although I searched desperately for any inconsistencies, I found none. She had lost the full use of her Gift only a couple orbits ago. This was before that. All I did know about the event had been told to me by her. I had thought I couldn't remember it because it was an agonizing experience. *No, I couldn't remember it because she is an Oblivion Telepath. How stupid can I be?*

I sat on my bed, feeling abandoned. Zentha had practically become a mother to me. *Only after killing my actual mother.*

Now, I could remember it all. Even before the event.

My father and I had worked on building that treehouse every day since my fifth birthday. Of course, we rarely made actual progress. Most of it was fooling around.

Then, at night, he would swap out with my mother when she got home. I almost never had both at the same time. She cared for me, telling me stories and acting out scenes with my seven-orbit-old self.

I squeezed the pillow beside me while resentment grew. They had taken me from my life and my family, yet I didn't understand why.

"Whoa…What treason did your pillow commit?" Wyn asked, snapping me out of my mind.

I looked at my lap. I had been tearing my pillow apart with my dagger.

"Naak, you look like hell. What the actual Ether happened to you?" He grimaced, as if he was disgusted by looking at me.

Wyn was my mentor. My brother. He was diligent, fun, and always exceptional. Everything I wanted to be.

"Is it true?" My voice was dark and hoarse, barely audible.

He squinted at me with a smug smile. "Is what true? Come on. Are you going to be cryptic—"

"Zentha killed my parents, didn't she?"

His cheery demeanor froze, but he just stared at me. He chuckled, trying to hide it. "Humans came when you were a kid. *They* killed them. Where in Rishi's name did you hear—"

"I remembered, Wyn. So let me rephrase. *Did you know?*" Bitter bile spewed with my words.

I began to understand. He wasn't confident; he was prideful. Wyn wasn't diligent; he was a pawn. I was just looking through a red-tinted glass all these orbits, wanting to have someone to look up to. The fae standing before me wasn't a brother; he was a forced companion.

The second youngest in the Ambition. Only person the kid could possibly relate to.

His expression flattened. "Your mother was a Petrifying Empath. Your father was a Descendent and an Ember Igniter. There was no doubt you would have a Gift we needed."

I had felt pain before. Endurance training and gashing wounds came quite often. Yet nothing compared to this.

"Prodigy—" he stammered with his words.

"Stop. I don't want to hear anymore 'justification' for this." I grabbed my dagger from the pillow. "Get out of my room."

That haughty demeanor of his waivered. He muttered, "It's my room, too. Onvyr—"

"I said, get out!" The blade flew, sticking in the wall a couple of inches from his head.

Wyn stared at it. "You can't tell a single soul here

anything about this." He glanced at me. "You know that, right? They won't kill you. There are things worse than death." He traced the bridge of his nose, mirroring where my scar laid. "But you also know that."

My hands trembled. *They wouldn't do that again...*

But he was right. What he said was true.

"Let this pass, Prodigy. Whether what happened to them was true or not, you can't deny the horrors humans have done. We've been on missions together. You've seen it for yourself." He opened the door. "I don't know how you remember, but please. Heed my words. You don't want to be on the wrong side of the Ambition."

***

That night, while Wyn slept deeply above me—snoring the entire time—I laid awake, my mind unable to calm down. *Why* do *we have to kill humans?* I tossed and turned, restless. I questioned everything the Ambition had taught me.

Something had never felt right whenever I would do anything for them. Joy came at a shadowed cost.

I had only killed one human, personally, but I had also created plenty of soldiers to do exactly that. And I listened to everyone, thinking they only wanted me to persuade so many people because civilians were just afraid to do what was right. Yet, now I doubted what was "right."

They killed my family, innocent people, without batting an eye and using stupid reasons to justify it. What else are they doing under the belief that it's what has to be done? The answer came to me like a stone hurled at my stomach.

Quietly, I got up, knowing what I needed to do.

"There are things worse than death."

Fear lingered, I decided to put on my armor and a concealed weapon. Although I now despised wearing anything the Ambition had given me, I had a good feeling I would need it all. I grabbed Wyn's shards and headed to the Ambition's holding cells.

There was a girl I needed to repay a favor to.

Untethered

Getting around security was easy enough. Zentha had taught me the quickest way to slip a fae a flash of the neutralizer. Of course, knowing where they liked to goof off in the first place probably helped.

These soldiers were always sent down to the cells for grunt work, usually to help atone for small slip-ups. No one ever wanted to stand here, doing nothing, so it was easy to catch them off-guard.

I peered through each of the windows, looking for her. My Essence built up in my chest, and the fear of being caught controlled me. I moved as fast as possible.

Thankfully, I was able to find her after only a little searching.

I unlocked the door with my Matrix gloves and rushed over, looking for how to unbind her. Her skin was a clammy blue, sticking to the metal cuffs on her wrists.

"Wake up. Please, I need you to wake up," I said,

quivering, finally undoing her cuffs. I shook her shoulders. "Please wake up."

I noticed the Lull Tap on her neck and disarmed it, finding it hard not to slap myself in stupidity. There was no way she could have woken up with that on.

Blood started dripping from it immediately after I plucked it out. *I didn't prepare for this.*

I kept pressure on the wound and scanned the cell for something to create a makeshift bandage. *I'm not even wearing cloth. Just armor. By Rishi's wrath, what else have I forgotten about?* I tore a piece off one of her sleeves and pressed it against her neck.

She began to blink awake. Since I was trying to stop the blood, I was awkwardly close to her face. I gave a crooked smile. The girl gasped and jolted backward in the chair. I followed her neck, trying to keep even pressure.

"Wait, wait, wait. I'm trying to stop the blood," I nervously explained in blurts. "Hold still."

Her face cringed when the pain set in. Her eyes never let up the cold stare she gave me. I tried my best to focus on the wound.

"Why? Why help? Wouldn't everything be easier for you if I bled out?" she spat at me.

The words seeped into my ears like poison. For a while after I met her, some part of me had wanted something similar to occur.

"Not anymore," I murmured.

Slowly, I lifted my hands off, causing her to take a sharp breath. The blood flow had stopped. *It didn't hit an artery. Good.*

Unable to avoid her any longer, I stepped back and met her eyes. She looked like a waking corpse, with shadows below her eyes and tears coating her clearly tired irises.

Her voice croaked. "I thought that my father was paranoid. I kept hanging out with you, even when he fervently protested! And for what? To be with a murderer? Isn't that right, Prodigy?"

I shook my head. "I-I thought they were my family. I thought they...What did you do? When I was using my Gift, what did you do to me?"

"What?" She scoffed. "I didn't do anything except suffer."

My eyes drifted. "Something happened. I stopped because a memory that I lost came back to me."

I bit my lip to hold back my emotions.

"Zentha was the reason my parents died. Not humans. She used her Gift on me to make me forget. But we have to go now, before they realize the guards are unconscious. I'm breaking you and me out of this hell."

Her hair hung in strands, the only thing between her eyes and mine. Yet something stirred in them. I couldn't tell if she was furious, hurt, or trying to understand me.

"How can I trust you?"

I met her gaze. "They hurt blameless people. They're doing the same with you. Something told me you were innocent, but I ignored it because of my...loyalties."

My tongue searched for the words to express my contrition. "Sorry" wouldn't be enough. Not after everything I had put her through. Syndra placed her hand on my shoulder. With a determined nod, I could tell she understood what I meant.

"Okay, but if I'm being honest..." Her head lolled forward. She wryly laughed. "I can barely sit up, let alone walk."

I made her wrap an arm around my shoulders, and I lifted her off the chair by her left side. "That's fine. I got you."

She reminded me of dragging weighted bags. Her

other arm dangled, hitting the chair. She winced.

"What? What's wrong?"

"My arm... That stupid lady broke it," she said through gritted teeth.

A ticking sounded from the hall. *Oh disperse it.*

"Are you going to be okay?"

She weakly nodded. "Yeah, just...maybe don't let it hit anything." Syndra looked at the cell door. "What is that sound?"

I began to walk her to the door, peering so I could check the halls.

"The alarm." I looked at her deep in those exhausted eyes. "They'll find us here. We're gonna need to move fast to a safe spot so I can use the shards. Can you do that?"

Another nod. "As long as you're good with dragging me a little."

Yeah, that's not gonna be the problem. The skilled soldiers on our tail on the other hand... I quickly sped down the hall, desperately trying not to trip her up or have her arm hit anything. We ran past the guards lying on the floor.

"Are...Are they—" she asked.

"No," I said. "They're unconscious, not dead."

Break room. Break room. Finally, at the end of the hall, I found where the guards went on their off time. *No one should be there right now.* I carefully stuck my hand out, trying not to drop her. The door unlocked with my glove.

"Prodigy!" Teidove bolted down the hall toward us.

Of course, it had to be him on duty tonight.

I was never gladder that he was a Polymorph and not a Limb Enhancer. With a swing, I flung the door shut and leaned against it. Syndra began slipping from my grip.

"Who was that?" she asked quietly. "Where did he come from? I didn't see him."

"He was working further on down. One of my prefects."

Pounding hit my back through the door. *We need to get out of here.* The shards were in a pouch on my belt, but I couldn't reach it with her still relying on me for support.

I took her to a wall and leaned her against it. "Gotta get my shards. Try to stay standing for a bit longer. We'll get you to a healer once we get out of here."

"Kaylessa can help—"

Teidove burst through the door, yet it wasn't him who came forward.

Zentha ambled out from behind him. "Prodigy, what do you think you're doing?"

Her thin smile sent a jolt of pain through me. It was the same as the one she had worn when she "rescued" my younger self. Words abandoned me. My heart raced with panic.

"Leave her there. Stay still. We'll take care of this," she cooed.

My hand drifted to my hidden dagger. "I won't let you hurt any more innocent people."

Her laugh was cold and sharp with Essence. "No one is innocent. Especially not her. She's been corrupted by them."

"No. She's done nothing." I hardened myself, swearing silently that not a single one of them would get through me.

Zentha sighed. "I really did try to help you."

The two of them lunged at me, with Zentha trying to knock me off balance and Teidove wielding a blade to my chest.

I flipped out my dagger, dodging Zentha and

redirecting Teidove's blade to cut her. When I kicked him aside, he hit against a nearby table. Just enough for a little distance. Zentha grabbed my arm, pulling me close.

"Are you really going to vie with *me*?" she mocked, her eyes wide with Essence-enhanced excitement.

She's right. I can't fight her off. I feigned a go at stabbing her, causing her to block her side. Swiftly, I grabbed my neutralizer with my free arm, shutting my eyes and flashing it before she could attack again.

She stumbled away, having shielded her eyes enough to avoid unconsciousness. But she was still disoriented.

I searched for my shards, finding them in her hands.

Zentha rubbed her blazing eyes. "Hope you aren't looking for these," she said, dangling the pouch.

Teidove, muddled, leaned against a wall, having caught a bit of the light as well. Syndra grabbed my arm from behind.

"What?" I blurted, a little higher pitched than I would have liked.

"Let's go," Syndra whispered, with equally contempt and determined eyes. Opalescent eyes. Energy flowed from her, collecting into a rift beside me.

Teidove regained balance first and headed for us.

Left with no other option, I snatched Syndra's hand and pulled her through the portal.

This is Fine

Despite my best wishes, I couldn't find peace after I went through the rift. Instead, I found myself in the Ether. The Elements had brought me to the realm again.

Yet, this time felt different than before.

"You should thank us," Jeongsin said. "Had we kept your consciousness in your body, you'd be in great pain."

I looked down at my hands. They were almost as blurred out as the surroundings. "Whoa, am I a ghost?"

"No!" Uli snapped. "We do not talk of ghosts, not even as a joke. They're much too troublesome for the four of us to deal with."

Sentir crossed his arms. "But technically, yup. Your body is just over there."

I glanced toward two orange blobs a little further from us. One of them was moving around, dragging the other into a giant cyan blotch. I assumed the one being dragged was probably me.

"You will want to stay here for a bit longer until you

heal," Svitlo said.

My blurry arms self-refracted different colors yet gray in nature. By that point, I was easily able to recognize my Blessing. I sighed, sitting on what seemed to be the ground.

"Why did he do it?" I mumbled, leaning my face on my fist.

"Do which?" Alegria sat beside me. "Harm you, or save you?"

"Ugh...both." I covered my face with my hands. "I need a vacation or something."

She giggled. "Well, if he doesn't get you help, you'll get to have a permanent vacation."

I jerked my head up. "What do you mean?"

"Ignore her." Sentir knelt beside us. "My sister likes creating panic sometimes. He can definitely get you help. We know this boy. We're the ones who gave him his Gift, after all."

"Yeah...What's up with that, man?" I groaned. "What kind of Gift does *that*?"

"A Gift honed in by his family line. His mother was a powerful Empath, and when we saw how much power he harbored..." Sentir whistled. "We knew he'd be the perfect fit for Perspective Empathy."

"It created just a little havoc," Alegria added, putting

her fingers together.

I rolled my eyes. "A little? I have no idea what's wrong with you guys."

Jharana cleared her throat. "The thing we should be focusing on is you. Why the Ether did you use your Gift without calling one of us to help you? You did it twice!"

I hugged my knees. "I trusted him. I thought using just a little would be fine. And it certainly saved us in the end." I laid my head on my knees and looked at them. "Do any of you know what Onvyr was talking about? About me making him remember a memory?"

Jeongsin nodded. "Memories are echoes of time, held in mind by a neural connection and interpreted through mental perspective. Oblivion Telepaths can break that connection, causing the memory to drift away." A sly smile grew on his face. "Your Blessing recreated that connection. From nothing. It found the echo of time and linked it back to his mind."

I shook my head. "But I didn't do anything."

He laughed. "Have you not heard of the subconscious? Looks like that's where your Blessing resides and works from."

Exhaustion gradually pulsed through me. I didn't have the energy to deal with them. "I just want to sleep."

Aithalis came up beside me. "You better avoid doing so. Give the fae a bit more time to figure out how to heal you."

Alegria agreed. "And he surely can. That's for certain. He just needs to realize it."

I laid down and rolled my head toward Aithalis . "So, how did I create the rifts?"

She shrugged. "Your Blessing."

"You all are great at explaining things. Did it work, though?" I glanced back to where the orange colors had entered the cyan. "Did it bring us to Kaylessa?"

The Element of Nature grinned. "Yup."

Good. I sighed. *I just want to sleep.* I tried to think of conversation to keep me awake. "So, I notice one of you isn't here. He never introduced himself to me before. Who is that?"

Svitlo started, "He—"

"That's the Element of Technology," Riah interrupted. "Nolo doesn't quite care about mortal matters, though. He can be...what's the word?"

"A menace," Aithalis said, with hatred in her words. "All Teknolojia wants is to cut down my forests. Replace it all with metal and cement."

"Doesn't metal come from the Earth?" I asked, attempting to be interested. "Shouldn't you have control over that?"

"Once it's processed by mortal hands, it becomes his. The cyan Essence you see is him," she told me with a bit of a pout.

My mind wandered while I stared into the distance. The Elements talked and chattered, but I didn't have the focus to hear their words any more. After having been through so much, I needed to rest.

I just want to sleep.

Something grabbed my hand. My eyes drifted to it, trying to make it out. None of the Elements were touching me. But someone was holding my hand. With a flash, I briefly saw Onvyr.

A sentence from Sentir broke through my daze: "Finally. He realized it."

Pure Essence swirled, immediately turning into my Blessing's Essence. Adrenaline pumped through me. I was pulled back out of the Ether.

Pulse

We fell into a bush on the other side. I froze to stone as Teidove followed us through before it closed. Thankfully, the bush concealed us both. He ran away, searching for us. A breath of relief filled my lungs, and I pulled her out.

"He's gone. Come on," I said.

While I exited the leaves, I noticed Syndra had fallen unconscious. Bits of her began dispersing.

She's out of Essence.

I scanned the area for a solution. We were in a human city in front of a building. The thick air smelled of pollution. Big foreign runes hung above the doors. Never had I wished I knew any human language so much.

Unfortunately, she had been lighter when she was helping herself walk alongside me. I was forced to drag her. While I didn't know what to do, I knew I needed to get to someone. *Anyone.* Even if they were a human.

The doors automatically slid open. Inside, a bunch of humans were sitting down or behind a clean white desk. Everyone seemed concerned at the sight of Syndra in my arms. A few came and surrounded me, muttering things in their nasally language. It matched Syndra's accent.

"Please, she needs help," I tried telling them. I remembered the healer Syndra had mentioned. *It's worth a shot.* "Kaylessa. Do you know a Kaylessa?"

A few humans in dark clothes came in and tried taking her from me. I kicked them off. No way was I letting her go with humans alone.

After I took out my dagger, they pulled out black metal boxes. Hand size. Each of them clicked once they reached the humans' fingers. It took a beat before I recognized what they were, something I had only ever seen once before: guns.

"*Healer*," I said, emphasizing each syllable. "She needs a *healer*. Please, bring her one."

A human in a white coat came rushing in. Her blond curls bounced as she tried talking to the humans with weapons. The woman fell to the ground, examining Syndra.

"Elena needs immediate attention," she told me in Voliun.

She's a fae in disguise.

Her gaze was strong and protective. "You're from the Ambition."

I glanced down at my armor. "Please, I just need her to get better. She's dispersing."

"I can see that." The lady picked her up. "You're lucky I heard how they described you before things escalated. I'm the only fae here."

"Wait, you can't take her away."

Although she was a fae, I still didn't know her. I needed to stay by Syndra.

"Listen, if you want to come with me, then you will have to put that blade away." She looked around and spoke to the humans in dark clothes. The lady turned to me. "They think you're a danger. I can't disagree, but if you're as desperate to come as you sound, drop the blade. Kick it to them."

I didn't want to be defenseless, but I needed to be with Syndra, so I kicked my dagger to them. They lowered their guns.

"Okay, follow me." The fae ran off with the girl in her arms.

Everything blurred by while we sprinted through

the place. She led me into a room filled with odd things, like a bed with railings and boxes of gloves beside a sink.

It wasn't until we stopped that I noticed the dark-clothed humans had followed us. After putting Syndra down, the lady came to the door and forced them out. She frantically spun around the room, grabbing more familiar fae physician tools from hiding spots. I spotted a pouch of shards hidden in the corner of a desk, keeping note of them in case I needed a quick getaway.

"What in Rishi's name gave you the idea to come to a human hospital in search for a healer?" she asked, analyzing Syndra. "Especially when her problem deals with Essence?"

"I didn't. She did. She created a rift after being on a Lull Tap for a while. Are you Kaylessa?"

She glared at me. "Yeah. I'm her aunt," she said. "How long was she on that?"

I shook my head. "Phases? I don't know. Since last evening."

Kaylessa shot me a cold stare. "You understand what a Lull Tap does, right?"

"Puts people to sleep?"

She scoffed. "It saps the user of Essence to force

them into slumber. It's not supposed to be used for long periods of time. And then, after waking up, she used a rift?" Kaylessa took a step back and clenched the bed railing. "There's nothing left for me to work with."

I shakily walked over to her. "What are you saying?"

Her eyes were dark and somber. "I can't save her."

"No." The memory of my dead parents flashed before me. "No, no. You're a healer. Heal her!"

"In these situations, the only solution would be to give her more pure Essence or Essence tainted by the same Gift she has. She doesn't have any more to live off of, and she has no Gift. Nothing we can match. Although I can transfer Essence, we have no access to pure Essence, and what we can give is only Essence tainted by *our* Gifts." Kaylessa stroked Syndra's pale face. "It's too late, young one."

I had felt helplessness like this only once before, when I couldn't do anything to save my parents. Just watch. And now, I was being forced to do the same with Syndra, with nothing I could do to save her. My emotions burned inside me, intense with the rage of my Essence. *Wait.* I stared at my hands. *My Essence.*

I turned to the healer. "If I had pure Essence, could you channel it to her?"

Kaylessa solemnly chuckled. "In theory, sure. But it's like I said…Our Gifts taint any pure Essence our bodies make."

I grabbed her hand. "No, listen. Something has always been different with me. We've been testing me to try to understand. My body makes too much Essence to be used."

She drew her brows together. "Like Darunia? That means—"

"I have a ton of pure Essence in me."

Hope reawakened. Kaylessa shot up and grabbed a ribbon. She placed me beside Syndra.

"Hold her hand and hold it tight."

I obeyed, standing still while she wrapped the girl's cold hand together with mine.

"Alright hon. Give it your all, as if you are playing Essence Erupting, but focus only on the pure Essence, not your Gift."

My Essence knew exactly what to do. I stopped trying to restrain it. The floodgate opened. The patterns on the ribbon glowed as the energy reached it. It exploded out of me—anchored by the ribbon—and tunnelled into Syndra.

The strain of harboring it all left my chest. My hair fell out of place. An optimistic relief created a smile on my face.

Once I felt myself beginning to use my Empathic Essence, I pulled away. The ribbon fell when I let go. Her dispersing body pulled all of itself together, and pearly gray particles danced around her. Color tinted her skin. Her arm shifted when the Essence healed it back into place.

Dizzy, I fell into a chair Kaylessa had pulled out for me. After inspecting the girl once more, the healer knelt and hugged me.

"You did it," she whispered in my ear.

The pride that warmed me was different than anything I had ever experienced before. It felt good. Stainless. Like it was the first right thing I had done.

I hugged her back.

Cost

Time ticked away while I watched Syndra get better. Maliei Kaylessa kept herself busy, checking on Syndra and periodically leaving to attend to humans—apparently, that was her human job.

"All right, things are settled." Kaylessa closed the door behind her. "My patients are in the hands of other doctors, I finally got security off of your back—which was crazy hard since they thought you were a terrorist—and I called her father. He should be here any beat now to take her back home."

She leaned against the sink.

"Now, I'm still quite curious what a member of the Ambition was doing with my niece and why he would risk so much for her. Doesn't seem like you're here on their commands."

My chest felt light now that I knew I had left it all behind. I looked up at her. "Didn't want innocent people to pay for made-up crimes." I glanced back at the recovering girl. "Lives aren't just collateral damage."

A knock came at the door. Kaylessa headed over and let them in.

"This is Leorn," she said. "Her father."

He had starkly dark hair, contrasting against his white skin. His eyes were gray, akin to hers but well-worn and without her idealism. It was clear he was related, but something felt off. Familiar. Like a connection.

"Leorn, this is—" She stopped with a chuckle. "I'm so sorry. I don't think I ever caught your name, sweetie."

I stared at him. "It's Onvyr, but you know that don't you?"

The fae headed toward 'his daughter.' "I don't know what you're talking about." He turned to Kaylessa. "Thank you for caring for her. We all can talk about this when we get home." He looked at me. "I'll take you and her. We'll leave Kaylessa to her duties here. Come."

I darted my eyes to the rift shards. *"They wouldn't have still come to the bag if I had kept it closed, though, right? I mean, I would be standing in the way."*

In one motion, I leapt up and flung the shards at him, stopping him from getting to Syndra.

"You aren't touching her."

He ducked from them, but when I tugged the seam, the shards flew back. Some of them sliced into the back of his head.

The fae bent over in pain and clutched his scalp, grumbling. "You're gonna regret that."

"Hey!" Kaylessa shouted. "What are you guys doing?"

My attention remained on him. "I was wrong. You don't know me by that name. No, you know me as Prodigy."

I tackled the fae, moving him away from Syndra. He pulled out of my grasp and instead pinned me to the floor. From an unseen sheath, he flung out a dagger. It took all my strength to avoid the weapon from puncturing my chest when he pushed it toward me.

"The both of you, stop it!" Kaylessa tried separating us.

"He isn't who you think he is," I said through gritted teeth.

I rolled and got him off me, then flung him to the door.

"What are you talking about, boy? I've known Kaylessa for over half a century," he growled.

Chains appeared around his wrists, dragging him to the ground.

"No, but *I* have." A fae bearing the same face came into the room. Essence made his eyes glow golden. "And you should know better than to impersonate an Illusionist."

The real Leorn Lavadan glanced at me with a scowl. "Kaylessa, give me one good reason why I shouldn't incapacitate him as well. His armor gives him away as a puppet of the Ambition."

"That boy saved your daughter's life, that's why," she said with confidence.

The imposter changed faces, now looking like Zentha, although the expression was flat. "You have to return, Prodigy. If you don't, the punishment we will dole out will surely make you regret ever turning your back to us. Threads never break clean."

I rolled my eyes at him. "Quit it, Teidove. You've never been good at pretending to show emotion. I'm not going back."

"Teidove?" Kaylessa echoed, concern melting her voice. "Onas?"

His face morphed back to his own. Cold and monotone, he mocked, "Aw, Meia, did you miss me?"

She covered her mouth with her hands. "I don't understand. Why…Sweet boy, what have you done?"

He stared at me, still struggling with his chains. "Why don't you ask Nim Innocent?" An unnerving grin cracked unnaturally on his face.

Everyone's eyes fell on me. Almost everyone. *I wish you were awake….*

I remembered the first time I had seen him, trying to accumulate an explanation. "I-I am a Perspective Empath. They…had me change those they considered strong candidates to believe in our goal. To have a passion for our ambition."

"A Perspective Empath…" Lavadan repeated in apprehensive wonder. "There aren't many of those."

"But that means you changed him orbits ago," Kaylessa said. "To keep him in this state requires an empathic connection. A constant flow of Essence."

I shared a look with her.

"You mean… You've done this to multiple people, over orbits, and still have an overflow of Essence?" A mixture of fear and curiosity swirled in her eyes.

"Perspective Empaths can create and break links." Lavadan shot me the same look of determination and contempt Syndra had only moments before we went through the rift.

"You can fix him."

"I don't—I don't know how," I replied, backing up.

Even if I knew how, after all the damage I've done with my Gift, there's no way I'm using it ever again.

Shame and regret began to create a rock in my chest.

Many wouldn't have died had I just told the Ambition no.

"As if Prodigy could do anything more than what he is told." Teidove scoffed.

"Honey..." Kaylessa twirled me around and knelt to my height. "This fae is like a son to me. He is my daughter's betrothed. This... this is not him. Please. I've seen what you can do." Hope flashed from within her again. "Please."

I turned to the chained fae on the floor. The thought of using my Gift made me hesitant.

She was right. This wasn't him. Right before I used my Gift on him all those orbits ago, he had whispered to me "I forgive you." We had imprisoned him, tortured him...And then I put him through unbelievable pain. Yet he forgave me. I would never forget those words.

With a sigh, I walked over to him and placed my hand on the base of his throat. He spat in my face.

"You'll always be the dirt under our shoes. Never anything more," he snarled, his voice low.

I wiped my face and closed my eyes. I focused on the connection between us, the string of Essence keeping him so different. It was old, hardened. I flooded it with Essence, but I couldn't figure out how to snap it.

"I can't cut it," I said. "It's too strong."

Maliei Kaylessa's voice hovered by me. "Then don't cut it. Unravel it."

I nodded, reigning back my Essence. If the brute force of it wouldn't work, then I would have to pick it apart. Each emotion intertwined in the string was snipped one by one. Teidove shook and fought while they each reverted. Resentment. Devotion. He screamed in pain. Anger. Loyalty.

It came undone.

I observed the true him for the first time. I had always believed he felt little to nothing. No, he had felt it all. It was a web of beautiful intricacies. Nothing erratic or out of place. *He has composure. Maturity.*

I pulled away from him.

His head lulled forward and he panted. Kaylessa placed a hand on my shoulder. She, Lavadan, and I shared one thought: *Did it work?*

Teidove looked up and around. "I never thought I'd be in a human hospital." He stared at his hands. "Did a lot of things I never thought I'd do." His eyes drifted up with a contrition I was beginning to know all too well.

"Leorn, let him go," Kaylessa said,

Lavadan got rid of the illusion immediately.

Kaylessa rushed to hug Teidove, and Lavadan helped him stand.

"Just don't go around with my face again, okay? Not a good look for you." Leorn chuckled, patting him on the back.

"Yes, Jeerei," Onas said.

Remorse stung my eyes. I had been the reason why so many were in the same condition Onas was in.

"I'm so sorry." My voice cracked. "It's my fault. I—"

Onas came up and hugged me. "I already forgave you." He pulled back, ruffling my hair. "Just need a little help learning wrong from right."

How? How is this the same person that scolded me for snacking between training sessions? That abhorred it whenever I wasn't on my feet? But he wasn't.

No. He was the same person who knew how to manage every aspect of himself. How to embrace every emotion without being torn apart. *How can I be like him?*

"They won't like this," I said. "Both of us, gone."

"Oh, they might grumble at my absence. It's you that I can see them hunting down," he said.

"What? I'm just a kid."

He shook his head. "You were their Prodigy. I don't think you understand. They *need* you to be able to continue getting a constant flow of new members."

"He's in danger, isn't he?" Kaylessa asked.

Onas nodded gravely. "I would say so. It depends on what the Harbinger decides."

Dread bounced between my ribs, shaking me from the inside out. *All I wanted was to get away from them.* I hadn't expected all of this to follow me.

Lavadan asked, "The Harbinger?"

"'The outstretched hand of justice,'" Onas recited, hollow. "'The eye of untold truth. The crownless sovereign.

The spark of ambition.' The Harbinger is the head of the Ambition and the person that the rest of us both fear and revere the most."

I tucked my hands under my arms to stop them from shaking.

If the Harbinger had their mind set to something, it came true. Zentha had told me many stories about the meticulous methods they took, all of it unseen and nonsense until their outcome came to light.

I glanced up at Onas. "The Harbinger wouldn't devote attention just to me, right?"

"No," he said, turning his gaze to Syndra. "Not just to you. The both of you now pose a threat to the Ambition. The Forbidden and the Traitor."

Where Forgiveness Begins

Although I was back inside my body, I had no idea where I was. I wandered around the nothingness surrounding me. From behind, a trail of energy flew through the air, creating an opalescent silhouette.

"Hello?" I asked it.

Each movement it made seemed to mimic that of my own. It radiated the aura of the Elements.

"You're...my Blessing, aren't you?"

Despite its lack of features or voice, I could tell it smiled.

You helped us create that rift right when we needed it." Curious, I asked, "Why? Why did you help Onvyr?"

The gray around me twisted and turned. Pure crystalline Essence channeled to my Blessing from a pool behind. The pool was draining quickly.

"You…didn't have enough Essence?"

It nodded. The memory of what Onvyr did played before me—the pure Essence he had given me flowing straight into the pool.

"You used him." I glared at the silhouette. "You just needed more Essence, so you needed to keep him close. That's why you gave him that memory back. So he would stick around."

I didn't know how I felt about him. But whether we were still friends or not, using him was wrong. He had helped me…in the end.

Anger pricked from the silhouette. Images of Onvyr appeared in front of me. Not a memory, but closer to a vision.

He cradled his chest while pure Essence exploded within. Onvyr struggled harder to keep it at bay. Something in his eyes snapped. It filled every part of him, emanating an insatiable thirst.

I was immediately reminded of Zentha.

"Is that…what happens if it collects too much?"

It all washed back into the gray.

I pleaded, "Wait…But I just want some answers. I—"

My sentence began to echo, but the words twisted the more they bounced. The silhouette before me grew taller. Tanned skin appeared, along with long oak brown hair. A person I had never seen before, but I felt I knew them all too well.

It took hold of me by the arms. The echoes congregated into five distinct words in my own voice:

"It's time to wake up."

Light seared into my eyes. My body was stone when I tried to sit up. Every part of me felt like the lingering pain of a cramp gone past. Groans slipped from my mouth while I looked around.

I was back in a room I called my own. The dawning light shone on a fae waiting for me. Mr. Lavadan sat in the corner, having fallen asleep.

I never felt as relieved to see him as I did then and there.

"Mr. Lavadan…" I said.

Thankfully, he was a light sleeper. He woke up, groggy, caverns under his eyes from worry.

"My dear." He jumped up, ran to me, and began examining me. "How do you feel? Are you holding up fine? You were—"

I hugged him. He reciprocated with a laugh.

Realization seeped in. Everything clicked into place.

Since I came to the village, he had made sure he was there in my darkest moments. He cared for me in a way I hadn't experienced before. Whatever pain I harbored for him was purely out of my own unforgiving heart. Mr. Lavadan held none of it, even to the point of outing himself to an Ancient at my Ritual to protect me.

When I was in the Ambition's clutches, I had found myself alone with people who wanted to hurt me. That was what Mr. Lavadan tried keeping me from.

And when Onvyr had carried me out of my cell, I couldn't help but remember what Mr. Lavadan had said. *"I can't protect you if you're out of my reach."*

He was my provider, teacher…No. Father. *Appi.*

"Appi." It came out as a whisper filled with nothing but the gratitude I had for him.

I hadn't even realized I said it until it was spoken. I pulled back, a little embarrassed.

"I'm sorry. I-I'm not sure if you're okay with me calling you that. I…"

He knelt on one knee in front of me, joy radiating. His brows drew together. "My dear, what did I say? Do not be sorry for anything you have not done wrong. I storge you—"

"What?" *Is that another word in Voliun?* I rubbed my neck, feeling it empty of devices. *I don't have my translator on.*

Panic rose. I wasn't sure what he was saying, whether he was making fun or angry. For all I knew, it meant "hate."

He chuckled and explained, "It means a deep familial love. Is 'storge' not how you say it in English?"

I shrugged. *I've never heard it before.* The sentiment was touching me.

"My point is. You can call me anything you want. You could call me *naak* for all I care." He hugged me once more. "You are my *Baalih,* and I am truly sorry I was not there for you earlier."

I leaned my head on his shoulder. "You're here now."

Storge. Humans just used "love" for everything. But storge couldn't have been more spot-on. The resonation of the word filled me to the brim with belonging. He was the first person I storge'ed — or whatever the past tense of it was. I grinned. He was also the only person I had met who earned storge.

With a laugh, he looked at me. "Actually, maybe do not call me *naak*. It is a little insulting."

"We'll see how well you do as my Appi," I joked.

He stood up, fixing my hair. "Are you up for walking so we can see the others? Or should I just call them over? I can not keep you to myself."

"I don't know. Lemme see." I let my legs dangle from the side of the bed.

With a little courage, I tried standing up. Appi caught me when I stumbled, light headed. My vision was spotting. He picked me up and placed me back in bed.

"Let me go bring them over," he said, concerned.

I would have nodded in agreement had my head not been spinning. "Yeah, sounds fair."

He left to probably grab Kaylessa and Taelin. I couldn't think of Shaeli going out of her way to be here for…well, anything. But I remembered one fae. *Will he be here?*

Kaylessa came in, followed promptly by Taelin.

She hurried to me, holding my hand while her eyes glimmered orange. "How are you doing, sweetie?" Almost immediately, she answered her own question. "Light headed? Sounds right. *Somebody* shouldn't have let you try to stand up while you're still recovering." She glared at Appi, who in return just smiled nervously.

I looked around for Onvyr. Instead, I spotted a man I was all too familiar with. I squirmed backward in my bed. "That's…That's—"

Kaylessa turned around, understanding my fear. "Oh, yes. Onas."

He seemed just as stone-cold as ever, although his hair was quite oily and ruffled.

"What is *he* doing here?" I asked, keeping my eyes on

the first fae I had ever seen. Who had tried to kill me multiple times.

"I follow you through the rift," he said, hid accent heavy and his English a little spotty. "I not with Ambition anymore. Please do not be afraid."

I shook my head. "That was you? Teidove? How do I know you're not going to try to hurt me again?"

He glanced at Appi, only coming to me once given permission.

Onas stood at the foot of my bed. "I changed. Prod—*esh*, I mean, Onvyr—use his Gift on me. He change my perspective."

I recalled the pain the boy had put me through. Once more, I searched, finally finding him hiding in the shadows of the doorway. Pity twinged in me. *He probably feels uncomfortable around people he doesn't know.*

"He fix me. I sorry for it all," Onas explained, although his face didn't quite show any signs that was what he felt.

On the other hand, I couldn't tell what he felt at all.

Slowly, I nodded. "It's...okay." Thinking of my father, I told myself, *I need to be quicker to forgive.*

Kaylessa came up to me. "Before we go any further, I'm sure *everyone* would like to understand you. I'm certain my husband and a certain someone in the corner here can't.

Here's a translator. I had wanted you to recover without being hooked up to any gadgets, so we had taken it off."

I equipped it and turned my attention to Onvyr. "Why are you hiding?"

Appi directed his line of sight to the doorway. "No, no. I said to stay out of here," he growled.

"What?" I moved myself to the foot of my bed, and Onas walked out of the way. "Why can't he come in?"

Appi turned to me. "He's from the Ambition. And he's yet to tell us what happened or why he came into that hospital carrying my dying daughter. I do *not* trust him."

Dying? I almost died. I looked at the shameful boy, even more grateful.

Onas cleared his throat. "To be honest, *Jeerei*, we've been talking with him since we got here. The boy hasn't been given a chance to explain. He's even still in his armor, of which I can attest is useful but quite uncomfortable."

"What are you complaining about?" I scoffed. "Onas was in the Ambition before too, but here *he* is."

Appi shook his head. "*He* was not given a choice. *He* was forced into it."

"And so was Onvyr, if you'd just let him speak!" I looked at the doorway. "Onvyr, you deserve to get to talk. Ignore him. This is my room. Come in."

He shuffled in, hesitant, his amber eyes glued to the floor. His blond hair, once gelled into a bullet casing, now hung loose. Some strands even covered a quarter of his face.

"Tell them how you started with the Ambition," I said. "They'll understand."

He looked up, obviously overwhelmed by the moment. *Maybe I shouldn't have put him on the spot.*

I nodded at him, trying to encourage the mute boy. Onvyr returned the gesture, keeping his eyes on me while he explained everything. His family. Zentha. His Gift and role.

I wondered what I would have done in his place. I liked to think I would have acted on what felt off, especially because killing was wrong. But I was different from him. I often followed my gut.

How we think we would react in situations versus the truth of what we would do in reality lies on two opposing sides of the same coin. A coin rubbed raw enough to blur the images. I see that now.

Kaylessa reached out to Onvyr. "I am so sorry you had to go through that."

Taelin rubbed his neck, mumbling, "Sounds a little like a sob story."

His wife elbowed him. "Taelin!"

The fae shrugged. "What? It's true." He looked down at Onvyr. "Don't get me wrong. No one should have to go through losing their whole family. That's just unimaginable. But it doesn't explain how the two of you ended where you did."

Everyone seemed to look at us, searching for an answer.

I scratched the back of my head. "Okay, sooo, you know how I would leave the house often?"

Appi gave me a flat look. "Yes. I very much do." He crossed his arms.

"Welllll, I never went too far from the house, but…I *might've* been meeting up with him in the woods." I gave him a toothy grin, wincing in anticipation.

"*What?*" he snapped. "This is why I told you to stay home! Did you not find it at least a little suspicious to find a boy in the woods?" He rubbed the bridge of his nose. "My daughter. Meeting up with a member of the Ambition! An assassin!"

"Hey, he didn't ever kill anyone," I said, turning to Onvyr. "Right?"

The boy seemed solemn. He returned to looking at the ground. "Only one directly…"

Onas interjected. "It wasn't entirely her fault she did what she did. Go ahead. Tell them how it all went down," he said, prompting Onvyr.

With a gentle sigh, he nodded. The boy peered at

Appi. "We thought…We thought she was corrupt because of how she grew up. That she would harm fae society. We saw her as nothing different than a human in fae clothing."

"The Forbidden," Onas added.

Onvyr continued. "But after a bit, I was told that she had parents with powerful Gifts." Something clicked as he went on. "So she would have a powerful Gift." He wrung his wrists. "Like how they thought I would…"

Sympathy ached in me. "So, you never wanted to kill me?" I asked, knowing he needed to get back on topic.

He snapped out of it. "Oh, um, well…The plan was to wait until we knew for sure what Gift you had. If it was powerful, then we'd bring you in, hopefully by choice. Force if not."

"And if she didn't have an acceptable Gift?" Appi asked, scowling.

Onvyr flinched. "Then…I was to kill her." He looked to me, somber. "I was the youngest they had. They wanted me to convince you to join…if things went well. So I purposely ran into you in the forest. To meet you. Get close. When you came back to me, off guard with how your Ritual went, I waivered. I couldn't kill you. You were my friend."

It all made sense, and I believed him. He seemed conflicted with himself when I looked back on any of his lies. Like his outward appearance vied with the truth.

Here, he stared at me with guilt-ridden eyes and

sounded genuine, like he had finally stopped lying to everyone, including himself.

"That's why you pressed me to try to use my Blessing." I turned to the others. "Despite the Elements' warning, I tried using it. I somehow created a rift."

Kaylessa tilted her head. "No Gift can do that."

"It's not a Gift. It's a Blessing," I stated, pretending like I knew how it all worked.

And I had never been more grateful for it than when we escaped. I still remembered how it took over, speaking through me. Yet I hadn't felt out of control. My will and its own overlapped, perfectly in sync.

Inseparable.

"I didn't believe anything you said about the Elements," Onvyr told me.

I nodded, already knowing this.

"But I can't think of another reason to explain it. After I saw what you could do, I was relieved that we could continue on. But, um, when I tried using my Gift, your Blessing brought that memory back."

I remembered what I had seen only moments before waking up. *It used him, right?* I recalled the prediction, the pain he would go through with the enveloping pure Essence.

Something clung me to him while he continued

describing how we escaped. *My will overlapped with my Blessing…*

It hadn't used him. If its goal was the same as mine, it wouldn't want to hurt him.

"…so it brought me to the hospital. Then, I met *Maliei* Kaylessa," he said.

Clearly, he seemed drained, like although he knew what happened next, he was running out of words to say. I grinned. It was the most I had ever heard him talk. And it wasn't entirely by choice as much as pressure.

"Kaylessa, Appi said that I was dying. Is that true?" I asked, taking the weight of explaining off Onvyr.

The boy's eyes thanked me.

"Oh? 'Appi'?" She eyed him with a smile and turned back to me. Kaylessa put her hands on her hips. "Uh, yes, that's right. You were dispersing before our eyes. Had it not been for Onvyr *Gee*, you assuredly wouldn't have made it."

Kaylessa looked at Taelin. "He naturally makes tenfold the Essence of a normal fae. The boy donated excess to her to save her."

Taelin straightened. "Just like…?"

Kaylessa nodded.

Onvyr looked at the couple, confused and curious. I finally saw him for what he was. He truly was a lost little boy, out of his element, his comfort, and haunted by his past.

Displaced

I sat in their living room, fidgeting with my soft chainmail. Onas had convinced me to take off my armor, but halfway through the process, we realized there were no normal clothes for me to change into. So, I just sat in my chainmail and my armored greaves, exhausted and stressed.

After I took Syndra from the Ambition, it was a never ending series of events: going to the hospital, fending off Onas, moving Syndra home…Oh my Ether, was I tired.

Thankfully, ever since I gave Syndra all my extra Essence, I hadn't seemed to be overly sensitive or overwhelmed, except of course when she called me out to explain everything. I mean, had she met me? *Why did I save the kid, again?*

I rubbed my eyes. *I must have been awake for over a revolution now.* Curious, I instinctively went to check my leather Mat gloves to find out.

Fear stung when I realized I still had them on. The Ambition could track me and everything I did if I used them. I immediately took them off and threw them to the ground, unsure what to do.

"You littering in someone else's house?" Nim Taelin walked over. He sat beside me on the couch and picked up my gloves.

"Sorry, I didn't—I don't know—" I stammered.

He analyzed them. "Are these the Ambition's?"

I nodded.

Nim chuckled. "You just don't know how to turn them off. Simple solution." He held them up, his eyes flashing cyan. "Off." He tossed them back to me. "There. Now you got nothing to worry about. We can disconnect them from the Ambition's database later on so you can still use them."

I held them in wonder, not having been with someone with a Technological Gift before. "Speech Hacker?"

"Sure thing." He gave me a small smile, a little proud.

Maliei Kaylessa, Nim Onas, Lavadan and Syndra came into the room. The girl walked in, relying on her father for balance.

Never before had I felt so out of place. Like obsidian among diamonds. Yet, I found relief with Syndra around. She knew me. And that's all I needed.

Kaylessa hugged her husband from behind. "I called Shaeli. She should be here any beat now."

"Did you tell her who we found?" Syndra asked, smiling at Onas.

"No," Kaylessa said, giggling. "She's gonna—"

A girl came through the door, distracted by her Mat gloves. "Meiaa," she groaned. "What in Rishi's name could be so important that you pull me out from school?"

Kaylessa clicked her tongue. "You weren't at school, were you?"

The fae shrugged. "Technically, I was still on campus. It's not my fault that I—"

She caught sight of Onas. For the first time, I saw a soft smile stretch genuinely on his face. Shaeli ran toward Onas, nearly tackling him.

"Onas! Where did you—How did they—" Tears leaked from her eyes.

With a laugh, he picked her up and twirled her

around. "Missed you too, love."

Taelin guffawed beside me. "Baalih, don't strangle him. We just got him back!"

Shaeli stepped back, gazing at her betrothed. She leaned in close to his face, held him close to her, and slapped the living Essence out of him. "Where the Ether have you been the last few orbits?"

He rubbed the handprint on his cheek. "Somewhere I couldn't escape." Onas glanced at me. "But thanks to Onvyr, I'm back...for good."

"I saw Elena's memories. Did you do that?"

Onas sighed. "Not by choice."

Shaeli nodded and grabbed his arm. "Well, hear me now. You are *not* allowed to leave me for more than twelve phases without a legitimate reason."

He cocked his head to the side. "Not even a revolution?"

Shaeli kissed him. "Not even for twelve and a half phases."

I looked away. Onas had given me credit for his return, although I had as much to do with that as I did his disappearance. He had missed out on orbits of his betrothal because of me.

Nim Taelin noticed that I had turned away, apparently assuming it was because of her kiss. He smiled and elbowed me. With a finger, he made a gagging motion, pretending like he was throwing up. I couldn't help but giggle. Syndra laughed as well from the other side of the room.

Kaylessa pulled his head backward from the other side of the couch. "How is my husband worse than the children?"

He shrugged, kissing her, still upside down.

Lavadan whispered something to Syndra before stepping out of the room. She meandered wearily over to me and leaned on the back of the couch.

"Where'd he go?" I whispered to her.

"Got no clue. He said he had a call to make. Soooo, you're gonna stick around now, right?"

Stick around? "What?"

"You lived with the Ambition, didn't you? Since you're not with them anymore, you have to live *somewhere*." She looked around. "Don't tell him I told you this, but my father has an empty guest room. We could hang out every day!"

I looked for what to say. *There's no way I'm gonna*

be able to stay with him. *He hates my guts.*

She was just trying to be generous, but I was hesitant. I didn't want to offend her by saying anything bad about her father. She seemed pretty close to him ever since had she gotten back.

"That's right. We gotta find you a place to stay," Taelin chimed in.

"He's not staying here," Lavadan coldly stated from a doorway.

Syndra whined. "But Appi...Where is he gonna be? I'm alone a lot of the day with my studies. It'd be nice to have a friend to help."

He shot daggers at me. "You already have friends, my dear. Good ones. Not him." Lavadan stood beside her. "And you won't be so alone soon. The condition was that you complete the Ritual before you get placed in a school. We can now work out the details to get you enrolled."

"So where will he live?" Onas asked.

A silence lingered in the air. A pit grew at the bottom of my stomach. *No one trusts the kid from the Ambition.*

"He'll stay with us," Maliei Kaylessa said, pulling her hair back. "We have room. We'll take care of him."

Taelin cleared his throat, obviously uncomfortable with her decision.

"You all need to take a breath." Maliei walked to me. "I've seen what lengths he'll go to atone. He is more than welcome in our home."

Onas nodded. "Sounds like it's decided."

Lavadan couldn't help but agree. "Your decisions are your own. It is good that we cleared this up, though. I was just in contact with a representative for the Ancients. They need to be updated with all that's occurred between him and my daughter." He looked at Syndra and me. "The representative set up a meeting in a few phases."

"The Ancients?" My intestines knotted. Bile accumulated. *I can't meet with the Ancients.*

Onas understood my opposition and stepped forward. "What the Ambition told you about them isn't all true."

I shot a glare at him. "So, they are ensuring their subjects are cared for? Even the Underprivileged?" Essence returned to me, and resentment amplified in my words. "So they *aren't* trying to figure out ways to replace the Underprivileged? To isolate their own?"

Onas looked away, unable to speak for them.

But Kaylessa tried. "Hon, none of those things are proven true. Those are only theories and—"

"So they've been proven wrong?" I snapped.

Everyone around me tensed with my spiked anger.

Like I could hurt them at any given beat. Except Onas, who just avoided my eyes, knowing the words I spoke weren't false. Syndra looked at me, subtly mouthing, *Calm down.*

I took a deep breath. *She's right. I have no room to be assertive about anything.*

"Sorry," I mumbled, trying to sound composed. "I just can't meet the Ancients."

Lavadan scowled. "Either you go, or you are taken to them by force. They certainly do not like being ignored."

"You'll be okay. We'll all be there," Syndra said, lighthearted.

"Actually, Onas and Shaeli will be going in tomorrow, since they are in their later decades and thus deserve a separate meeting," Lavadan explained.

Syndra shrugged. "Okay, so *most* of us will be there. Sounds like they'll be questioning me as much as you. I know they can be scary, but if I can do it, you can."

She seemed so certain. Determined.

I was just tired. Anxious and tired. *Fine. Whatever. Just want to get this over with.*

Begrudgingly, I said, "Okay. I'll go."

She seemed proud of me. This was all just wrong timing, though. My Essence was stirring up again, accumulating. Although it wasn't as full as it usually was, it was clear to me that controlling any emotions would be difficult.

Just because I had left the Ambition didn't mean I was buddies with the rulers who had ignored our biggest problems for centuries and had instigated the modern struggles we faced. And I wasn't going to be.

***

The Pantheon.

I had never imagined I would ever step foot inside such a well known place. Yet there I was, walking alongside Syndra, down the halls. *Most or all of them will be present.* Poison seeped in my veins while I waited to see how it would go down.

When I glanced at Syndra, I felt jealous. She was calm and prepared. Even if I hadn't been from the Ambition, even if I had been in her place instead, I would never find that courage. I mean, even our differences in clothing probably didn't help me.

No new clothes, plus only a few phases since I had fled the Ambition, equaled chainmail and a couple pieces of armor left on my legs. Meanwhile, she looked like an actual normal fae.

There was no way they'll see me as anything other than a thorn from the Ambition now.

"Are you okay?" she asked, taking my mind off the surely upcoming drama.

I nodded, not wanting to explain it all quite yet. "I was wondering..." I whispered, "You told me your name is Syndra. But I was told you go by Elena."

"Oh, that's right." She looked at me. "You know, Elena was pushed around a lot. Let herself be kicked around by whoever. Syndra was able to stand up for herself. Almost everything holding me back just went out the window since my world turned inside out. Now, it's like...why the heck not?" With a nod, she said, "Call me Syndra. It'll be weird for me, but I think I can start best if you are the one calling me that."

Easy enough for me. A little pride for her sparked in me. She had started choosing fae over humans.

We entered the attendant's area with all ten

Ancients looking from above. Intricate markings embellished each of them, with every Ancient's being different in style and placement.

Hypocrites. *"We care for our people, no matter the Gift. Let's just place our Underprivileged Ancients out of immediate eyeshot. Oh, and give them minimal adornment."*

I barely heard the surrounding crowd of fae murmur at my appearance over my surging thoughts. Surely, my mouth was at a slight frown. In hindsight, I didn't help my image, but emotions really controlled me more than I controlled them.

Syndra spoke with them. She was as calm as I was disgusted.

My Essence accumulated, hitting against my reign of control. I was so preoccupied with keeping it in the safe range and trying to hide what I felt, that I barely heard anything they were talking about.

"...So is he just mute or purposely refusing to answer us?"

I snapped out of it. Rosandoral was talking to me. I glanced at Syndra, unsure of the question. She just motioned for me to speak.

With my voice amplified by the magnifier, I turned

to them. "Sorry. Didn't hear the question."

Tanila Sarkis rubbed her face with the base of her palm. "First, he doesn't kneel at all, just stares at us. Then, he lets all of our questions go in one ear and out the other."

When did everyone kneel?

She scoffed. "We *asked*: Have you committed any crimes? Mind you, we can also find out for ourselves if you're telling the truth or not."

Her husband, Nylian, beside her added, "And before you continue, know that this isn't going well as a first impression. The two of you seem to have that tendency in common."

I tried hard to keep myself from snarling. *Why in the Rishi's name would I care what my impression is to you?*

Syndra stepped beside me. She turned off the magnifier and said, "It's okay. You got this."

My Essence simmered down, as if she had literally taken a bit of anxiety off my chest. Of course, she wasn't an Empathic Transfer, but somehow she definitely helped me gain a bit more self-control.

"Just one human. I killed one human. No more. No fae. Mainly, I just worked behind the scenes for the Ambition."

Syndra said to them, "He would just use his Gift as they asked. Using your Gift isn't a crime, right?"

Rosandoral seemed a bit more patient with her than me. "It all depends on the Gift and usage."

Inamenor placed his head on his hand, watching attentively. "Syndra Bee, you have to let him speak for himself." He looked at me, playing with his Gift and snapping his fingers to create small sparks. "What is your Gift and how did you use it?"

"Perspective Empathy." *Gonna call me out on being Underprivileged directly, or just passively?* "I used my Gift to persuade fae to join the Ambition."

Rosandoral noted, "That's a pretty rare Gift. But that usage..."

"But he didn't use his Gift like that because he thought it was right. It's more like he was misled," Syndra said. "They stole him from his family and erased his memories. They basically brainwashed—"

"Bee, you must *stop*," Faphine said, stern but advising. "He must be the one explaining. You've already had your turn."

She did? I can't believe I missed that. I shifted my posture, trying a little to seem less cocky or however they saw me. I had to admit they were right about one thing:

This wasn't going well.

They talked amongst themselves, deciding my fate. Kaylessa came up behind me.

"*My family* will take full responsibility of him in our *Independent* village. Please remember that," she sweetly told them.

Awkwardly, Rosandoral nodded. "We understand." They went back to deliberating, typing to each other using their Mat gloves.

I glanced at Maliei Kaylessa, wondering where she had gotten the guts to speak up how she did. *Even I know it's dangerous to interrupt the Ancients.*

After deliberation was over, Rosandoral turned to us, "Syndra Bee will pursue formal education despite the conundrum of her Gift. The schools may either accept her or reject her at their own discretion. The boy will reside with Kaylessa, Taelin, and Shaeli Heiwys. The Institute of Relational Empathy will either accept or reject him at their own discretion. If rejected, he will be taught by the Heiwyses. The boy will require an emissary, just the same as Syndra Bee."

She shot a sly look at Kaylessa.

"We only require so much because although two of them are Independents and technically out of our full jurisdiction, they are still both special cases."

"Taelin and I can fill in for emissaries, just as Leorn is doing for Syndra," Kaylessa said.

Rosandoral nodded. "It is decided. Council adjourned."

My tension lessened when we began to leave. Maliei Kaylessa was very happy with the outcome, practically bouncing with every step.

When we got outside, Nim Taelin pulled me aside. "Go on," he told his wife. "We will just be a beat."

Nim kneeled at my level, as serious as I have ever seen him—within the last couple of phases that I had known him, of course.

"I want you to understand. Kaylessa is very kind and, frankly, just loves nurturing others. I wasn't there when you helped Elena, but she surely was, and what you did touched her deeply."

I rubbed my arm. "You don't want me to live with your family."

He shook his head. "The problem isn't that taking care of you will be an issue, although I expect dealing with Ambition matters won't be the easiest. I'm fine with being one of your guardians. Thing is... Kiddo, I have a rather unpredictable daughter. I love her dearly and want to be sure she is safe and prepared once she gets married soon. She only has a few more orbits left in her betrothal."

Taelin's dark eyes pleaded, standing out against his tanned skin. "Please, don't complicate anything for her. For my family."

It was a reasonable request, especially considering where I came from. "I promise."

He smiled. "Okay, champ. Let's catch up with the others. I'm sure you'll want to hang around Elena before Leorn builds a wall between you two." He chuckled. "It's not that you're a bad kid. I think. Leorn can just be...very protective. He doesn't want you being friends with his daughter because he fears losing her again. I mean, she *did* almost die last night."

I spotted Syndra talking with a few others.

Taelin patted me on the back.

"Go on. You can meet us back at the entrance," he told me, walking away.

I attempted to join her but stopped midway, stunned by the company she was with.

First up was the Descendent conversing with her. He had sleek, unkempt but immaculate hair, startling against his light green toga. It had to be a Cainaris. They were the only Descendents nowadays who didn't have higher Gifts, like Illusionists or Tenebrals. They had Gifts from Nature, shown by his clothing. I remembered her talking about him before. *So this is her crush...*

But it wasn't purely him who kept me from joining them.

The girl she was talking to was like me. She had an abundance of pure Essence. I could feel it.

This is the girl she was talking about that made a scene at Essence Erupting. Her features were soft but beautiful. Black braids woven into a low bun, adorned with metal embellishments. And her smile. Zentha wore a constant smile, but never before had I seen one so genuine and innocently uplifting as this girl's.

She looked at me, as if she had felt the same familiarity. My Essence caused blood to rush to my cheeks. I glanced away, feeling a bit like a stalker.

Did she recognize my Essence or just me looking at her? Was I staring? Oh my Ether, I was staring, wasn't I?

When I glanced back, the girl seemed to be talking with the others like nothing happened.

Meanwhile, Syndra seemed enthralled in the conversation. I lectured myself at the stupid unrealistic goals I had. *She already has friends and a family and...She has it all.* I needed her more than she needed me.

I began to walk away.

Obsidian Among Diamonds

Explaining my situation to the Ancients without describing how their entire belief system was skewed was definitely like trying to keep a cat in the bag. A very angry and insane cat. But I couldn't tell them about the Elements. They would have never believed me, and it would have caused a heck of a scene. Apparently, fae weren't the most flexible creatures.

On top of that, the Ancients, despite my desire to stick with Appi's teaching, had us start planning to enroll me into the different fae schools. Of which, each one would most assuredly turn me away and no one would care.

But in comparison, my side of the meeting was just fine. It was Onvyr's that worried me the most.

He was like a constantly annoyed statue, just staring at the Ancients, ignoring most of the questions thrown at him. I tried to cover for him, but the Ancients did *not* care for that.

After we got out, Darunia and Akkar were waiting for me by a tree just outside. Darunia was the first to see me.

"Oh my Ether, *Jeerei* Lavadan told me what happened to you last night." She looked at me, searching for anything out of place. Darunia sighed in relief. "You seem to be fine. How are you recovering?"

I shrugged. "I'm okay. Feeling a bit of mental inertia, but okay."

Akkar laughed, his head resting on his hand. "*Esh*…Look at all the attention you get just for narrowly surviving! Everyone's talking about you. I should try almost dying."

"Just tell me when. I can hook you up." I clicked my tongue and shot a finger gun at him. "Sounds like I'll have the crazy group of murderers on my tail now. Something about me being corrupt and no better than a human."

Darunia shook her head. "No, you're not a human! In no way are you corrupt or — "

"Welll, I don't know about that part." Akkar crossed his arms. "She *is* pretty rude. That would play into corruption, yeah?"

"Are you really going to tick off the girl with a mysterious power? I mean, I knew you weren't smart, but this is a new low," I said.

He scoffed. "Oh, I don't care what you say. There's no way you got as much power as me."

"Can I tell him the whole story?" Darunia asked. "He still hasn't heard exactly how your Ritual went."

I waved my hand, not wanting to have to deal with him myself. "Please do."

While the two discussed, I found myself once again left in a conversation where I was the odd man out. I was *that kid* who people needed to explain to understand. Who knew nothing about commonplace topics.

I looked around and I got a brief glance of Onvyr walking past us. My Blessing echoed my loneliness. *I wish he could just join us. He understands.*

I turned back, knowing he had everything set up for him. He had gotten himself a home, support, and soon, a school. A fancy institute I knew he would excel at. Onvyr always seemed to know any subject I brought up. He didn't need me as much as I needed him.

With a smile, I rejoined the conversation. As if I believed Darunia had stuck around with me out of friendship, even though I knew she was just curious about the fae who had grown up human. As if Akkar's teases didn't touch me, yet I could never quite tell what he truly thought of me. As if I knew how to be a fae.

Epilogue

I sat, anxious, knowing the only thing I had left of a family was still stuck in the Ambition.

Wyn might have known it all happened, but he still was the one to mentor me. To help me.

When I had approached him with the truth, he seemed to truly worry about me, telling me to avoid alerting the Ambition of my revelation. He knew what the consequences would be and wanted me to avoid them at all costs.

He's always stood by me. It's time I looked out for him.

The first night I stayed with the Heiwyses, I snuck out and borrowed one of their cycles. Determination brought me through the rift to the place I had risked it all to escape.

This base was hidden in a valley, so there were plenty of places to hide the cycle and sneak my way in.

I had put back on my full armor, hoping to blend in,

and followed a group of distracted trainees into the dorms, praying no one looked behind them. Never had I been gladder that the Ambition didn't believe in cameras. They thought too much reliance on anything was toxic.

But then again, you don't need to be a Technopath to fool mortal senses.

Swiftly, I made my way into my room, hoping my old roomie hadn't missed dinner. Sure enough, Wyn never skipped out on food.

"Prodigy." He stared at me, confused, hurt. Wyn glanced at my hair. "Taking advantage of Zentha not being around to gel it, I see. You never did like how she did your hair." Serious, he stood up. "You need to leave."

I shook my head. "No, *you* do. Tell me that what they're doing is right."

Wyn laughed. "Naak, this isn't a matter of right and wrong. Nothing can just...*fit* into those categories."

"Wyn, tell me."

He hesitated. Defeated, he grinned. "I can't."

"Then come on. I'll help you out. You don't have to stay here."

"And live a life on the run? It's like how I've seen human soldiers try to return to civilian life. They won't accept us." He scoffed. "No reputation equals no life. No one knows us."

"You're wrong. There's a family. They don't care about that. They're taking me in. And I'm not even in my decades yet! They'd do the same for you."

Wyn sat back down, playing with the food on his plate. "I can't go. This is all I know. My family has been with them—"

"For generations," I finished for him, rolling my eyes. "You know you're not close with your family. Please—"

"*No.*" Wyn snapped. He gave me the desperate look of a trapped bird. "My family has been doing this for generations. I don't know how to do anything else. However reliant you think you were with them, you were only here five orbits. *Five orbits.* I've been here for forty-two, all my life. It wasn't until they recruited a *child* did I even begin to question them." He returned to eating. "Just go, kid. I'm not someone who can be saved."

Although I didn't understand his reasoning, I knew I couldn't force him into anything. I swept aside some hairs that had fallen in front of my eyes.

"You are. You're just too scared to let yourself be saved," I noted coldly.

He winced, knowing the truth. I turned to the door.

"Wait." Wyn tossed me a shoulder cloak. "You'll need this."

I held it in my hands. I didn't want to use it; I didn't want anything of the Ambition's.

"Why?"

"I meant it when I said you'll have a life on the run. They don't take traitors lightly. Take this too." He flung a knife to my feet. It stuck in the ground only an inch from me. "You gotta tread lightly. You've already gotten the attention of the Harbinger. They've sent her."

I picked up the knife. "Who? Zentha?"

Wyn shook his head. "She's too involved with you, I think. No. Our former Cention."

I clasped my hands around the cloth, turning my knuckles white, and shuddered, remembering the fae who had given me most of my scars.

Wyn nodded grimly. "And she knows where you and the Forbidden live.

Innocence is a fantasy. Even for infants, who reach and cry for their mother yet would not to a stranger. As knowledge is analyzed and expanded, it is come to be known that all are born with inherent bias, no matter how much we try to deny this. All it takes is a simple push, a delicate tipping point, to dictate where that bias lies.

From bias comes persecution. Suffering.

How horrible it is to live in a world of suffering, stretching from the unheard screams in the womb to the variable death we all reach. But the ignorant rather let themselves suffer out of lethargy and indifference. That is the true epidemic: indifference. So, with a burning ambition, I carefully place each gear in deliberate positions within my mechanism to eradicate suffering.

Until a child comes along to loosen the screws.

Youth have no restraints. But admonishment does not just come in the form of pulling the child away and giving them a lecture. Where is the lesson in a talk that the young will only forget two beats later?

So I let her. Yes, she may have found a way to remove one of my most integral gears, but one must be elevated to be torn down. And that gear plucked? I knew his bias since the moment I took him in. It was only a matter of time before my blanket of protection over him was unraveled and his bias overcame him. Now, I must test the waters to determine the punishment to be doled. I must enter in one of my most apt pawns. Someone who will rattle the Traitor and the Forbidden. My most capable Writcaller.

For one must be elevated to be torn down.

— The Harbinger

Note From the
Author

It truly is a great blessing to evolve from reader to writer. But becoming a writer is not what most understand. Writing a story is the act of walking the microscopic line between insanity and eloquence. It is the careful skill of containing an entire universe with multitudinous narratives inside one's own mind and channeling it out through the fine tip of a pen. Or a keyboard, in most cases nowadays.

It needs a constant change in perspective. The ability to transform into one, three, twenty different people, each with their own unlimited complexities. Being a writer requires organized insanity and infinite empathy to even begin to understand what and why each person feels, thinks, and does what they do.

This is a skill I've always admired and tried to hone in on for years, for I've spent close to a decade with all those narratives already developed inside my head. All I needed was the ability to put it on paper. And all it took was a decade! (That's not a long time right?) But here I finally am, still a minor—yes, 17 still counts as being a kid—and having been able to begin my first series. I thank God for at last drilling into my head the focus and discipline to begin writing my stories rather than just daydream 24/7. Which, I can assure you, is the most difficult part of authoring, by far. Not publishing or editing. No, it was the initial writing that was the hardest. But now that I've begun, I don't plan on stopping.

So hang on tight. Because this is just the beginning.

SDG